PENGUIN 🐧 CLASSICS

AN AFRICAN MILLIONAIRE

GRANT ALLEN was born on February 24, 1848, near Kingston, Ontario. Though largely forgotten today, during his lifetime he was a prolific and popular writer who published widely in diverse areas, which were as various as his own intellectual pursuits, and ranged from the sciences to literature. Titles of several of his books reveal his breadth of interests, including *The Evolutionist at Large* (1881), *The Colours of Flowers as Illustrated in the British Flora* (1882), and *Biographies of Working Men* (1884). As a naturalist and professed socialist, he embraced a number of radical views for his time, such as the advancement of women's rights. For example, *The Woman Who Did* (1895) espoused a then controversial literary critique of sexual conventions and marriage. As a writer of popular fiction, Allen produced a number of successful, though now forgettable, potboilers. His best stories, which featured the notorious con artist and thief Colonel Clay, first appeared in the *Strand Magazine* and later were collected in the book *An African Millionaire: Episodes in the Life of the Illustrious Colonel Clay* (1897), regarded by many critics as the first fictional work to feature a criminal protagonist. Near the end of his life, Allen asked his friend Sir Arthur Conan Doyle—author of the Sherlock Holmes tales—to complete the final chapter of his novel *Hilda Wade: A Woman with Tenacity of Purpose* (1900), which was published posthumously. Allen died on October 28, 1899 (though some sources cite October 25, 1899, as the day he died).

GARY HOPPENSTAND is a professor of English at Michigan State University. He has published numerous scholarly books and articles about popular literature, and his editorial work has been nominated for the World Fantasy Award. He has twice won the Popular Culture Association's Best Book award in the Textbook/Reference category, and he is a former president of the national Popular Culture Association. He won the top scholarly honor given by the national Popular Culture Association—the Governing Board Award—in 2008 "for his contributions to popular culture studies and the Popular Culture Association." Currently, he is the editor of *The Journal of Popular Culture*.

GRANT ALLEN

An African Millionaire

EPISODES IN THE LIFE OF
THE ILLUSTRIOUS COLONEL CLAY

Introduction by
GARY HOPPENSTAND

PENGUIN BOOKS

PENGUIN BOOKS

Published by the Penguin Group

Penguin Group (USA) Inc., 375 Hudson Street, New York, New York 10014, U.S.A.
Penguin Group (Canada), 90 Eglinton Avenue East, Suite 700, Toronto,
Ontario, Canada M4P 2Y3 (a division of Pearson Penguin Canada Inc.)
Penguin Books Ltd, 80 Strand, London WC2R 0RL, England
Penguin Ireland, 25 St Stephen's Green, Dublin 2, Ireland (a division of Penguin Books Ltd)
Penguin Group (Australia), 250 Camberwell Road, Camberwell,
Victoria 3124, Australia (a division of Pearson Australia Group Pty Ltd)
Penguin Books India Pvt Ltd, 11 Community Centre, Panchsheel Park, New Delhi - 110 017, India
Penguin Group (NZ), 67 Apollo Drive, Rosedale, Auckland 0632,
New Zealand (a division of Pearson New Zealand Ltd)
Penguin Books (South Africa) (Pty) Ltd, 24 Sturdee Avenue,
Rosebank, Johannesburg 2196, South Africa

Penguin Books Ltd, Registered Offices:
80 Strand, London WC2R 0RL, England

First published in Great Britain by Grant Richards 1897
First published in the United States of America by Edward Arnold 1897
This edition with an introduction by Gary Hoppenstand published in Penguin Books 2012

Introduction copyright © Gary Hoppenstand, 2012
All rights reserved

LIBRARY OF CONGRESS CATALOGING IN PUBLICATION DATA
Allen, Grant, 1848-1899.
An African millionaire : episodes in the life of the illustrious
Colonel Clay / Grant Allen ; introduction by Gary Hoppenstand.
p. cm.
ISBN 978-0-14-310657-9 (pbk.)
I. Title.
PR4004.A2A62 2012
823'.8—dc23
2011045212

Set in Sabon

146122990

Contents

AN AFRICAN MILLIONAIRE

Introduction

Chris Steinbrunner and Otto Penzler argue in their *Encyclopedia of Mystery and Detection* that Colonel Clay was "the first important rogue in short crime fiction who is the hero, not a subsidiary character, villain, or antihero" (5). This statement represents the general assertion about Colonel Clay by various historians of crime fiction whenever the character is discussed in the critical texts of the genre. The claim is true, but perhaps not exactly in the way intended by Steinbrunner and Penzler. After all, the title of Grant Allen's book is *An African Millionaire* and not *The Adventures of Colonel Clay*. And the actual rogue protagonist is Sir Charles Vandrift, the African millionaire of the title, and not Colonel Clay. Still, there is no doubt that Colonel Clay is the hero. The character readily solicits the reader's compassion, and though he is a consummate thief and con man, his creator—Grant Allen— presents him in a highly sympathetic light.

The problem is that the reader does not see much of this rogue hero. Colonel Clay rarely makes an appearance out of disguise in any of the twelve linked stories in the collection until near the book's conclusion, while Sir Charles Vandrift is featured prominently throughout, always accompanied by his brother-in-law and the narrator of the stories, Seymour Wilbraham Wentworth, a lesser rogue who serves as Sir Charles's apparently less-than-honest personal secretary. Colonel Clay is the absentee rogue hero, while Sir Charles Vandrift commands the reader's point of view as a main protagonist. Allen even mimics (and mocks) the hero/sidekick relationship between Sir Charles and Seymour Wentworth that Sir Arthur Conan Doyle popularized in his adventures with Sherlock Holmes and Dr. Watson, a relationship also borrowed later by Conan Doyle's brother-in-law E. W. Hornung in *The Amateur Cracksman* (1899), featuring the gentleman thief, A. J. Raffles, and his companion in crime, "Bunny" Manders.

As a self-professed Communist (Clodd 41) and member of the Fabian Society (Clodd 131), at the very least Grant Allen entertained a hearty suspicion of capitalism and the captains of commerce. He was by trade a professional author who often encountered some difficulty in earning a livable income from his scientific writings, and no doubt this fact helped to encourage his suspicion of unrestricted capitalism in general; he despaired of the difficulty of writing for a living, in part because of the unscrupulous business practices of the publishers of his time, at one point stating: "the [writing] profession is overcrowded, and the competition keen. . . . I should say distinctly it's an excellent one to keep out of" (Morton 193).

Indeed, one of the main reasons why Allen turned to writing fiction such as *An African Millionaire* was that it earned more money than writing essays and books about natural science, philosophy, politics, or history, which were his typical literary stock-in-trade. Phyllis Rozendal notes that "Allen started writing fiction only after discovering that he could not make a living from his scientific writing" (6). Becoming a writer of popular fiction was a necessary decision that caused Allen a degree of unease. As Peter Morton notes in his *"The Busiest Man in England": Grant Allen and the Writing Trade, 1875–1900*: "Grant Allen, author of more than thirty novels and much short fiction, was notorious for his derogatory opinion of that important part of his trade. He wrote fiction for money, he said, and nothing more" (111). Allen himself states in the preface to *Strange Stories* (1890): "Being by trade a psychologist and scientific journeyman, I have been bold enough at times to stray surreptitiously and tentatively from my proper sphere into the flowery fields of pure fiction" (iii). No doubt the more substantial checks provided by editors and publishers of fiction periodicals and books helped to embolden Allen's efforts in the "flowery fields of pure fiction."

Charles Grant Blairfindie Allen was something of a political nonconformist and social rebel, and he was one of the most prolific and diverse writers of his time. Born on February 24, 1848, on Wolf Island near Kingston, Ontario, the second son of Joseph Antisell Allen, a Protestant clergyman at the Holy Trinity Church, and Charlotte Catherine Ann Grant, the daughter of the fifth baron of Longueuil, Quebec, the young Grant Allen possessed an early affection for nature that would later serve him well when he wrote on the natural sciences. He moved to the United States with his parents at age thirteen, and later received a scholarship to attend Merton College at Oxford in 1867. He graduated in 1871 and following the death of his first wife married Ellen Jerrard in 1873. Allen taught in Jamaica at Government College, Spanish Town, returning to England in 1876, where he became a professional author and essayist. He died at the age of fifty-one on October 25, 1899 (Merriman; a number of sources cite Allen's date of death as October 28, 1899), survived by his second wife, Ellen, and his only son, Jerrard Grant (Ruddick, 10).

"His colonial background gave Allen an outsider's perspective on late-Victorian England at the height of its imperial power, a perspective clarified by his own remarkable qualities of mind," claims Nicholas Ruddick. Ruddick goes on to say that "Little escaped his scrutiny: he had the trained eye of a naturalist or a detective" (10). Paul Matthew St. Pierre adds: "Prolific, versatile, original, even profound, Grant Allen dedicated his life to the quest for incontrovertible knowledge through the written word" (5). Unlike several of his literary peers who also penned thrillers featuring thief protagonists—authors such as Guy Boothby and E. W. Hornung—Allen was not primarily known as a writer of crime fiction. He was otherwise quite prolific, however, publishing nonfiction titles covering a wide range of topics, from history to science to philosophy to art and literary melodrama. His earliest efforts were in the natural sciences, and included such titles as *The Colour-Sense: Its Origin and Development* (1879), *Vignettes from Nature* (1881), and *Flowers and Their Pedigrees* (1883). Allen also tackled controversial subjects in politics and religion, as illustrated in his books *Individualism and Socialism* (1889; reprinted from *Contemporary Review* of May 1889) and *The Evolution of the Idea of God: An Inquiry into the Origins of Religion* (1897).

Apparently, writing about these topics failed to earn Allen a decent income, so he turned to producing fiction and subsequently published now forgotten efforts such as *This Mortal Coil: A Novel* (1888), *The Jaws of Death: A Novel* (1889), and *Dumaresq's Daughter: A Novel* (1891). Allen could, if he wanted, create some measure of scandal and controversy with his fiction. His novel *The Woman Who Did* (1895), for example, about a female protagonist who rebelled against the social norms of her time by having a child out of wedlock (a woman who was of the middle class and not a prostitute), created quite a stir among his more socially conservative readers. Few people today, however, have read *The Woman Who Did*, and even fewer would be shocked by its once scandalous content. In retrospect, reviewing the vast bulk of Allen's literary output, his single lasting contribution to literature is his escapist crime thriller *An African Millionaire*.

Sometimes the reading of popular crime fiction reveals nothing more than escapist entertainment—mere character, plot, and setting—but such is not the case with *An African Millionaire*. Allen's episodic novel offers its reader a humorous satire of unrestrained capitalism. Both Sir Charles Vandrift and Seymour Wentworth are comic figures, businessmen-rogues of dubious intelligence who, in their various encounters with the crafty Colonel Clay, are diminished in their arrogance and pride as well as their pocketbooks. Colonel Clay is a consummate trickster figure, a turn-of-the-twentieth-century Robin Hood who robs from the rich and unscrupulous South African capitalist (who himself basically robs and deceives others who trust in him and his business practices). In the story "The Episode of the Drawn Game," Colonel Clay proclaims to Sir Charles: "*You* are a capitalist and a millionaire. In *your* large way you prey upon society. . . . In *my* smaller way, again, *I* relieve you in turn of a portion of the plunder. I am a Robin Hood of my age."

   Allen's invention of the rogue protagonist resulted not only from his own desire to lampoon the capitalistic excesses of his time, but also indirectly from the evolving nature of the detective protagonist in the crime fiction of the nineteenth century. Indeed, by the turn of the twentieth century, the dilemma with the ever-expanding popularity of the detective story was that the detective hero had become too smart, too clever, too brave, and altogether too infallible. With the advent of serialized heroes (such as the detective protagonist) in mid- to late nineteenth-century popular fiction—especially as seen in the story papers of the middle decades of the nineteenth century, and in the development and growing popularity of American dime novels and British "penny dreadfuls"—a problem began to emerge as authors and publishers attempted to maintain their weekly, biweekly, or monthly publication schedules. They ascertained that in order to sustain and expand their working-class audience's interest in their serialized hero, they had to expand their hero's abilities, eventually to the point where heroes, including the detective heroes of crime fiction, were nearly superhuman and virtually unstoppable in their actions.

   And, as these authors of popular fiction and their publishers soon discovered, at that instant when the hero becomes too powerful for his adversaries, the narrative impact of the thriller diminishes and becomes less interesting to readers. One way that the writers of commercial serialized fiction sought to combat the use of a powerful hero was to create an adversary or villain who was nearly the hero's equal, so that the successful outcome of the hero's battle with evil could remain in doubt until a story's conclusion, and that dramatic tension could be maintained for a longer period and in a more entertaining fashion.

   In the final decade of the nineteenth century, Sir Arthur Conan Doyle helped to refine and focus the development of the villain in popular crime fiction. Conan Doyle intended to kill his popular detective, Sherlock Holmes, with the publication of "The Final Problem" in the December 1893 issue of the *Strand Magazine*. Holmes first appeared in the novel *A Study in Scarlet* in 1887, and though the character provided Conan Doyle with both a devoted readership and a decent income, by 1893 he was ready to move on to what he considered more important work: historical fiction. After he decided to end the profitable but artistically unsatisfying career of Sherlock Holmes, the next question for Conan Doyle was how to pull it off.

Conan Doyle devised a plot that would send Sherlock Holmes out in style. He created a nefarious foe who was an intellectual match for Holmes, and then had the two battle to the death. Conan Doyle's biographer Martin Booth adds that Conan Doyle had his "doubts over the morality" of the Raffles stories penned by his brother-in-law, E. W. Hornung (182). Conan Doyle may have disputed the wisdom of turning a master thief into a hero, but he had no difficulties in creating a master villain of pure evil. Thus, the conclusion of the short story "The Final Problem" finds Sherlock Holmes locked in mortal combat with the wicked professor James Moriarty, the "Napoleon of Crime," both tumbling to their demise in the churning waters of the Reichenbach Falls in Switzerland. If Conan Doyle was going to kill the greatest fictional detective of his time, he needed an opponent of nearly equal status to Holmes to add gravitas to the event.

Eventually, however, Conan Doyle was compelled by his many distraught readers (and perhaps by a much lighter pocketbook) to resurrect Sherlock Holmes, but in a way the Napoleon of Crime also had his moment of triumph. What Conan Doyle did not realize was that in creating Professor Moriarty, he was tapping into a subversive cultural mind-set in readers of popular crime fiction in the late Victorian era, an audience that not only was drawn to the detective hero—who embodied law, order, and social justice—but that also found a type of seditious pleasure in the archvillain—a character that embodied crime, anarchy, and social injustice.

No less a literary giant than George Orwell saw virtue in the rogue protagonist of popular crime fiction. In his essay "Raffles and Miss Blandish," Orwell offers a comparison between the Raffles stories by E. W. Hornung and the James Hadley Chase novel *No Orchids for Miss Blandish* (1939). The latter does not compare favorably in Orwell's view, because it embraces the "sadistic" and "masochistic" elements found in the American pulp magazines of that era, even though Chase was a British author writing for a British audience enduring the London blitz. Specifically, Orwell objects to the morally equivocal representation of crime in the story, where "being a criminal is only reprehensible in the sense that it does not pay" (33). The police employ criminal methods in Chase's novel, Orwell informs his reader, so that there is little difference between crook and cop. Orwell states: "This is a new departure for English sensational fiction, in which till recently there has always been a sharp distinction between right and wrong and a general agreement that virtue must triumph in the last chapter" (33). Grant Allen's Colonel Clay, along with many of the gentlemen crooks and tender con artists inspired by Allen's creation, decidedly avoid the hearty strain of violence found, with a few exceptions, in the dime novels and early pulp fiction magazines of the late nineteenth and early twentieth centuries.

Indeed, during the decades immediately preceding World War I, a number of thief and con-artist protagonists populated the magazines and bookstalls of the day in Great Britain, America, and France: disreputable yet lovable rogues such as E. W. Hornung's A. J. Raffles, Guy Boothby's Simon Carne, Maurice Leblanc's Arsène Lupin, George Randolph Chester's Get-Rich-Quick Wallingford, O. Henry's Jeff Peters, Frederick Irving Anderson's Infallible Godahl, and Edgar Wallace's Four Square Jane, among others. And, as illustrious as is this literary rogues gallery, none of these charming villains holds the distinction of being the first important thief protagonist in popular crime fiction; that honor belongs to Grant Allen's Colonel Cuthbert Clay.

As his professional surname indicates, Colonel Clay is a man of clay, readily transformed into any number of undetectable disguises so that he can better torment and fleece Sir Charles Vandrift. And yet, it is not without accident that the first great rogue protagonist in crime fiction should be a master of disguise. Raffles and Simon Carne were notable gentlemen crooks, Jeff Peters and J. Rufus Wallingford were consummate con artists, while Colonel Clay was fundamentally a master of disguise. Grant Allen readily adopted a prevalent literary motif from nineteenth-century popular fiction in the creation of Colonel Clay. Disguise and elements of deception were common staples in the gothic tales of the late eighteenth century and in the story papers of the early to mid-nineteenth century. Characters in disguise appeared throughout the genres of romance fiction and crime fiction, especially in the detective dime novels and pulp magazines of the late nineteenth and early twentieth centuries. The literary device of disguise that is so pervasive in the developing years of popular fiction can be explained by examining the audience of this type of fiction. The working class and middle class in Europe and America composed the bulk of the readership of mass-produced, mass-consumed escapist fiction, and many professional authors who sought to sell their stories to this readership understood what that audience desired: action, predictable storytelling, easily recognizable protagonists and villains, and plot twists that revolved around disguise and deception. One of the driving ambitions of an evolving working class and middle class, especially in America, was the desire to achieve a higher level of wealth and social status. The motif of disguise in popular fiction catered to this ambition in stories purchased for escapist entertainment. Readers, especially readers of crime tales, could thrill to the adventures of heroes, villains, and other characters who were not what they appeared to be, thus satisfying a deep psychological desire to be someone different, better, more exciting, and ultimately more fulfilling. Grant Allen, it seems, understood this essential psychological need in his audience, and therefore when he fabricated a rogue protagonist in Colonel Clay for what he hoped would be a popular series of crime stories, he developed a fascinating master of disguise to meet that need.

Colonel Clay appeared in twelve linked short stories that first ran in the pages of *The Strand Magazine* between 1896 and 1897. These stories were later collected in a single hardcover volume published in 1897 entitled *An African Millionaire: Episodes in the Life of the Illustrious Colonel Clay*, as a type of novel—a common practice among professional authors of fiction who sought to enhance their income by first publishing their thematically linked stories in periodicals such as the *Strand Magazine* and then collecting the stories into a hardcover book for a new round of sales and royalty checks.

The reader is told in the first story of *An African Millionaire*, entitled "The Episode of the Mexican Seer," that Colonel Clay is both feared and admired by the police. In the various settings of the rich and famous (or infamous), emblematic of the wealthy capitalists' undeserved economic privilege, he is a wolf disguised in sheep's clothing among sheep who need to be sheared of their jewelry and cash. He is a con artist who outcons a notorious capitalist con artist. The irony in all the Colonel Clay stories is that Sir Charles is aware that he is about to be conned and sees the crime as a challenge, with a presupposition that, as a successful capitalist, he is a better con artist than Colonel Clay. Typically, Sir Charles expects one con, but to his surprise gets another that completely fools him.

The supporting cast of characters in *An African Millionaire* is as amusing, and as flawed, as Sir Charles. Seymour Wentworth, or Sey, is a marvelous narrator, offering a number of astute and humorous asides about his employer and his employer's ego, all while simultaneously keeping in the good graces of his arrogant brother-in-law. As a minor crook himself, he is less than successful in his own financial schemes, as seen in "The Episode of the Tyrolean Castle" when Sey attempts to profit via commission from the sale of a castle as part of a scheme by Colonel Clay. Of course, the castle in question is not really up for sale, and Sey is embarrassed when he realizes that his employer and benefactor may later discover his greedy deception. (In several of the later stories, Colonel Clay uses Sey's fear of being found out to taunt and ridicule the hapless secretary and personal assistant.)

Sir Charles's wife, Lady Amelia Vandrift, is likewise comical as Sir Charles's occasional coconspirator in unethical business ventures. In "The Episode of the Tyrolean Castle," Sey informs the reader in his at times acidic tongue that the seemingly highborn wife of the wealthy South African millionaire and financier is "a confirmed Cockney." Later, Sey goes on to note that Amelia professes an aristocratic and romantic fancy, all of which paints her as a hypocrite and a social climber—faults that Colonel Clay takes advantage of with glee. In "The Episode of the Old Bailey," for example, following the capture of Colonel Clay and his unmasking as the plebeian-sounding Paul Finglemore, Amelia pleads with Sey to help her see that Césarine, her maid (who turns out to be one of Colonel Clay's two female accomplices), not be arrested, because of the embarrassment it may cause. "I assure you, Seymour, the thing's not to be dreamt of," Amelia proclaims. "There are details of a lady's life—known only to her maid—which *cannot* be made public." The reader wonders at this point what juicy secrets Amelia is attempting to hide. And, amusingly, this conversation occurs just after Sir Charles similarly informs Sey that he, Sir Charles, "cannot consent to be a party to the arrest of White Heather," the other female accomplice of Colonel Clay's, an attractive woman who has in the past manipulated the South African millionaire with her wiles. Sir Charles does not want to be humiliated in court by exposure of his attraction to White Heather. Sey informs the reader: "Indeed, I must allow that under whatever disguise White Heather appeared to us, Charles was always that disguise's devoted slave from the first moment he met it. It occurred to me, therefore, that the clever little woman—call her what you will—might be the holder of more than one indiscreet communication." Though both husband and wife feel guilty about their indiscretions with Colonel Clay's female accomplices, they each condemn the actions of the other woman not directly involved with their indiscretions. Yes, Sir Charles is a romantic fool where love is concerned, and is exploited by Colonel Clay for being something of a cad, but Amelia is equally guilty of unstated indiscretions. Crass hypocrisy is thus drolly layered on Charles's and Amelia's feelings of culpability and shame.

In the end, Colonel Clay is never caught by his adversary, Charles Vandrift. Sey almost nabs him at one point in "The Episode of the Game of Poker," but literally cannot hold his grasp on the fleeing rogue. Both Sir Charles and Sey continually fail in their assorted comical attempts to capture him. The only thing that finally brings Colonel Clay's career to an end is science or, more specifically, the application of a scientific method of personal identification. Since the author of *An African Millionaire* was himself a proponent of science and an author of numerous scientific texts, it makes perfect sense in the Colonel Clay stories that lesser intellects cannot capture a greater intellect. Only science can achieve what mere human ingenuity fails to accomplish. In "The Episode of the Bertillon Method," when the scientist, Dr. Beddersley, helps to detect the slippery Colonel Clay, the scoundrel announces: "If *you've* tracked me strictly in accordance with Bertillon's methods, I don't mind so much. I will not yield to fools; I yield to science." The statement is meant to be both an insult to Sir Charles and homage paid to scientific knowledge (or what was then considered scientific knowledge: Alphonse Bertillon [1853–1914] was a French criminologist who devised a system by which individuals could be identified and recorded by their physical measurements.)

The final chapter of *An African Millionaire* and the resolution of Colonel Clay's escapades, entitled "The Episode of the Old Bailey," resounds with the author's condemnation of Sir Charles and with the martyrdom of Paul Finglemore, Colonel Clay's actual name. Ostensibly on trial for his crimes, Colonel Clay assumes his own defense and cross-examines his nemesis, Sir Charles Vandrift, essentially turning the tables and placing Sir Charles on trial in the court of public opinion for his various transgressions in the world of cutthroat finance. Sir Charles is made to face his unethical attempt to purchase fine diamonds for the price of worthless paste ("The Episode of the Diamond Links"), his desire to acquire the rights to a lucrative gold mine by amalgamating his essentially worthless section of the mine with a rival's valuable section ("The Episode of the Seldon Gold-Mine"), and his vile effort to unload what he thought was worthless stock in his diamond mine before stockholders were alerted to the danger of their holdings ("The Episode of the German Professor"). In each instance, Colonel Clay outfoxes the real crook, Sir Charles, humiliating the greedy financier as well as fleecing him of his ill-gotten wealth. The judge sums up the case against Colonel Clay by saying that even the "richest— and vilest—of men must be protected" and that if a "rogue cheated a rogue, he must still be punished." Colonel Clay faces his fate bravely, while the disgraced and humbled Sir Charles yet envies the loving devotion of Colonel Clay's two female assistants—a devotion that he himself will never know from others.

Ultimately, Grant Allen's *An African Millionaire* offers a type of working-class fantasy of revenge, packaged within the innocuous wrappings of popular crime fiction. Though the detective hero, as a symbol of law and order, reigned in the popular press of the late-Victorian and Edwardian periods in Europe and America, during the decade and a half before World War I, the rogue, the gentleman thief, and the con artist lurked prominently nearby in the shadows of the police station, just out of direct sight and ready to foil the designs of both society and the authorities. These heroic villains held a kind of bipolar, divergent, yet strangely intertwined appeal for their audiences, who were attracted not only to law and the detective, but also to crime and the criminal. And yet, in creating Colonel Clay as the first rogue protagonist in crime fiction, Grant Allen also placed his own unique stamp on the character. As you read the various Colonel Clay adventures, you will note that Allen employs a sophisticated game metaphor throughout in which there exists a battle of minds between rogues of different classes and social standing, where Colonel Clay, as an emblem of the oppressed working class, triumphs time and again against his idiotic counterpart, Sir Charles Vandrift, who is emblematic of the obtuse capitalist exploiter—until the conclusion of *An African Millionaire*, during which Allen finally submits to the social expectations of his readers by having Colonel Clay apprehended and tried for his various crimes. As escapist and satiric fiction, *An African Millionaire* stops short of being entirely subversive.

Summarizing Grant Allen's place in literature, Peter Morton states: "He straddles so many different areas in the literary culture of his day. He is the skilled marketer of popular fiction; the dedicated but unaffiliated scholar, reckless of his time and energy. . . . And, most dramatic of all, the idealistic social reformer half-willing to immolate his own career for the sake of having his radical say" (3–4). Speaking directly about *An African Millionaire*, Nick Freeman notes that "Allen was not known as a humorous writer although he had explored most genres of popular fiction and would later show a facility for caddish wit in his 'Colonel Clay' stories" (112). And as his biographer, Edward Clodd, summarizes in *Grant Allen: A Memoir*: "Few living men have undertaken so bewildering a range of studies—ever had, to use a homely expression, so many irons in the fire—irons, be it said, of strange incongruity and divergence. . . . His eagerness to be ever learning was equaled only by his willingness to impart all that he knew" (205–6). Grant Allen possessed a complex and diverse intellect. Sadly, much of the knowledge that Allen conveyed to his readers during his lifetime now resides in the dim obscurity of the past, a mere historical footnote, but at least one of his books has achieved lasting fame among those who admire a well-told story that has long outlived the naturalist, the scientist, the historian, and the writer of ephemeral melodrama.

Certainly, Grant Allen's *An African Millionaire* is variously comical, satirical, subversive, and humorous, but primarily it is entertaining. Each story builds on the previous one, and the reader is as challenged as the befuddled Sir Charles as to how the infinitely resourceful Colonel Clay will carry out his next ingenious scheme. Allen has created in the book you now hold his single lasting work of fiction: an influential, episodic literary masterpiece that established an archetypal literary character in Colonel Clay, a lovable rogue who helped to influence a generation of crime writers to follow. *An African Millionaire* also recalls for the contemporary reader an era of both ostentatious wealth and great economic disparity, and a protagonist who sought to gently mock the intellectually dull champion of unrestrained capitalism and pretentious aspirations to social class—Sir Charles Vandrift—and the rather silly excesses of wealth and privilege that Sir Charles represented in the British Empire at the turn of the twentieth century. Perhaps its message from over a hundred years ago still holds relevance today as a metaphor for unrestrained and unrepentant Wall Street greed. If not, *An African Millionaire* undoubtedly remains a vastly engaging and amusing read and a beloved classic in the field of crime fiction. Enjoy.

GARY HOPPENSTAND

Works Cited

Allen, Grant. "Preface." *Strange Stories*. London: Chatto & Windus, 1890.

Booth, Martin. *The Doctor and the Detective: A Biography of Sir Arthur Conan Diyle*. New York: Thomas Dunne Books / St. Martin's Minotaur, 1997.

Clodd, Edward. *Grant Allen: A Memoir (with a Bibliography)*. London: Grant Richards, 1900.

Freeman, Nick. "'Intentional Rudeness'? *The British Barbarians* and the Cultural Politics of 1895." In *Grant Allen: Literature and Cultural Politics at the Fin de Siècle*. Edited by William Greenslade and Terence Rodgers. Aldershot, Hants, England: Ashgate, 2005.

Merriman, C. D. "Grant Allen." *The Literature Network*. June 17, 2011. http://www.online-literature.com/grant-allen/.

Morton, Peter. *"The Busiest Man in England": Grant Allen and the Writing Trade, 1875–1900*. New York: Palgrave Macmillan, 2005.

Orwell, George. "Raffles and Miss Blandish." In *The Complete Short Stories of Raffles—the Amateur Cracksman*. By E. W. Hornung. New York: St. Martin's Press, 1984.

Rozendal, Phyllis. "Grant Allen." *Dictionary of Literary Biography*. Vol. 70, *British Mystery Writers, 1860–1919*. Edited by Bernard Benstock and Thomas F. Staley. Detroit: Gale Research, 1988.

Ruddick, Nicholas. "Grant Allen." *Dictionary of Literary Biography*. Vol. 178, *British Fantasy and Science-Fiction Writers Before World War I*. Edited by Darren Harris-Fain. Detroit: Gale Research, 1997.

St. Pierre, Paul Matthew. "Grant Allen." *Dictionary of Literary Biography*. Vol. 92, *Canadian Writers, 1890–1920*. Edited by William H. New. Detroit: Gale Research, 1990.

Steinbrunner, Chris, and Otto Penzler. *Encyclopedia of Mystery and Detection*. San Diego, CA: Harvest/HBJ, 1976.

Suggestions for Further Reading

William L. DeAndrea, *Encyclopedia Mysteriosa: A Comprehensive Guide to the Art of Detection in Print, Film, Radio, and Television* (New York: Prentice Hall, 1994).

Ralph Harper, *The World of the Thriller* (Cleveland: Case Western Reserve University Press, 1969).

Howard Haycraft, *Murder for Pleasure: The Life and Times of the Detective Story* (D. Appleton-Century Company, 1941).

Tony Hilfer, *The Crime Novel: A Deviant Genre* (Austin, TX: University of Texas Press, 1990).

Jerry Palmer, *Thrillers: Genesis and Structure of a Popular Genre* (New York: St. Martin's Press, 1979).

Linden Peach, *Masquerade, Crime and Fiction: Criminal Deceptions* (New York: Palgrave Macmillan, 2006).

Charles J. Rzepka, *Detective Fiction* (Malden, MA: Polity Press, 2005).

Robert Sampson, *Yesterday's Faces: A Study of Series Characters in the Early Pulp Magazines, Volume I—Glory Figures* (Bowling Green, OH: Bowling Green University Popular Press, 1983).

Michael Sims, ed. *The Penguin Book of Gaslight Crime* (New York: Penguin Books, 2009).

Colin Watson, *Snobbery with Violence: Crime Stories and Their Audience* (New York: St. Martin's Press, 1971).

An African Millionaire

I

THE EPISODE OF THE MEXICAN SEER

My name is Seymour Wilbraham Wentworth. I am brother-in-law and secretary to Sir Charles Vandrift, the South African millionaire and famous financier. Many years ago, when Charlie Vandrift was a small lawyer in Cape Town, I had the (qualified) good fortune to marry his sister. Much later, when the Vandrift estate and farm near Kimberley developed by degrees into the Cloetedorp Golcondas, Limited, my brother-in-law offered me the not unremunerative post of secretary; in which capacity I have ever since been his constant and attached companion.

He is not a man whom any common sharper can take in, is Charles Vandrift. Middle height, square build, firm mouth, keen eyes—the very picture of a sharp and successful business genius. I have only known one rogue impose upon Sir Charles, and that one rogue, as the Commissary of Police at Nice remarked, would doubtless have imposed upon a syndicate of Vidocq, Robert Houdin, and Cagliostro.

We had run across to the Riviera for a few weeks in the season. Our object being strictly rest and recreation from the arduous duties of financial combination, we did not think it necessary to take our wives out with us. Indeed, Lady Vandrift is absolutely wedded to the joys of London, and does not appreciate the rural delights of the Mediterranean littoral. But Sir Charles and I, though immersed in affairs when at home, both thoroughly enjoy the complete change from the City to the charming vegetation and pellucid air on the terrace at Monte Carlo. We *are* so fond of scenery. That delicious view over the rocks of Monaco, with the Maritime Alps in the rear, and the blue sea in front, not to mention the imposing Casino in the foreground, appeals to me as one of the most beautiful prospects in all Europe. Sir Charles has a sentimental attachment for the place. He finds it restores and freshens him, after the turmoil of London, to win a few hundreds at roulette in the course of an afternoon among the palms and cactuses and pure breezes of Monte Carlo. The country, say I, for a jaded intellect! However, we never on any account actually stop in the Principality itself. Sir Charles thinks Monte Carlo is not a sound address for a financier's letters. He prefers a comfortable hotel on the Promenade des Anglais at Nice, where he recovers health and renovates his nervous system by taking daily excursions along the coast to the Casino.

This particular season we were snugly ensconced at the Hôtel des Anglais. We had capital quarters on the first floor—salon, study, and bedrooms—and found on the spot a most agreeable cosmopolitan society. All Nice, just then, was ringing with talk about a curious impostor, known to his followers as the Great Mexican Seer, and supposed to be gifted with second sight, as well as with endless other supernatural powers. Now, it is a peculiarity of my able brother-in-law's that, when he meets with a quack, he burns to expose him; he is so keen a man of business himself that it gives him, so to speak, a disinterested pleasure to unmask and detect imposture in others. Many ladies at the hotel, some of whom had met and conversed with the Mexican Seer, were constantly telling us strange stories of his doings. He had disclosed to one the present whereabouts of a runaway husband; he had pointed out to another the numbers that would win at roulette next evening; he had shown a third the image on a screen of the man she had for years adored without his knowledge. Of course, Sir Charles didn't believe a word of it; but his curiosity was roused; he wished to see and judge for himself of the wonderful thought-reader.

'What would be his terms, do you think, for a private *séance*?' he asked of Madame Picardet, the lady to whom the Seer had successfully predicted the winning numbers.

'He does not work for money,' Madame Picardet answered,

'but for the good of humanity. I'm sure he would gladly come and exhibit for nothing his miraculous faculties.'

'Nonsense!' Sir Charles answered. 'The man must live. I'd pay him five guineas, though, to see him alone. What hotel is he stopping at?'

'The Cosmopolitan, I think,' the lady answered. 'Oh no; I remember now, the Westminster.'

Sir Charles turned to me quietly. 'Look here, Seymour,' he whispered. 'Go round to this fellow's place immediately after dinner, and offer him five pounds to give a private *séance* at once in my rooms, without mentioning who I am to him; keep the name quite quiet. Bring him back with you, too, and come straight upstairs with him, so that there may be no collusion. We'll see just how much the fellow can tell us.'

I went as directed. I found the Seer a very remarkable and interesting person. He stood about Sir Charles's own height, but was slimmer and straighter, with an aquiline nose, strangely piercing eyes, very large black pupils, and a finely-chiselled close-shaven face, like the bust of Antinous in our hall in Mayfair. What gave him his most characteristic touch, however, was his odd head of hair, curly and wavy like Paderewski's, standing out in a halo round his high white forehead and his delicate profile. I could see at a glance why he succeeded so well in impressing women; he had the look of a poet, a singer, a prophet.

'I have come round,' I said, 'to ask whether you will consent to give a *séance* at once in a friend's rooms; and my principal wishes me to add that he is prepared to pay five pounds as the price of the entertainment.'

Señor Antonio Herrera—that was what he called himself—bowed to me with impressive Spanish politeness. His dusky olive cheeks were wrinkled with a smile of gentle contempt as he answered gravely—

'I do not sell my gifts; I bestow them freely. If your friend—your anonymous friend—desires to behold the cosmic wonders that are wrought through my hands, I am glad to show them to him. Fortunately, as often happens when it is necessary to convince and confound a sceptic (for that your friend is a sceptic I feel instinctively), I chance to have no engagements at all this evening.' He ran his hand through his fine, long hair reflectively. 'Yes, I go,' he continued, as if addressing some unknown presence that hovered about the ceiling; 'I go; come with me!' Then he put on his broad sombrero, with its crimson ribbon, wrapped a cloak round his shoulders, lighted a cigarette, and strode forth by my side towards the Hôtel des Anglais.

He talked little by the way, and that little in curt sentences. He seemed buried in deep thought; indeed, when we reached the door and I turned in, he walked a step or two farther on, as if not noticing to what place I had brought him. Then he drew himself up short, and gazed around him for a moment. 'Ha, the Anglais,' he said—and I may mention in passing that his English, in spite of a slight southern accent, was idiomatic and excellent. 'It is here, then; it is here!' He was addressing once more the unseen presence.

I smiled to think that these childish devices were intended to deceive Sir Charles Vandrift. Not quite the sort of man (as the City of London knows) to be taken in by hocus-pocus. And all this, I saw, was the cheapest and most commonplace conjurer's patter.

We went upstairs to our rooms. Charles had gathered together a few friends to watch the performance. The Seer entered, wrapt in thought. He was in evening dress, but a red sash round his waist gave a touch of picturesqueness and a dash of colour. He paused for a moment in the middle of the salon, without letting his eyes rest on anybody or anything. Then he walked straight up to Charles, and held out his dark hand.

'Good-evening,' he said. 'You are the host. My soul's sight tells me so.'

'Good shot,' Sir Charles answered. 'These fellows have to be quick-witted, you know, Mrs. Mackenzie, or they'd never get on at it.'

The Seer gazed about him, and smiled blankly at a person or two whose faces he seemed to recognise from a previous existence. Then Charles began to ask him a few simple questions, not about himself, but about me, just to test him. He answered most of them with surprising correctness. 'His name? His name begins with an *S* I think:—You call him Seymour.' He paused long between each clause, as if the facts were revealed to him slowly. 'Seymour—Wilbraham—Earl of Strafford. No, not Earl of Strafford! Seymour Wilbraham Wentworth. There seems to be some connection in somebody's mind now present between Wentworth and Strafford. I am not English. I do not know what it means. But they are somehow the same name, Wentworth and Strafford.'

He gazed around, apparently for confirmation. A lady came to his rescue.

'Wentworth was the surname of the great Earl of Strafford,' she murmured gently; 'and I was wondering, as you spoke, whether Mr. Wentworth might possibly be descended from him.'

'He is,' the Seer replied instantly, with a flash of those dark eyes. And I thought this curious; for though my father always maintained the reality of the relationship, there was one link wanting to complete the pedigree. He could not make sure that the Hon. Thomas Wilbraham Wentworth was the father of Jonathan Wentworth, the Bristol horse-dealer, from whom we are descended.

'Where was I born?' Sir Charles interrupted, coming suddenly to his own case.

The Seer clapped his two hands to his forehead and held it between them, as if to prevent it from bursting. 'Africa,' he said slowly, as the facts narrowed down, so to speak. 'South Africa; Cape of Good Hope; Jansenville; De Witt Street. 1840.'

'By Jove, he's correct,' Sir Charles muttered. 'He seems really to do it. Still, he may have found me out. He may have known where he was coming.'

'I never gave a hint,' I answered; 'till he reached the door, he didn't even know to what hotel I was piloting him.'

The Seer stroked his chin softly. His eye appeared to me to have a furtive gleam in it. 'Would you like me to tell you the number of a bank-note inclosed in an envelope?' he asked casually.

'Go out of the room,' Sir Charles said, 'while I pass it round the company.'

Señor Herrera disappeared. Sir Charles passed it round cautiously, holding it all the time in his own hand, but letting his guests see the number. Then he placed it in an envelope and gummed it down firmly.

The Seer returned. His keen eyes swept the company with a comprehensive glance. He shook his shaggy mane. Then he took the envelope in his hands and gazed at it fixedly. 'AF, 73549,' he answered, in a slow tone. 'A Bank of England note for fifty pounds—exchanged at the Casino for gold won yesterday at Monte Carlo.'

'I see how he did that,' Sir Charles said triumphantly. 'He must have changed it there himself; and then I changed it back again. In point of fact, I remember seeing a fellow with long hair loafing about. Still, it's capital conjuring.'

'He can see through matter,' one of the ladies interposed. It was Madame Picardet. 'He can see through a box.' She drew a little gold vinaigrette, such as our grandmothers used, from her dress-pocket. 'What is in this?' she inquired, holding it up to him.

Señor Herrera gazed through it. 'Three gold coins,' he replied, knitting his brows with the effort of seeing into the box: 'one, an American five dollars; one, a French ten-franc piece; one, twenty marks, German, of the old Emperor William.'

She opened the box and passed it round. Sir Charles smiled a quiet smile.

'Confederacy!' he muttered, half to himself. 'Confederacy!'

The Seer turned to him with a sullen air. 'You want a better sign?' he said, in a very impressive voice. 'A sign that will convince you! Very well: you have a letter in your left waistcoat pocket—a crumpled-up letter. Do you wish me to read it out? I will, if you desire it.'

It may seem to those who know Sir Charles incredible, but, I am bound to admit, my brother-in-law coloured. What that letter contained I cannot say; he only answered, very testily and evasively, 'No, thank you; I won't trouble you. The exhibition you have already given us of your skill in this kind more than amply suffices.' And his fingers strayed nervously to his waistcoat pocket, as if he was half afraid, even then, Señor Herrera would read it.

I fancied, too, he glanced somewhat anxiously towards Madame Picardet.

The Seer bowed courteously. 'Your will, señor, is law,' he said. 'I make it a principle, though I can see through all things, invariably to respect the secrecies and sanctities. If it were not so, I might dissolve society. For which of us is there who could bear the whole truth being told about him?' He gazed around the room. An unpleasant thrill supervened. Most of us felt this uncanny Spanish American knew really too much. And some of us were engaged in financial operations.

'For example,' the Seer continued blandly, 'I happened a few weeks ago to travel down here from Paris by train with a very intelligent man, a company promoter. He had in his bag some documents—some confidential documents.' He glanced at Sir Charles. 'You know the kind of thing, my dear sir: reports from experts—from mining engineers. You may have seen some such; marked *strictly private*.'

'They form an element in high finance,' Sir Charles admitted coldly.

'Pre-cisely,' the Seer murmured, his accent for a moment less Spanish than before. 'And, as they were marked *strictly private*, I respect, of course, the seal of confidence. That's all I wish to say. I hold it a duty, being intrusted with such powers, not to use them in a manner which may annoy or incommode my fellow-creatures.'

'Your feeling does you honour,' Sir Charles answered, with some acerbity. Then he whispered in my ear: 'Confounded clever scoundrel, Sey; rather wish we hadn't brought him here.'

Señor Herrera seemed intuitively to divine this wish, for he interposed, in a lighter and gayer tone—

'I will now show you a different and more interesting embodiment of occult power, for which we shall need a somewhat subdued arrangement of surrounding lights. Would you mind, señor host—for I have purposely abstained from reading

your name on the brain of any one present—would you mind
my turning down this lamp just a little? . . . So! That will do.
Now, this one; and this one. Exactly! That's right.' He poured
a few grains of powder out of a packet into a saucer. 'Next, a
match, if you please. Thank you!' It burnt with a strange green
light. He drew from his pocket a card, and produced a little
ink-bottle. 'Have you a pen?' he asked.

I instantly brought one. He handed it to Sir Charles. 'Oblige
me,' he said, 'by writing your name there.' And he indicated a
place in the centre of the card, which had an embossed edge,
with a small middle square of a different colour.

Sir Charles has a natural disinclination to signing his name
without knowing why. 'What do you want with it?' he asked.
(A millionaire's signature has so many uses.)

'I want you to put the card in an envelope,' the Seer replied,
'and then to burn it. After that, I shall show you your own
name written in letters of blood on my arm, in your own handwriting.'

Sir Charles took the pen. If the signature was to be burned
as soon as finished, he didn't mind giving it. He wrote his
name in his usual firm clear style—the writing of a man who
knows his worth and is not afraid of drawing a cheque for five
thousand.

'Look at it long,' the Seer said, from the other side of the
room. He had not watched him write it.

Sir Charles stared at it fixedly. The Seer was really beginning to produce an impression.

'Now, put it in that envelope,' the Seer exclaimed.

Sir Charles, like a lamb, placed it as directed.

The Seer strode forward. 'Give me the envelope,' he said. He
took it in his hand, walked over towards the fireplace, and solemnly burnt it. 'See—it crumbles into ashes,' he cried. Then he
came back to the middle of the room, close to the green light,
rolled up his sleeve, and held his arm before Sir Charles. There,
in blood-red letters, my brother-in-law read the name, 'Charles
Vandrift,' in his own handwriting!

'I see how that's done,' Sir Charles murmured, drawing back.
'It's a clever delusion; but still, I see through it. It's like that

ghost-book. Your ink was deep green; your light was green; you made me look at it long; and then I saw the same thing written on the skin of your arm in complementary colours.'

'You think so?' the Seer replied, with a curious curl of the lip.

'I'm sure of it,' Sir Charles answered.

Quick as lightning the Seer again rolled up his sleeve. 'That's your name,' he cried, in a very clear voice, 'but not your whole name. What do you say, then, to my right? Is this one also a complementary colour?' He held his other arm out. There, in sea-green letters, I read the name, 'Charles O'Sullivan Vandrift.' It is my brother-in-law's full baptismal designation; but he has dropped the O'Sullivan for many years past, and, to say the truth, doesn't like it. He is a little bit ashamed of his mother's family.

Charles glanced at it hurriedly. 'Quite right,' he said, 'quite right!' But his voice was hollow. I could guess he didn't care to continue the *séance*. He could see through the man, of course; but it was clear the fellow knew too much about us to be entirely pleasant.

'Turn up the lights,' I said, and a servant turned them. 'Shall I say coffee and benedictine?' I whispered to Vandrift.

'By all means,' he answered. 'Anything to keep this fellow from further impertinences! And, I say, don't you think you'd better suggest at the same time that the men should smoke? Even these ladies are not above a cigarette—some of them.'

There was a sigh of relief. The lights burned brightly. The Seer for the moment retired from business, so to speak. He accepted a partaga with a very good grace, sipped his coffee in a corner, and chatted to the lady who had suggested Strafford with marked politeness. He was a polished gentleman.

Next morning, in the hall of the hotel, I saw Madame Picardet again, in a neat tailor-made travelling dress, evidently bound for the railway-station.

'What, off, Madame Picardet?' I cried.

She smiled, and held out her prettily-gloved hand. 'Yes, I'm off,' she answered archly. 'Florence, or Rome, or somewhere. I've drained Nice dry—like a sucked orange. Got all the fun I can out of it. Now I'm away again to my beloved Italy.'

But it struck me as odd that, if Italy was her game, she went by the omnibus which takes down to the *train de luxe* for Paris. However, a man of the world accepts what a lady tells him, no matter how improbable; and I confess, for ten days or so, I thought no more about her, or the Seer either.

At the end of that time our fortnightly pass-book came in from the bank in London. It is part of my duty, as the millionaire's secretary, to make up this book once a fortnight, and to compare the cancelled cheques with Sir Charles's counterfoils. On this particular occasion I happened to observe what I can only describe as a very grave discrepancy,—in fact, a discrepancy of £5000. On the wrong side, too. Sir Charles was debited with £5000 more than the total amount that was shown on the counterfoils.

I examined the book with care. The source of the error was obvious. It lay in a cheque to Self or Bearer, for £5000, signed by Sir Charles, and evidently paid across the counter in London, as it bore on its face no stamp or indication of any other office.

I called in my brother-in-law from the salon to the study. 'Look here, Charles,' I said, 'there's a cheque in the book which you haven't entered.' And I handed it to him without comment, for I thought it might have been drawn to settle some little loss on the turf or at cards, or to make up some other affair he didn't desire to mention to me. These things will happen.

He looked at it and stared hard. Then he pursed up his mouth and gave a long low 'Whew!' At last he turned it over and remarked, 'I say, Sey, my boy, we've just been done jolly well brown, haven't we?'

I glanced at the cheque. 'How do you mean?' I inquired.

'Why, the Seer,' he replied, still staring at it ruefully. 'I don't mind the five thou., but to think the fellow should have gammoned the pair of us like that—ignominious, I call it!'

'How do you know it's the Seer?' I asked.

'Look at the green ink,' he answered. 'Besides, I recollect the very shape of the last flourish. I flourished a bit like that in the excitement of the moment, which I don't always do with my regular signature.'

'He's done us,' I answered, recognising it. 'But how the dickens did he manage to transfer it to the cheque? This looks like your own handwriting, Charles, not a clever forgery.'

'It is,' he said. 'I admit it—I can't deny it. Only fancy his bamboozling me when I was most on my guard! I wasn't to be taken in by any of his silly occult tricks and catch-words; but it never occurred to me he was going to victimise me financially in this way. I expected attempts at a loan or an extortion; but to collar my signature to a blank cheque—atrocious!'

'How did he manage it?' I asked.

'I haven't the faintest conception. I only know those are the words I wrote. I could swear to them anywhere.'

'Then you can't protest the cheque?'

'Unfortunately, no; it's my own true signature.'

We went that afternoon without delay to see the Chief Commissary of Police at the office. He was a gentlemanly Frenchman, much less formal and red-tapey than usual, and he spoke excellent English with an American accent, having acted, in fact, as a detective in New York for about ten years in his early manhood.

'I guess,' he said slowly, after hearing our story, 'you've been victimised right here by Colonel Clay, gentlemen.'

'Who is Colonel Clay?' Sir Charles asked.

'That's just what I want to know,' the Commissary answered, in his curious American-French-English. 'He is a Colonel, because he occasionally gives himself a commission; he is called Colonel Clay, because he appears to possess an india-rubber face, and he can mould it like clay in the hands of the potter. Real name, unknown. Nationality, equally French and English. Address, usually Europe. Profession, former maker of wax figures to the Musée Grévin. Age, what he chooses. Employs his knowledge to mould his own nose and cheeks, with wax additions, to the character he desires to personate. Aquiline this time, you say. *Hein!* Anything like these photographs?'

He rummaged in his desk and handed us two.

'Not in the least,' Sir Charles answered. 'Except, perhaps, as to the neck, everything here is quite unlike him.'

'Then that's the Colonel!' the Commissary answered, with decision, rubbing his hands in glee. 'Look here,' and he took out a pencil and rapidly sketched the outline of one of the two faces—that of a bland-looking young man, with no expression worth mentioning. 'There's the Colonel in his simple disguise. Very good. Now watch me: figure to yourself that he adds here a tiny patch of wax to his nose—an aquiline bridge—just so; well, you have him right there; and the chin, ah, one touch: now, for hair, a wig: for complexion, nothing easier: that's the profile of your rascal, isn't it?'

'Exactly,' we both murmured. By two curves of the pencil, and a shock of false hair, the face was transmuted.

'He had very large eyes, with very big pupils, though,' I objected, looking close; 'and the man in the photograph here has them small and boiled-fishy.'

'That's so,' the Commissary answered. 'A drop of bella-donna expands—and produces the Seer; five grains of opium contract—and give a dead-alive, stupidly-innocent appear-ance. Well, you leave this affair to me, gentlemen. I'll see the fun out. I don't say I'll catch him for you; nobody ever yet has caught Colonel Clay; but I'll explain how he did the trick; and that ought to be consolation enough to a man of your means for a trifle of five thousand!'

'You are not the conventional French office-holder, M. le Commissaire,' I ventured to interpose.

'You bet!' the Commissary replied, and drew himself up like a captain of infantry. 'Messieurs,' he continued, in French, with the utmost dignity, 'I shall devote the resources of this office to tracing out the crime, and, if possible, to effectuating the arrest of the culpable.'

We telegraphed to London, of course, and we wrote to the bank, with a full description of the suspected person. But I need hardly add that nothing came of it.

Three days later the Commissary called at our hotel. 'Well, gentlemen,' he said, 'I am glad to say I have discovered every-thing!'

'What? Arrested the Seer?' Sir Charles cried.

The Commissary drew back, almost horrified at the suggestion.

'Arrested Colonel Clay?' he exclaimed. '*Mais*, monsieur, we are only human! Arrested him? No, not quite. But tracked out how he did it. That is already much—to unravel Colonel Clay, gentlemen!'

'Well, what do you make of it?' Sir Charles asked, crestfallen.

The Commissary sat down and gloated over his discovery. It was clear a well-planned crime amused him vastly. 'In the first place, monsieur,' he said, 'disabuse your mind of the idea that when monsieur your secretary went out to fetch Señor Herrera that night, Señor Herrera didn't know to whose rooms he was coming. Quite otherwise, in point of fact. I do not doubt myself that Señor Herrera, or Colonel Clay (call him which you like), came to Nice this winter for no other purpose than just to rob you.'

'But I sent for him,' my brother-in-law interposed.

'Yes; he *meant* you to send for him. He forced a card, so to speak. If he couldn't do that I guess he would be a pretty poor conjurer. He had a lady of his own—his wife, let us say, or his sister—stopping here at this hotel; a certain Madame Picardet. Through her he induced several ladies of your circle to attend his *séances*. She and they spoke to you about him, and aroused your curiosity. You may bet your bottom dollar that when he came to this room he came ready primed and prepared with endless facts about both of you.'

'What fools we have been, Sey,' my brother-in-law exclaimed. 'I see it all now. That designing woman sent round before dinner to say I wanted to meet him; and by the time you got there he was ready for bamboozling me.'

'That's so,' the Commissary answered. 'He had your name ready painted on both his arms; and he had made other preparations of still greater importance.'

'You mean the cheque. Well, how did he get it?'

The Commissary opened the door. 'Come in,' he said. And a young man entered whom we recognised at once as the chief clerk in the Foreign Department of the Crédit Marseillais, the principal bank all along the Riviera.

'State what you know of this cheque,' the Commissary said, showing it to him, for we had handed it over to the police as a piece of evidence.

'About four weeks since——' the clerk began.

'Say ten days before your *séance*,' the Commissary interposed.

'A gentleman with very long hair and an aquiline nose, dark, strange, and handsome, called in at my department and asked if I could tell him the name of Sir Charles Vandrift's London banker. He said he had a sum to pay in to your credit, and asked if we would forward it for him. I told him it was irregular for us to receive the money, as you had no account with us, but that your London bankers were Darby, Drummond, and Rothenberg, Limited.'

'Quite right,' Sir Charles murmured.

'Two days later a lady, Madame Picardet, who was a customer of ours, brought in a good cheque for three hundred pounds, signed by a first-rate name, and asked us to pay it in on her behalf to Darby, Drummond, and Rothenberg's, and to open a London account with them for her. We did so, and received in reply a cheque-book.'

'From which this cheque was taken, as I learn from the number, by telegram from London,' the Commissary put in. 'Also, that on the same day on which your cheque was cashed, Madame Picardet, in London, withdrew her balance.'

'But how did the fellow get me to sign the cheque?' Sir Charles cried. 'How did he manage the card trick?'

The Commissary produced a similar card from his pocket. 'Was that the sort of thing?' he asked.

'Precisely! A facsimile.'

'I thought so. Well, our Colonel, I find, bought a packet of such cards, intended for admission to a religious function, at a shop in the Quai Masséna. He cut out the centre, and, see here——' The Commissary turned it over, and showed a piece of paper pasted neatly over the back; this he tore off, and there, concealed behind it, lay a folded cheque, with only the place where the signature should be written showing through on the face which the Seer had presented to us. 'I call that a neat trick,' the Commissary remarked, with professional enjoyment of a really good deception.

'But he burnt the envelope before my eyes,' Sir Charles exclaimed.

'Pooh!' the Commissary answered. 'What would he be worth as a conjurer, anyway, if he couldn't substitute one envelope for another between the table and the fireplace without your noticing it? And Colonel Clay, you must remember, is a prince among conjurers.'

'Well, it's a comfort to know we've identified our man, and the woman who was with him,' Sir Charles said, with a slight sigh of relief. 'The next thing will be, of course, you'll follow them up on these clues in England and arrest them?'

The Commissary shrugged his shoulders. 'Arrest them!' he exclaimed, much amused. 'Ah, monsieur, but you are sanguine! No officer of justice has ever succeeded in arresting le Colonel Caoutchouc, as we call him in French. He is as slippery as an eel, that man. He wriggles through our fingers. Suppose even we caught him, what could we prove? I ask you. Nobody who has seen him once can ever swear to him again in his next impersonation. He is *impayable*, this good Colonel. On the day when I arrest him, I assure you, monsieur, I shall consider myself the smartest police-officer in Europe.'

'Well, I shall catch him yet,' Sir Charles answered, and relapsed into silence.

THE EPISODE OF THE
DIAMOND LINKS

'Let us take a trip to Switzerland,' said Lady Vandrift. And any one who knows Amelia will not be surprised to learn that we *did* take a trip to Switzerland accordingly. Nobody can drive Sir Charles, except his wife. And nobody at all can drive Amelia.

There were difficulties at the outset, because we had not ordered rooms at the hotels beforehand, and it was well on in the season; but they were overcome at last by the usual application of a golden key; and we found ourselves in due time pleasantly quartered in Lucerne, at that most comfortable of European hostelries, the Schweitzerhof.

We were a square party of four—Sir Charles and Amelia, myself and Isabel. We had nice big rooms, on the first floor, overlooking the lake; and as none of us was possessed with the faintest symptom of that incipient mania which shows itself in the form of an insane desire to climb mountain heights of disagreeable steepness and unnecessary snowiness, I will venture to assert we all enjoyed ourselves. We spent most of our time sensibly in lounging about the lake on the jolly little steamers; and when we did a mountain climb, it was on the Rigi or Pilatus— where an engine undertook all the muscular work for us.

As usual, at the hotel, a great many miscellaneous people showed a burning desire to be specially nice to us. If you wish to see how friendly and charming humanity is, just try being a well-known millionaire for a week, and you'll learn a thing or two. Wherever Sir Charles goes he is surrounded by charming and disinterested people, all eager to make his distinguished acquaintance, and all familiar with several excellent investments, or several deserving objects of Christian charity. It is my business in life, as his brother-in-law and secretary, to decline with thanks the excellent investments, and to throw judicious cold water on the objects of charity. Even I myself, as the great man's almoner, am very much sought after. People casually allude before me to artless stories of 'poor curates in Cumberland, you know, Mr. Wentworth,' or widows in Cornwall, penniless poets with epics in their desks, and young painters who need but the breath of a patron to open to them the doors of an admiring Academy. I smile and look wise, while I administer cold water in minute doses; but I never report one of these cases to Sir Charles, except in the rare or almost unheard-of event where I think there is really something in them.

Ever since our little adventure with the Seer at Nice, Sir Charles, who is constitutionally cautious, had been even more careful than usual about possible sharpers. And, as chance would have it, there sat just opposite us at *table d'hôte* at the Schweitzerhof—'tis a fad of Amelia's to dine at *table d'hôte*; she says she can't bear to be boxed up all day in private rooms with 'too much family'—a sinister-looking man with dark hair and eyes, conspicuous by his bushy overhanging eyebrows. My attention was first called to the eyebrows in question by a nice little parson who sat at our side, and who observed that they were made up of certain large and bristly hairs, which (he told us) had been traced by Darwin to our monkey ancestors. Very pleasant little fellow, this fresh-faced young parson, on his honeymoon tour with a nice wee wife, a bonnie Scotch lassie with a charming accent.

I looked at the eyebrows close. Then a sudden thought struck me. 'Do you believe they're his own?' I asked of the curate; 'or are they only stuck on—a make-up disguise? They really almost look like it.'

'You don't suppose——' Charles began, and checked himself suddenly.

'Yes, I do,' I answered; 'the Seer!' Then I recollected my blunder, and looked down sheepishly. For, to say the truth, Vandrift had straightly enjoined on me long before to say nothing of our painful little episode at Nice to Amelia; he was afraid if *she* once heard of it, *he* would hear of it for ever after.

'What Seer?' the little parson inquired, with parsonical curiosity.

I noticed the man with the overhanging eyebrows give a queer sort of start. Charles's glance was fixed upon me. I hardly knew what to answer.

'Oh, a man who was at Nice with us last year,' I stammered out, trying hard to look unconcerned. 'A fellow they talked about, that's all.' And I turned the subject.

But the curate, like a donkey, wouldn't let me turn it.

'Had he eyebrows like that?' he inquired, in an undertone. I was really angry. If this *was* Colonel Clay, the curate was obviously giving him the cue, and making it much more difficult for us to catch him, now we might possibly have lighted on the chance of doing so.

'No, he hadn't,' I answered testily; 'it was a passing expression. But this is not the man. I was mistaken, no doubt.' And I nudged him gently.

The little curate was too innocent for anything. 'Oh, I see,' he replied, nodding hard and looking wise. Then he turned to his wife and made an obvious face, which the man with the eyebrows couldn't fail to notice.

Fortunately, a political discussion going on a few places farther down the table spread up to us and diverted attention for a moment. The magical name of Gladstone saved us. Sir Charles flared up. I was truly pleased, for I could see Amelia was boiling over with curiosity by this time.

After dinner, in the billiard-room, however, the man with the big eyebrows sidled up and began to talk to me. If he *was* Colonel Clay, it was evident he bore us no grudge at all for the five thousand pounds he had done us out of. On the contrary, he seemed quite prepared to do us out of five thousand more when opportunity offered; for he introduced himself at once as Dr. Hector Macpherson, the exclusive grantee of extensive concessions from the Brazilian Government on the Upper Amazons. He dived into conversation with me at once as to the splendid mineral resources of his Brazilian estate—the silver, the platinum, the actual rubies, the possible diamonds. I listened and smiled; I knew what was coming. All he needed to develop this magnificent concession was a little more capital. It was sad to see thousands of pounds' worth of platinum and car-loads of rubies just crumbling in the soil or carried away by the river, for want of a few hundreds to work them with properly. If he knew of anybody, now, with money to invest, he could recommend him—nay, offer him—a unique opportunity of earning, say, 40 per cent on his capital, on unimpeachable security.

'I wouldn't do it for every man,' Dr. Hector Macpherson remarked, drawing himself up; 'but if I took a fancy to a fellow who had command of ready cash, I might choose to put him in the way of feathering his nest with unexampled rapidity.'

'Exceedingly disinterested of you,' I answered drily, fixing my eyes on his eyebrows.

The little curate, meanwhile, was playing billiards with Sir Charles. His glance followed mine as it rested for a moment on the monkey-like hairs.

'False, obviously false,' he remarked with his lips; and I'm bound to confess I never saw any man speak so well by movement alone; you could follow every word though not a sound escaped him.

During the rest of that evening Dr. Hector Macpherson stuck to me as close as a mustard-plaster. And he was almost as irritating. I got heartily sick of the Upper Amazons. I have positively waded in my time through ruby mines (in prospectuses, I mean) till the mere sight of a ruby absolutely sickens me. When Charles, in an unwonted fit of generosity, once gave his sister Isabel (whom I had the honour to marry) a ruby necklet (inferior stones), I made Isabel change it for sapphires and amethysts, on the judicious plea that they suited her complexion better. (I scored one, incidentally, for having considered Isabel's complexion.) By the time I went to bed I was prepared to sink the Upper Amazons in the sea, and to stab, shoot, poison, or otherwise seriously damage the man with the concession and the false eyebrows.

For the next three days, at intervals, he returned to the charge. He bored me to death with his platinum and his rubies. He didn't want a capitalist who would personally exploit the thing; he would prefer to do it all on his own account, giving the capitalist preference debentures of his bogus company, and a lien on the concession. I listened and smiled; I listened and yawned; I listened and was rude; I ceased to listen at all; but still he droned on with it. I fell asleep on the steamer one day, and woke up in ten minutes to hear him droning yet, 'And the yield of platinum per ton was certified to be——' I forget how many pounds, or ounces, or penny-weights. These details of assays have ceased to interest me: like the man who 'didn't believe in ghosts,' I have seen too many of them.

The fresh-faced little curate and his wife, however, were quite different people. He was a cricketing Oxford man; she was a breezy Scotch lass, with a wholesome breath of the High-lands about her. I called her 'White Heather.' Their name was Brabazon. Millionaires are so accustomed to being beset by harpies of every description, that when they come across a young couple who are simple and natural, they delight in the purely human relation. We picnicked and went excursions a great deal with the honeymooners. They were so frank in their young love, and so proof against chaff, that we all really liked them. But whenever I called the pretty girl 'White Heather,' she looked so shocked, and cried: 'Oh, Mr. Wentworth!' Still, we were the best of friends. The curate offered to row us in a boat on the lake one day, while the Scotch lassie assured us she could take an oar almost as well as he did. However, we did not accept their offer, as row-boats exert an unfavourable influence upon Amelia's digestive organs.

'Nice young fellow, that man Brabazon,' Sir Charles said to me one day, as we lounged together along the quay; 'never talks about advowsons or next presentations. Doesn't seem to me to care two pins about promotion. Says he's quite content in his country curacy; enough to five upon, and needs no more; and his wife has a little, a very little, money. I asked him about his poor to day, on purpose to test him: these parsons are always trying to screw something out of one for their poor; men in my position know the truth of the saying that we have that class of the population always with us. Would you believe it, he says he hasn't any poor at all in his parish! They're all well-to-do farmers or else able-bodied labourers, and his one terror is that somebody will come and try to pauperise them. "If a philanthropist were to give me fifty pounds to-day for use at Empingham," he said, "I assure you, Sir Charles, I shouldn't know what to do with it. I think I should buy new dresses for Jessie, who wants them about as much as anybody else in the village—that is to say, not at all." There's a parson for you, Sey, my boy. Only wish we had one of his sort at Seldon.'

'He certainly doesn't want to get anything out of you,' I answered.

That evening at dinner a queer little episode happened. The man with the eyebrows began talking to me across the table in his usual fashion, full of his wearisome concession on the Upper Amazons. I was trying to squash him as politely as possible, when I caught Amelia's eye. Her look amused me. She was engaged in making signals to Charles at her side to observe the little curate's curious sleeve-links. I glanced at them, and saw at once they were a singular possession for so unobtrusive a person. They consisted each of a short gold bar for one arm of the link, fastened by a tiny chain of the same material to what seemed to my tolerably experienced eye—a first-rate diamond. Pretty big diamonds, too, and of remarkable shape, brilliancy, and cutting. In a moment I knew what Amelia meant. She owned a diamond *rivière*, said to be of Indian origin, but short by two stones for the circumference of her tolerably ample neck. Now, she had long been wanting two diamonds like these to match her set; but owing to the unusual shape and antiquated cutting of her own gems, she had never been able to complete the necklet, at least without removing an extravagant amount from a much larger stone of the first water.

The Scotch lassie's eyes caught Amelia's at the same time, and she broke into a pretty smile of good-humoured amusement. 'Taken in another person, Dick, dear!' she exclaimed, in her breezy way, turning to her husband. 'Lady Vandrift is observing your diamond sleeve-links.'

'They're very fine gems,' Amelia observed incautiously. (A most unwise admission if she desired to buy them.)

But the pleasant little curate was too transparently simple a soul to take advantage of her slip of judgment. 'They *are* good stones,' he replied; 'very good stones—considering. They're not diamonds at all, to tell you the truth. They're best old-fashioned Oriental paste. My great-grandfather bought them, after the siege of Seringapatam, for a few rupees, from a Sepoy who had looted them from Tippoo Sultan's palace. He thought, like you, he had got a good thing. But it turned out, when they came to be examined by experts, they were only paste—very wonderful paste; it is supposed they had even imposed upon Tippoo himself, so fine is the imitation. But they are worth—well, say, fifty shillings at the utmost.'

While he spoke Charles looked at Amelia, and Amelia looked at Charles. Their eyes spoke volumes. The *rivière* was also supposed to have come from Tippoo's collection. Both drew at once an identical conclusion. These were two of the same stones, very likely torn apart and disengaged from the rest in the *mêlée* at the capture of the Indian palace.

'Can you take them off?' Sir Charles asked blandly. He spoke in the tone that indicates business.

'Certainly,' the little curate answered, smiling. 'I'm accustomed to taking them off. They're always noticed. They've been kept in the family ever since the siege, as a sort of valueless heir-loom, for the sake of the picturesqueness of the story, you know; and nobody ever sees them without asking, as you do, to examine them closely. They deceive even experts at first. But they're paste, all the same; unmitigated Oriental paste, for all that.'

He took them both off, and handed them to Charles. No man in England is a finer judge of gems than my brother-in-law. I watched him narrowly. He examined them close, first with the naked eye, then with the little pocket-lens which he always carries. 'Admirable imitation,' he muttered, passing them on to Amelia. 'I'm not surprised they should impose upon inexperienced observers.'

But from the tone in which he said it, I could see at once he had satisfied himself they were real gems of unusual value. I know Charles's way of doing business so well. His glance to Amelia meant, 'These are the very stones you have so long been in search of.'

The Scotch lassie laughed a merry laugh. 'He sees through them now, Dick,' she cried. 'I felt sure Sir Charles would be a judge of diamonds.'

Amelia turned them over. I know Amelia, too; and I knew from the way Amelia looked at them that she meant to have them. And when Amelia means to have anything, people who stand in the way may just as well spare themselves the trouble of opposing her.

They were beautiful diamonds. We found out afterwards the little curate's account was quite correct: these stones *had* come from the same necklet as Amelia's *rivière*, made for a favourite wife of Tippoo's, who had presumably as expansive personal charms as our beloved sister-in-law's. More perfect diamonds have seldom been seen. They have excited the universal admiration of thieves and connoisseurs. Amelia told me afterwards that, according to legend, a Sepoy stole the necklet at the sack of the palace, and then fought with another for it. It was believed that two stones got spilt in the scuffle, and were picked up and sold by a third person—a looker-on—who had no idea of the value of his booty. Amelia had been hunting for them for several years to complete her necklet.

'They are excellent paste,' Sir Charles observed, handing them back. 'It takes a first-rate judge to detect them from the reality. Lady Vandrift has a necklet much the same in character, but composed of genuine stones; and as these are so much like them, and would complete her set, to all outer appearance, I wouldn't mind giving you, say, £10 for the pair of them.'

Mrs. Brabazon looked delighted. 'Oh, sell them to him, Dick,' she cried, 'and buy me a brooch with the money! A pair of common links would do for you just as well. Ten pounds for two paste stones! It's quite a lot of money.'

She said it so sweetly, with her pretty Scotch accent, that I couldn't imagine how Dick had the heart to refuse her. But he did, all the same.

'No, Jess, darling,' he answered. 'They're worthless, I know; but they have for me a certain sentimental value, as I've often told you. My dear mother wore them, while she lived, as earrings; and as soon as she died I had them set as links in order that I might always keep them about me. Besides, they have historical and family interest. Even a worthless heirloom, after all, *is* an heirloom.'

Dr. Hector Macpherson looked across and intervened. 'There is a part of my concession,' he said, 'where we have reason to believe a perfect new Kimberley will soon be discovered. If at any time you would care, Sir Charles, to look at my diamonds— when I get them—it would afford me the greatest pleasure in life to submit them to your consideration.'

Sir Charles could stand it no longer. 'Sir,' he said, gazing across at him with his sternest air, 'if your concession were as full of diamonds as Sindbad the Sailor's valley, I would not care to turn my head to look at them. I am acquainted with the nature and practice of salting.' And he glared at the man with the overhanging eyebrows as if he would devour him raw. Poor Dr. Hector Macpherson subsided instantly. We learnt a little later that he was a harmless lunatic, who went about the world with successive concessions for ruby mines and platinum reefs, because he had been ruined and driven mad by speculations in the two, and now recouped himself by imaginary grants in Burmah and Brazil, or anywhere else that turned up handy. And his eyebrows, after all, were of Nature's handicraft. We were sorry for the incident; but a man in Sir Charles's position is such a mark for rogues that, if he did not take means to protect himself promptly, he would be for ever overrun by them.

When we went up to our *salon* that evening, Amelia flung herself on the sofa. 'Charles,' she broke out in the voice of a tragedy queen, 'those are real diamonds, and I shall never be happy again till I get them.'

'They are real diamonds,' Charles echoed. 'And you shall have them, Amelia. They're worth not less than three thousand pounds. But I shall bid them up gently.'

So, next day, Charles set to work to higgle with the curate. Brabazon, however, didn't care to part with them. He was no money-grubber, he said. He cared more for his mother's gift and a family tradition than for a hundred pounds, if Sir Charles were to offer it. Charles's eye gleamed. 'But if I give you *two* hundred!' he said insinuatingly. 'What opportunities for good! You could build a new wing to your village school-house!'

'We have ample accommodation,' the curate answered. 'No, I don't think I'll sell them.'

Still, his voice faltered somewhat, and he looked down at them inquiringly.

Charles was too precipitate.

'A hundred pounds more or less matters little to me,' he said; 'and my wife has set her heart on them. It's every man's duty to please his wife—isn't it, Mrs. Brabazon?—I offer you three hundred.'

The little Scotch girl clasped her hands.

'Three hundred pounds! Oh, Dick, just think what fun we could have, and what good we could do with it! Do let him have them.'

Her accent was irresistible. But the curate shook his head.

'Impossible,' he answered. 'My dear mother's ear-rings! Uncle Aubrey would be so angry if he knew I'd sold them. I daren't face Uncle Aubrey.'

'Has he expectations from Uncle Aubrey?' Sir Charles asked of White Heather.

Mrs. Brabazon laughed. 'Uncle Aubrey! Oh, dear, no. Poor dear old Uncle Aubrey! Why, the darling old soul hasn't a penny to bless himself with, except his pension. He's a retired post captain.' And she laughed melodiously. She was a charming woman.

'Then I should disregard Uncle Aubrey's feelings,' Sir Charles said decisively.

'No, no,' the curate answered. 'Poor dear old Uncle Aubrey! I wouldn't do anything for the world to annoy him. And he'd be sure to notice it.'

We went back to Amelia. 'Well, have you got them?' she asked.

'No,' Sir Charles answered. 'Not yet. But he's coming round, I think. He's hesitating now. Would rather like to sell them himself, but is afraid what "Uncle Aubrey" would say about the matter. His wife will talk him out of his needless consideration for Uncle Aubrey's feelings; and to-morrow we'll finally clench the bargain.'

Next morning we stayed late in our *salon*, where we always breakfasted, and did not come down to the public rooms till just before *déjeûner*, Sir Charles being busy with me over arrears of correspondence. When we *did* come down the *concierge* stepped forward with a twisted little feminine note for Amelia. She took it and read it. Her countenance fell. 'There, Charles,' she cried, handing it to him, 'you've let the chance slip. I shall *never* be happy now! They've gone off with the diamonds.'

Charles seized the note and read it. Then he passed it on to me. It was short, but final:—

'*Thursday, 6 a.m.*

'DEAR LADY VANDRIFT—*Will* you kindly excuse our having gone off hurriedly without bidding you good-bye? We have just had a horrid telegram to say that Dick's favourite sister is *dangerously* ill of fever in Paris. I wanted to shake hands with you before we left—you have all been so sweet to us—but we go by the morning train, absurdly early, and I wouldn't for worlds disturb you. Perhaps some day we may meet again—though, buried as we are in a North-country village, it isn't likely; but in any case, you have secured the grateful recollection of Yours very cordially,   JESSIE BRABAZON.

'P.S.—Kindest regards to Sir Charles and those *dear* Wentworths, and a kiss for yourself, if I may venture to send you one.'

'She doesn't even mention where they've gone,' Amelia exclaimed, in a very bad humour.

'The *concierge* may know,' Isabel suggested, looking over my shoulder.

We asked at his office.

Yes, the gentleman's address was the Rev. Richard Peploe Brabazon, Holme Bush Cottage, Empingham, Northumberland.

Any address where letters might be sent at once, in Paris?

For the next ten days, or till further notice, Hôtel des Deux Mondes, Avenue de l'Opéra.

Amelia's mind was made up at once.

'Strike while the iron's hot,' she cried. 'This sudden illness, coming at the end of their honeymoon, and involving ten days' more stay at an expensive hotel, will probably upset the curate's budget. He'll be glad to sell now. You'll get them for three hundred. It was absurd of Charles to offer so much at first; but offered once, of course we must stick to it.'

'What do you propose to do?' Charles asked. 'Write, or telegraph?'

'Oh, how silly men are!' Amelia cried. 'Is this the sort of business to be arranged by letter, still less by telegram? No. Seymour must start off at once, taking the night train to Paris; and the moment he gets there, he must interview the curate or Mrs. Brabazon. Mrs. Brabazon's the best. She has none of this stupid, sentimental nonsense about Uncle Aubrey.'

It is no part of a secretary's duties to act as a diamond broker. But when Amelia puts her foot down, she puts her foot down—a fact which she is unnecessarily fond of emphasising in that identical proposition. So the self-same evening saw me safe in the train on my way to Paris; and next morning I turned out of my comfortable sleeping-car at the Gare de Strasbourg. My orders were to bring back those diamonds, alive or dead, so to speak, in my pocket to Lucerne; and to offer any needful sum, up to two thousand five hundred pounds, for their immediate purchase.

When I arrived at the Deux Mondes I found the poor little curate and his wife both greatly agitated. They had sat up all night, they said, with their invalid sister; and the sleeplessness and suspense had certainly told upon them after their long railway journey. They were pale and tired, Mrs. Brabazon, in particular, looking ill and worried—too much like White Heather. I was more than half ashamed of bothering them about the diamonds at such a moment, but it occurred to me that Amelia was probably right—they would now have reached the end of the sum set apart for their Continental trip, and a little ready cash might be far from unwelcome.

I broached the subject delicately. It was a fad of Lady Vandrift's, I said. She had set her heart upon those useless trinkets.

And she wouldn't go without them. She must and would have them. But the curate was obdurate. He threw Uncle Aubrey still in my teeth. Three hundred?—no, never! A mother's present; impossible, dear Jessie! Jessie begged and prayed; she had grown really attached to Lady Vandrift, she said; but the curate wouldn't hear of it. I went up tentatively to four hundred. He shook his head gloomily. It wasn't a question of money, he said. It was a question of affection. I saw it was no use trying that tack any longer. I struck out a new line. 'These stones,' I said, 'I think I ought to inform you, are really diamonds. Sir Charles is certain of it. Now, is it right for a man of your profession and position to be wearing a pair of big gems like those, worth several hundred pounds, as ordinary sleeve-links? A woman?—yes, I grant you. But for a man, is it manly?' And you a cricketer!'

He looked at me and laughed. 'Will nothing convince you?' he cried. 'They have been examined and tested by half a dozen jewellers, and we know them to be paste. It wouldn't be right of me to sell them to you under false pretences, however unwilling on my side. I *couldn't* do it.'

'Well, then,' I said, going up a bit in my bids to meet him, 'I'll put it like this. These gems are paste. But Lady Vandrift has an unconquerable and unaccountable desire to possess them. Money doesn't matter to her. She is a friend of your wife's. As a personal favour, won't you sell them to her for a thousand?'

He shook his head. 'It would be wrong,' he said,—'I might even add, criminal.'

'But we take all risk,' I cried.

He was absolute adamant. 'As a clergyman,' he answered, 'I feel I cannot do it.'

'Will *you* try, Mrs. Brabazon?' I asked.

The pretty little Scotchwoman leant over and whispered. She coaxed and cajoled him. Her ways were winsome. I couldn't hear what she said, but he seemed to give way at last. 'I should love Lady Vandrift to have them,' she murmured, turning to me. 'She *is* such a dear!' And she took out the links from her husband's cuffs and handed them across to me.

'How much?' I asked.

'Two thousand?' she answered, interrogatively. It was a big rise, all at once; but such are the ways of women.

'Done!' I replied. 'Do you consent?'

The curate looked up as if ashamed of himself.

'I consent,' he said slowly, 'since Jessie wishes it. But as a clergyman, and to prevent any future misunderstanding, I should like you to give me a statement in writing that you buy them on my distinct and positive declaration that they are made of paste—old Oriental paste—not genuine stones, and that I do not claim any other qualities for them.'

I popped the gems into my purse, well pleased.

'Certainly,' I said, pulling out a paper. Charles, with his unerring business instinct, had anticipated the request, and given me a signed agreement to that effect.

'You will take a cheque?' I inquired.

He hesitated.

'Notes of the Bank of France would suit me better,' he answered.

'Very well,' I replied. 'I will go out and get them.'

How very unsuspicious some people are! He allowed me to go off—with the stones in my pocket!

Sir Charles had given me a blank cheque, not exceeding two thousand five hundred pounds. I took it to our agents and cashed it for notes of the Bank of France. The curate clasped them with pleasure. And right glad I was to go back to Lucerne that night, feeling that I had got those diamonds into my hands for about a thousand pounds under their real value!

At Lucerne railway station Amelia met me. She was positively agitated.

'Have you bought them, Seymour?' she asked.

'Yes,' I answered, producing my spoils in triumph.

'Oh, how dreadful!' she cried, drawing back. 'Do you think they're real? Are you sure he hasn't cheated you?'

'Certain of it,' I replied, examining them. 'No one can take me in, in the matter of diamonds. Why on earth should you doubt them?'

'Because I've been talking to Mrs. O'Hagan, at the hotel, and she says there's a well-known trick just like that—she's read of it in a book. A swindler has two sets—one real, one false; and he makes you buy the false ones by showing you the real, and pretending he sells them as a special favour.'

'You needn't be alarmed,' I answered. 'I am a judge of diamonds.'

'I shan't be satisfied,' Amelia murmured, 'till Charles has seen them.'

We went up to the hotel. For the first time in her life I saw Amelia really nervous as I handed the stones to Charles to examine. Her doubt was contagious. I half feared, myself, he might break out into a deep monosyllabic interjection, losing his temper in haste, as he often does when things go wrong. But he looked at them with a smile, while I told him the price.

'Eight hundred pounds less than their value,' he answered, well satisfied.

'You have no doubt of their reality?' I asked.

'Not the slightest,' he replied, gazing at them. 'They are genuine stones, precisely the same in quality and type as Amelia's necklet.'

Amelia drew a sigh of relief. 'I'll go upstairs,' she said slowly, 'and bring down my own for you both to compare with them.'

One minute later she rushed down again, breathless. Amelia is far from slim, and I never before knew her exert herself so actively.

'Charles, Charles!' she cried, 'do you know what dreadful thing has happened? Two of my own stones are gone. He's stolen a couple of diamonds from my necklet, and sold them back to me.'

She held out the *rivière*. It was all too true. Two gems were missing—and these two just fitted the empty places!

A light broke in upon me. I clapped my hand to my head. 'By Jove,' I exclaimed, 'the little curate is—Colonel Clay!'

Charles clapped his own hand to his brow in turn. 'And Jessie,' he cried, 'White Heather—that innocent little Scotchwoman! I often detected a familiar ring in her voice, in spite of the charming Highland accent. Jessie is—Madame Picardet!'

We had absolutely no evidence; but, like the Commissary at Nice, we felt instinctively sure of it.

Sir Charles was determined to catch the rogue. This second deception put him on his mettle. 'The worst of the man is,' he said, 'he has a method. He doesn't go out of his way to cheat us; he makes us go out of ours to be cheated. He lays a trap, and we tumble headlong into it. To-morrow, Sey, we must follow him on to Paris.'

Amelia explained to him what Mrs. O'Hagan had said. Charles took it all in at once, with his usual sagacity. 'That explains,' he said, 'why the rascal used this particular trick to draw us on by. If we had suspected him he could have shown the diamonds were real, and so escaped detection. It was a blind to draw us off from the fact of the robbery. He went to Paris to be out of the way when the discovery was made, and to get a clear day's start of us. What a consummate rogue! And to do me twice running!'

'How did he get at my jewel - case, though?' Amelia exclaimed.

'That's the question,' Charles answered. 'You *do* leave it about so!'

'And why didn't he steal the whole *rivière* at once, and sell the gems?' I inquired.

'Too cunning,' Charles replied. 'This was much better business. It isn't easy to dispose of a big thing like that. In the first place, the stones are large and valuable; in the second place, they're well known—every dealer has heard of the Vandrift *rivière*, and seen pictures of the shape of them. They're marked gems, so to speak. No, he played a better game—took a couple of them off, and offered them to the only one person on earth who was likely to buy them without suspicion. He came here, meaning to work this very trick; he had the links made right to the shape beforehand, and then he stole the stones and slipped them into their places. It's a wonderfully clever trick. Upon my soul, I almost admire the fellow.'

For Charles is a business man himself, and can appreciate business capacity in others.

How Colonel Clay came to know about that necklet, and to appropriate two of the stones, we only discovered much later. I will not here anticipate that disclosure. One thing at a time is a good rule in life. For the moment he succeeded in baffling us altogether.

However, we followed him on to Paris, telegraphing beforehand to the Bank of France to stop the notes. It was all in vain. They had been cashed within half an hour of my paying them. The curate and his wife, we found, quitted the Hôtel des Deux Mondes for parts unknown that same afternoon. And, as usual with Colonel Clay, they vanished into space, leaving no clue behind them. In other words, they changed their disguise, no doubt, and reappeared somewhere else that night in altered characters. At any rate, no such person as the Reverend Richard Peploe Brabazon was ever afterwards heard of—and, for the matter of that, no such village exists as Empingham, Northumberland.

We communicated the matter to the Parisian police. They were *most* unsympathetic. 'It is no doubt Colonel Clay,' said the official whom we saw; 'but you seem to have little just ground of complaint against him. As far as I can see, messieurs, there is not much to choose between you. You, Monsieur le Chevalier, desired to buy diamonds at the price of paste. You, madame, feared you had bought paste at the price of diamonds. You, monsieur the secretary, tried to get the stones from an unsuspecting person for half their value. He took you all in, that brave Colonel Caoutchouc—it was diamond cut diamond.'

Which was true, no doubt, but by no means consoling.

We returned to the Grand Hotel. Charles was fuming with indignation. 'This is really too much,' he exclaimed. 'What an audacious rascal! But he will never again take me in, my dear Sey. I only hope he'll try it on. I should love to catch him. I'd know him another time, I'm sure, in spite of his disguises. It's absurd my being tricked twice running like this. But never again while I live! Never again, I declare to you!'

'*Jamais de la vie!*' a courier in the hall close by murmured responsive. We stood under the verandah of the Grand Hotel, in the big glass courtyard. And I verily believe that courier was really Colonel Clay himself in one of his disguises.

But perhaps we were beginning to suspect him everywhere.

III

THE EPISODE OF
THE OLD MASTER

Like most South Africans, Sir Charles Vandrift is anything but sedentary. He hates sitting down. He must always 'trek.' He cannot live without moving about freely. Six weeks in Mayfair at a time is as much as he can stand. Then he must run away incontinently for rest and change to Scotland, Homburg, Monte Carlo, Biarritz. 'I won't be a limpet on the rock,' he says. Thus it came to pass that in the early autumn we found ourselves stopping at the Métropole at Brighton. We were the accustomed nice little family party—Sir Charles and Amelia, myself and Isabel, with the suite as usual.

On the first Sunday morning after our arrival we strolled out, Charles and I—I regret to say during the hours allotted for Divine service—on to the King's Road, to get a whiff of fresh air, and a glimpse of the waves that were churning the Channel. The two ladies (with their bonnets) had gone to church; but Sir Charles had risen late, fatigued from the week's toil, while I myself was suffering from a matutinal headache, which I attributed to the close air in the billiard-room overnight, combined, perhaps, with the insidious effect of a brand of soda-water to which I was little accustomed; I had used it to dilute my evening whisky. We were to meet our wives afterwards at the church parade—an institution to which I believe both Amelia and Isabel attach even greater importance than to the sermon which precedes it.

We sat down on a glass seat. Charles gazed inquiringly up and down the King's Road, on the look-out for a boy with Sunday papers. At last one passed. '*Observer*,' my brother-in-law called out laconically.

'Ain't got none,' the boy answered, brandishing his bundle in our faces. "Ave a *Referee* or a *Pink 'Un?*'

Charles, however, is not a Refereader, while as to the *Pink 'Un*, he considers it unsuitable for public perusal on Sunday morning. It may be read indoors, but in the open air its blush betrays it. So he shook his head, and muttered, 'If you pass an *Observer*, send him on here at once to me.'

A polite stranger who sat close to us turned round with a pleasant smile. 'Would you allow me to offer you one?' he said, drawing a copy from his pocket. 'I fancy I bought the last. There's a run on them to-day, you see. Important news this morning from the Transvaal.'

Charles raised his eyebrows, and accepted it, as I thought, just a trifle grumpily. So, to remove the false impression his surliness might produce on so benevolent a mind, I entered into conversation with the polite stranger. He was a man of middle age, and medium height, with a cultivated air, and a pair of gold *pince-nez*; his eyes were sharp; his voice was refined; he dropped into talk before long about distinguished people just then in Brighton. It was clear at once that he was hand in glove with many of the very best kind. We compared notes as to Nice, Rome, Florence, Cairo. Our new acquaintance had scores of friends in common with us, it seemed; indeed, our circles so largely coincided, that I wondered we had never happened till then to knock up against one another.

'And Sir Charles Vandrift, the great African millionaire,' he said at last, 'do you know anything of *him?* I'm told he's at present down here at the Métropole.'

I waved my hand towards the person in question.

'*This* is Sir Charles Vandrift,' I answered, with proprietary pride; 'and *I* am his brother-in-law, Mr. Seymour Wentworth.'

'Oh, indeed!' the stranger answered, with a curious air of drawing in his horns. I wondered whether he had just been going to pretend he knew Sir Charles, or whether perchance he was on the point of saying something highly uncomplimentary, and was glad to have escaped it.

By this time, however, Charles laid down the paper and chimed into our conversation. I could see at once from his

mollified tone that the news from the Transvaal was favour-
able to his operations in Cloetedorp Golcondas. He was therefore in a friendly and affable temper. His whole manner
changed at once. He grew polite in return to the polite stranger.
Besides, we knew the man moved in the best society; he had
acquaintances whom Amelia was most anxious to secure for
her 'At Homes' in Mayfair—young Faith, the novelist, and Sir
Richard Montrose, the great Arctic traveller. As for the painters, it was clear that he was sworn friends with the whole lot
of them. He dined with Academicians, and gave weekly break-
fasts to the members of the Institute. Now, Amelia is particularly desirous that her *salon* should not be considered too
exclusively financial and political in character: with a solid
basis of M.P.'s and millionaires, she loves a delicate undercurrent of literature, art, and the musical glasses. Our new
acquaintance was extremely communicative: 'Knows his place
in society, Sey,' Sir Charles said to me afterwards, 'and is
therefore not afraid of talking freely, as so many people are
who have doubts about their position.' We exchanged cards
before we rose. Our new friend's name turned out to be Dr.
Edward Polperro.

'In practice here?' I inquired, though his garb belied it.

'Oh, not medical,' he answered. 'I am an LL.D. don't you
know. I interest myself in art, and buy to some extent for the
National Gallery.'

The very man for Amelia's 'At Homes'! Sir Charles snapped
at him instantly. 'I've brought my four-in-hand down here
with me,' he said, in his best friendly manner, 'and we think of
tooling over to-morrow to Lewes. If you'd care to take a seat
I'm sure Lady Vandrift would be charmed to see you.'

'You're very kind,' the Doctor said, 'on so casual an introduction. I'm sure I shall be delighted.'

'We start from the Métropole at ten-thirty,' Charles went on.

'I shall be there. Good morning!' And, with a satisfied smile,
he rose and left us, nodding.

We returned to the lawn, to Amelia and Isabel. Our new
friend passed us once or twice. Charles stopped him and introduced him. He was walking with two ladies, most elegantly

dressed in rather peculiar artistic dresses. Amelia was taken at first sight by his manner. 'One could see at a glance,' she said, 'he was a person of culture and of real distinction. I wonder whether he could bring the P.R.A. to my Parliamentary "At Home" on Wednesday fortnight?'

Next day, at ten-thirty, we started on our drive. Our team has been considered the best in Sussex. Charles is an excellent, though somewhat anxious—or, might I say better, somewhat careful?—whip. He finds the management of two leaders and two wheelers fills his hands for the moment, both literally and figuratively, leaving very little time for general conversation. Lady Belleisle of Beacon bloomed beside him on the box (her bloom is perennial, and applied by her maid); Dr. Polperro occupied the seat just behind with myself and Amelia. The Doctor talked most of the time to Lady Vandrift: his discourse was of picture-galleries, which Amelia detests, but in which she thinks it incumbent upon her, as Sir Charles's wife, to affect now and then a cultivated interest. *Noblesse oblige;* and the walls of Castle Seldon, our place in Ross-shire, are almost covered now with Leaders and with Orchardsons. This result was first arrived at by a singular accident. Sir Charles wanted a leader—for his coach, you understand—and told an artistic friend so. The artistic friend brought him a Leader next week with a capital L; and Sir Charles was so taken aback that he felt ashamed to confess the error. So he was turned unawares into a patron of painting.

Dr. Polperro, in spite of his too pronouncedly artistic talk, proved on closer view a most agreeable companion. He diversified his art cleverly with anecdotes and scandals; he told us exactly which famous painters had married their cooks, and which had only married their models; and otherwise showed himself a most diverting talker. Among other things, however, he happened to mention once that he had recently discovered a genuine Rembrandt—a quite undoubted Rembrandt, which had remained for years in the keeping of a certain obscure Dutch family. It had always been allowed to be a masterpiece of the painter, but it had seldom been seen for the last half-century save by a few intimate acquaintances. It was a portrait of one Maria Vanrenen of Haarlem, and he had bought it of her descendants at Gouda, in Holland.

I saw Charles prick up his ears, though he took no open notice. This Maria Vanrenen, as it happened, was a remote collateral ancestress of the Vandrifts, before they emigrated to the Cape in 1780; and the existence of the portrait, though not its whereabouts, was well known in the family. Isabel had often mentioned it. If it was to be had at anything like a reasonable price, it would be a splendid thing for the boys (Sir Charles, I ought to say, has two sons at Eton) to possess an undoubted portrait of an ancestress by Rembrandt.

Dr. Polperro talked a good deal after that about this valuable find. He had tried to sell it at first to the National Gallery; but though the Directors admired the work immensely, and admitted its genuineness, they regretted that the funds at their disposal this year did not permit them to acquire so important a canvas at a proper figure. South Kensington again was too poor; but the Doctor was in treaty at present with the Louvre and with Berlin. Still, it was a pity a fine work of art like that, once brought into the country, should be allowed to go out of it. Some patriotic patron of the fine arts ought to buy it for his own house, or else munificently present it to the nation.

All the time Charles said nothing. But I could feel him cogitating. He even looked behind him once, near a difficult corner (while the guard was actually engaged in tootling his horn to let passers-by know that the coach was coming), and gave Amelia a warning glance to say nothing committing, which had at once the requisite effect of sealing her mouth for the moment. It is a very unusual thing for Charles to look back while driving. I gathered from his doing so that he was inordinately anxious to possess this Rembrandt.

When we arrived at Lewes we put up our horses at the inn, and Charles ordered a lunch on his wonted scale of princely magnificence. Meanwhile we wandered, two and two, about the town and castle. I annexed Lady Belleisle, who is at least amusing. Charles drew me aside before starting. 'Look here, Sey,' he said, 'we must be *very* careful. This man, Polperro, is a chance acquaintance. There's nothing an astute rogue can take one in over more easily than an Old Master. If the Rembrandt is genuine I ought to have it; if it really represents Maria Vanrenen, it's a duty I owe to the boys to buy it. But I've been done twice lately, and I won't be done a third time. We must go to work cautiously.'

'You are right,' I answered. 'No more seers and curates!'

'If this man's an impostor,' Charles went on—'and in spite of what he says about the National Gallery and so forth, we know nothing of him—the story he tells is just the sort of one such a fellow would trump up in a moment to deceive me. He could easily learn who I was—I'm a well-known figure; he knew I was in Brighton, and he may have been sitting on that glass seat on Sunday on purpose to entrap me.'

'He introduced your name,' I said, 'and the moment he found out who I was he plunged into talk with me.'

'Yes,' Charles continued. 'He may have learned about the portrait of Maria Vanrenen, which my grandmother always said was preserved at Gouda; and, indeed, I myself have often mentioned it, as you doubtless remember. If so, what more natural, say, for a rogue than to begin talking about the portrait in that innocent way to Amelia? If he wants a Rembrandt, I believe they can be turned out to order to any amount in Birmingham. The moral of all which is, it behoves us to be careful.'

'Right you are,' I answered; 'and I am keeping my eye upon him.'

We drove back by another road, overshadowed by beech-trees in autumnal gold. It was a delightful excursion. Dr. Polperro's heart was elated by lunch and the excellent dry Monopole. He talked amazingly. I never heard a man with a greater or more varied flow of anecdote. He had been everywhere and knew all about everybody. Amelia booked him at once for her 'At Home' on Wednesday week, and he promised to introduce her to several artistic and literary celebrities.

That evening, however, about half-past seven, Charles and I strolled out together on the King's Road for a blow before dinner. We dine at eight. The air was delicious. We passed a small new hotel, very smart and exclusive, with a big bow window.

There, in evening dress, lights burning and blind up, sat our friend, Dr. Polperro, with a lady facing him, young, graceful, and pretty. A bottle of champagne stood open before him. He was helping himself plentifully to hot-house grapes, and full of good humour. It was clear he and the lady were occupied in the intense enjoyment of some capital joke; for they looked queerly at one another, and burst now and again into merry peals of laughter.

I drew back. So did Sir Charles. One idea passed at once through both our minds. I murmured, 'Colonel Clay!' He answered, '*And* Madame Picardet!'

They were not in the least like the Reverend Richard and Mrs. Brabazon. But that clinched the matter. Nor did I see a sign of the aquiline nose of the Mexican Seer. Still, I had learnt by then to discount appearances. If these were indeed the famous sharper and his wife or accomplice, we must be very careful. We were forewarned this time. Supposing he had the audacity to try a third trick of the sort upon us we had him under our thumbs. Only, we must take steps to prevent his dexterously slipping through our fingers.

'He can wriggle like an eel,' said the Commissary at Nice. We both recalled those words, and laid our plans deep to prevent the man's wriggling away from us on this third occasion.

'I tell you what it is, Sey,' my brother-in-law said, with impressive slowness. 'This time we must deliberately lay ourselves out to be swindled. We must propose of our own accord to buy the picture, making him guarantee it in writing as a genuine Rembrandt, and taking care to tie him down by most stringent conditions. But we must seem at the same time to be unsuspicious and innocent as babes; we must swallow whole whatever lies he tells us; pay his price—nominally—by cheque for the portrait; and then, arrest him the moment the bargain is complete, with the proofs of his guilt then and there upon him. Of course, what he'll try to do will be to vanish into thin air at once, as he did at Nice and Paris; but, this time, we'll have the police in waiting and everything ready. We'll avoid precipitancy, but we'll avoid delay too. We must hold our hands off till he's actually accepted and pocketed the money;

and then, we must nab him instantly, and walk him off to the local Bow Street. That's my plan of campaign. Meanwhile, we should appear all trustful innocence and confiding guileless-ness.'

In pursuance of this well-laid scheme, we called next day on Dr. Polperro at his hotel, and were introduced to his wife, a dainty little woman, in whom we affected not to recognise that arch Madame Picardet or that simple White Heather. The Doctor talked charmingly (as usual) about art—what a well-informed rascal he was, to be sure!—and Sir Charles expressed some interest in the supposed Rembrandt. Our new friend was delighted; we could see by his well-suppressed eagerness of tone that he knew us at once for probable purchasers. He would run up to town next day, he said, and bring down the portrait. And in effect, when Charles and I took our wonted places in the Pullman next morning, on our way up to the half-yearly meeting of Cloetedorp Golcondas, there was our Doctor, leaning back in his arm-chair as if the car belonged to him. Charles gave me an expressive look. 'Does it in style,' he whispered, 'doesn't he? Takes it out of my five thousand; or discounts the amount he means to chouse me of with his spuri-ous Rembrandt.'

Arrived in town, we went to work at once. We set a private detective from Marvillier's to watch our friend; and from him we learned that the so-called Doctor dropped in for a picture that day at a dealer's in the West-end (I suppress the name, having a judicious fear of the law of libel ever before my eyes), a dealer who was known to be mixed up before then in several shady or disreputable transactions. Though, to be sure, my experience has been that picture dealers are—picture dealers. Horses rank first in my mind as begetters and producers of unscrupulous agents, but pictures run them a very good sec-ond. Anyhow, we found out that our distinguished art-critic picked up his Rembrandt at this dealer's shop, and came down with it in his care the same night to Brighton.

In order not to act precipitately, and so ruin our plans, we induced Dr. Polperro (what a cleverly chosen name!) to bring the Rembrandt round to the Métropole for our inspection, and to leave it with us while we got the opinion of an expert from London.

The expert came down, and gave us a full report upon the alleged Old Master. In his judgment, it was not a Rembrandt at all, but a cunningly-painted and well-begrimed modern Dutch imitation. Moreover, he showed us by documentary evidence that the real portrait of Maria Vanrenen had, as a matter of fact, been brought to England five years before, and sold to Sir J. H. Tomlinson, the well-known connoisseur, for eight thousand pounds. Dr. Polperro's picture was, therefore, at best either a replica by Rembrandt; or else, more probably, a copy by a pupil; or, most likely of all, a mere modern forgery.

We were thus well prepared to fasten our charge of criminal conspiracy upon the self-styled Doctor. But in order to make assurance still more certain, we threw out vague hints to him that the portrait of Maria Vanrenen might really be elsewhere, and even suggested in his hearing that it might not improbably have got into the hands of that omnivorous collector, Sir J. H. Tomlinson. But the vendor was proof against all such attempts to decry his goods. He had the effrontery to brush away the documentary evidence, and to declare that Sir J. H. Tomlinson (one of the most learned and astute picture-buyers in England) had been smartly imposed upon by a needy Dutch artist with a talent for forgery. The real Maria Vanrenen, he declared and swore, was the one he offered us. 'Success has turned the man's head,' Charles said to me, well pleased. 'He thinks we will swallow any obvious lie he chooses to palm off upon us. But the bucket has come once too often to the well. This time we checkmate him.' It was a mixed metaphor, I admit; but Sir Charles's tropes are not always entirely superior to criticism.

So we pretended to believe our man, and accepted his assurances. Next came the question of price. This was warmly debated, for form's sake only. Sir J. H. Tomlinson had paid eight thousand for his genuine Maria. The Doctor demanded ten thousand for his spurious one. There was really no reason why we should higgle and dispute, for Charles meant merely to give his cheque for the sum and then arrest the fellow; but, still, we thought it best for the avoidance of suspicion to make

a show of resistance; and we at last beat him down to nine
thousand guineas. For this amount he was to give us a written
warranty that the work he sold us was a genuine Rembrandt,
that it represented Maria Vanrenen of Haarlem, and that he
had bought it direct, without doubt or question, from that
good lady's descendants at Gouda, in Holland.

It was capitally done. We arranged the thing to perfection.
We had a constable in waiting in our rooms at the Métropole,
and we settled that Dr. Polperro was to call at the hotel at a
certain fixed hour to sign the warranty and receive his money.
A regular agreement on sound stamped paper was drawn out
between us. At the appointed time the 'party of the first part'
came, having already given us over possession of the portrait.
Charles drew a cheque for the amount agreed upon, and
signed it. Then he handed it to the Doctor. Polperro just
clutched at it. Meanwhile, I took up my post by the door, while
two men in plain clothes, detectives from the police-station,
stood as men-servants and watched the windows. We feared
lest the impostor, once he had got the cheque, should dodge us
somehow, as he had already done at Nice and in Paris. The
moment he had pocketed his money with a smile of triumph, I
advanced to him rapidly. I had in my possession a pair of
handcuffs. Before he knew what was happening, I had slipped
them on his wrists and secured them dexterously, while the
constable stepped foward. 'We have got you this time!' I cried.
'We know who you are, Dr. Polperro. You are—Colonel Clay,
alias Señor Antonio Herrera, *alias* the Reverend Richard Peploe
Brabazon.'

I never saw any man so astonished in my life! He was utterly
flabbergasted. Charles thought he must have expected to get
clear away at once, and that this prompt action on our part
had taken the fellow so much by surprise as to simply unman
him. He gazed about him as if he hardly realised what was
happening.

'Are these two raving maniacs?' he asked at last, 'or what
do they mean by this nonsensical gibberish about Antonio
Herrera?'

The constable laid his hand on the prisoner's shoulder.

'It's all right, my man,' he said. 'We've got warrants out against you. I arrest you, Edward Polperro, *alias* the Reverend Richard Peploe Brabazon, on a charge of obtaining money under false pretences from Sir Charles Vandrift, K.C.M.G., M.P., on his sworn information, now here subscribed to.' For Charles had had the thing drawn out in readiness beforehand.

Our prisoner drew himself up. 'Look here, officer,' he said, in an offended tone, 'there's some mistake here in this matter. I have never given an *alias* at any time in my life. How do you know this is really Sir Charles Vandrift? It may be a case of bullying personation. My belief is, though, they're a pair of escaped lunatics.'

'We'll see about that to-morrow,' the constable said, collaring him. 'At present you've got to go off with me quietly to the station, where these gentlemen will enter up the charge against you.'

They carried him off, protesting. Charles and I signed the charge-sheet; and the officer locked him up to await his examination next day before the magistrate.

We were half afraid even now the fellow would manage somehow to get out on bail and give us the slip in spite of everything; and, indeed, he protested in the most violent manner against the treatment to which we were subjecting 'a gentleman in his position.' But Charles took care to tell the police it was all right; that he was a dangerous and peculiarly slippery criminal, and that on no account must they let him go on any pretext whatever, till he had been properly examined before the magistrates.

We learned at the hotel that night, curiously enough, that there really *was* a Dr. Polperro, a distinguished art critic, whose name, we didn't doubt, our impostor had been assuming.

Next morning, when we reached the court, an inspector met us with a very long face. 'Look here, gentlemen,' he said, 'I'm afraid you've committed a very serious blunder. You've made a precious bad mess of it. You've got yourselves into a scrape; and, what's worse, you've got us into one also. You were a deal too smart with your sworn information. We've made inquiries about this gentleman, and we find the account he gives of himself is perfectly correct. His name *is* Polperro; he's a well-known art critic and collector of pictures, employed abroad by the National Gallery. He was formerly an official in the South Kensington Museum, and he's a C.B. and LL.D., very highly respected. You've made a sad mistake, that's where it is; and you'll probably have to answer a charge of false imprisonment, in which I'm afraid you have also involved our own department.'

Charles gasped with horror. 'You haven't let him out,' he cried, 'on those absurd representations? You haven't let him slip through your hands as you did that murderer fellow?'

'Let him slip through our hands?' the inspector cried. 'I only wish he would. There's no chance of that, unfortunately. He's in the court there, this moment, breathing out fire and slaughter against you both; and we're here to protect you if he should happen to fall upon you. He's been locked up all night on your mistaken affidavits, and, naturally enough, he's mad with anger.'

'If you haven't let him go, I'm satisfied,' Charles answered. 'He's a fox for cunning. Where is he? Let me see him.'

We went into the court. There we saw our prisoner conversing amicably, in the most excited way, with the magistrate (who, it seems, was a personal friend of his); and Charles at once went up and spoke to them. Dr. Polperro turned round and glared at him through his *pince-nez*.

'The only possible explanation of this person's extraordinary and incredible conduct,' he said, 'is, that he must be mad—and his secretary equally so. He made my acquaintance, unasked, on a glass seat on the King's Road; invited me to go on his coach to Lewes; volunteered to buy a valuable picture of me; and then, at the last moment, unaccountably gave me in charge on this silly and preposterous trumped-up accusation. I demand a summons for false imprisonment.'

Suddenly it began to dawn upon us that the tables were turned. By degrees it came out that we had made a mistake. Dr. Polperro was really the person he represented himself to be, and had been always. His picture, we found out, was the real Maria Vanrenen, and a genuine Rembrandt, which he had merely deposited for cleaning and restoring at the suspicious dealer's. Sir J. H. Tomlinson had been imposed upon and cheated by a cunning Dutchman; *his* picture, though also an undoubted Rembrandt, was *not* the Maria, and was an inferior specimen in bad preservation. The authority we had consulted turned out to be an ignorant, self-sufficient quack. The Maria, moreover, was valued by other experts at no more than five or six thousand guineas. Charles wanted to cry off his bargain, but Dr. Polperro naturally wouldn't hear of it. The agreement was a legally binding instrument, and what passed in Charles's mind at the moment had nothing to do with the written contract. Our adversary only consented to forego the action for false imprisonment on condition that Charles inserted a printed apology in the *Times*, and paid him five hundred pounds compensation for damage to character. So that was the end of our well-planned attempt to arrest the swindler.

Not quite the end, however; for, of course, after this, the whole affair got by degrees into the papers. Dr. Polperro, who was a familiar person in literary and artistic society, as it turned out, brought an action against the so-called expert who had declared against the genuineness of his alleged Rembrandt, and convicted him of the grossest ignorance and misstatement. Then paragraphs got about. The *World* showed us up in a sarcastic article; and *Truth*, which has always been terribly severe upon Sir Charles and all the other South Africans, had a pungent set of verses on 'High Art in Kimberley.' By this means, as we suppose, the affair became known to Colonel Clay himself; for a week or two later my brother-in-law received a cheerful little note on scented paper from our persistent sharper. It was couched in these terms:—

'Oh, you innocent infant!

'Bless your ingenuous little heart! And did it believe, then, it had positively caught the redoubtable colonel? And had it ready a nice little pinch of salt to put upon his tail? And is it true its respected name is Sir Simple Simon? How heartily we have laughed, White Heather and I, at your neat little ruses! It would pay you, by the way, to take White Heather into your house for six months to instruct you in the agreeable sport of amateur detectives. Your charming *naïveté* quite moves our envy. So you actually imagined a man of my brains would condescend to anything so flat and stale as the silly and threadbare Old Master deception! And this in the so-called nineteenth century! *O sancta simplicitas!* When again shall such infantile transparency be mine? When, ah, when? But never mind, dear friend. Though you didn't catch me, we shall meet before long at some delightful Philippi.

'Yours, with the profoundest respect and gratitude,
'ANTONIO HERRERA,
'Otherwise RICHARD PEPLOE BRABAZON.'

Charles laid down the letter with a deep-drawn sigh. 'Sey, my boy,' he mused aloud, 'no fortune on earth—not even mine—can go on standing it. These perpetual drains begin really to terrify me. I foresee the end. I shall die in a workhouse. What with the money he robs me of when he *is* Colonel Clay, and the money I waste upon him when he *isn't* Colonel Clay, the man is beginning to tell upon my nervous system. I shall withdraw altogether from this worrying life. I shall retire from a scheming and polluted world to some untainted spot in the fresh, pure mountains.'

'You *must* need rest and change,' I said, 'when you talk like that. Let us try the Tyrol.'

IV

THE EPISODE OF THE
TYROLEAN CASTLE

We went to Meran. The place was practically decided for us by
Amelia's French maid, who really acts on such occasions as our
guide and courier.

She is *such* a clever girl, is Amelia's French maid. Whenever
we are going anywhere, Amelia generally asks (and accepts)
her advice as to choice of hotels and furnished villas. Césarine
has been all over the Continent in her time; and, being Alsa-
tian by birth, she of course speaks German as well as she
speaks French, while her long residence with Amelia has made
her at last almost equally at home in our native English. She is
a treasure, that girl; so neat and dexterous, and not above dab-
bling in anything on earth she may be asked to turn her hand
to. She walks the world with a needle-case in one hand and an
etna in the other. She can cook an omelette on occasion, or
drive a Norwegian cariole; she can sew, and knit, and make
dresses, and cure a cold, and do anything else on earth you ask
her. Her salads are the most savoury I ever tasted; while as for
her coffee (which she prepares for us in the train on long jour-
neys), there isn't a *chef de cuisine* at a West-end club to be
named in the same day with her.

So, when Amelia said, in her imperious way, 'Césarine, we
want to go to the Tyrol—now—at once—in mid-October,
where do you advise us to put up?'—Césarine answered, like a
shot, 'The Erzherzog Johann, of course, at Meran, for the
autumn, madame.'

'Is he . . . an archduke?' Amelia asked, a little staggered at
such apparent familiarity with Imperial personages.

'*Ma foi!* no, madame. He is an hotel—as you would say in

England, the "Victoria" or the "Prince of Wales's"—the most comfortable hotel in all South Tyrol; and at this time of year, naturally, you must go beyond the Alps; it begins already to be cold at Innsbruck.'

So to Meran we went; and a prettier or more picturesque place, I confess, I have seldom set eyes on. A rushing torrent; high hills and mountain peaks; terraced vineyard slopes; old walls and towers; quaint, arcaded streets; a craggy waterfall; a promenade after the fashion of a German Spa; and when you lift your eyes from the ground, jagged summits of Dolomites: it was a combination such as I had never before beheld; a Rhine town plumped down among green Alpine heights, and threaded by the cool colonnades of Italy.

I approved Césarine's choice; and I was particularly glad she had pronounced for an hotel, where all is plain sailing, instead of advising a furnished villa, the arrangements for which would naturally have fallen in large part upon the shoulders of the wretched secretary. As in any case I have to do three hours' work a day, I feel that such additions to my normal burden may well be spared me. I tipped Césarine half a sovereign, in fact, for her judicious choice. Césarine glanced at it on her palm in her mysterious, curious, half-smiling way, and pocketed it at once with a 'Merci, monsieur!' that had a touch of contempt in it. I always fancy Césarine has large ideas of her own on the subject of tipping, and thinks very small beer of the modest sums a mere secretary can alone afford to bestow upon her.

The great peculiarity of Meran is the number of schlosses (I believe my plural is strictly irregular, but very convenient to English ears) which you can see in every direction from its out-skirts. A statistical eye, it is supposed, can count to fewer than forty of these picturesque, ramshackled old castles from a point on the Küchelberg. For myself, I hate statistics (except as an element in financial prospectuses), and I really don't know how many ruinous piles Isabel and Amelia counted under Césarine's guidance; but I remember that most of them were quaint and beautiful, and that their variety of architecture seemed positively bewildering. One would be square, with funny little turrets stuck out at each angle; while another would rejoice in a big round keep, and spread on either side long, ivyclad walls and delightful bastions. Charles was immensely taken with them. He loves the picturesque, and has a poet hidden in that financial soul of his. (Very effectually hidden, though, I am ready to grant you.) From the moment he came he felt at once he would love to possess a castle of his own among these romantic mountains. 'Seldon!' he exclaimed contemptuously. 'They call Seldon a castle! But you and I know very well, Sey, it was built in 1860, with sham antique stones, for Macpherson of Seldon, at market rates, by Cubitt and Co., worshipful contractors of London. Macpherson charged me for that sham antiquity a preposterous price, at which one ought to procure a real ancestral mansion. Now, *these* castles are real. They are hoary with antiquity. Schloss Tyrol is Romanesque— tenth or eleventh century.' (He had been reading it up in *Baedeker*.) 'That's the sort of place for *me!*—tenth or eleventh century. I could live here, remote from stocks and shares, for ever; and in these sequestered glens, recollect, Sey, my boy, there are no Colonel Clays, and no arch Madame Picardets!'

As a matter of fact, he could have lived there six weeks, and then tired for Park Lane, Monte Carlo, Brighton.

As for Amelia, strange to say, she was equally taken with this new fad of Charles's. As a rule she hates everywhere on earth save London, except during the time when no respectable person can be seen in town, and when modest blinds shade the scandalised face of Mayfair and Belgravia. She bores herself to death even at Seldon. Castle, Rossshire, and yawns all day long in Paris or Vienna. She is a confirmed Cockney. Yet, for some occult reason, my amiable sister-in-law fell in love with South Tyrol. She wanted to vegetate in that lush vegetation. The grapes were being picked; pumpkins hung over the walls; Virginia creeper draped the quaint gray schlosses with crimson cloaks; and everything was as beautiful as a dream of Burne-Jones's. (I know I am quite right in mentioning Burne-Jones, especially in connection with Romanesque architecture, because I heard him highly praised on that very ground by our friend and enemy, Dr. Edward Polperro.) So perhaps it was excusable that Amelia should fall in love with it all, under the circumstances; besides, she is largely influenced by what Césarine says, and Césarine declares there is no climate in Europe like Meran in winter. I do not agree with her. The sun sets behind the hills at three in the afternoon, and a nasty warm wind blows moist over the snow in January and February.

However, Amelia set Césarine to inquire of the people at the hotel about the market price of tumbledown ruins, and the number of such eligible family mausoleums just then for sale in the immediate neighbourhood. Césarine returned with a full, true, and particular list, adorned with flowers of rhetoric which would have delighted the soul of good old John Robins. They were all picturesque, all Romanesque, all richly ivy-clad, all commodious, all historical, and all the property of high well-born Grafs and very honourable Freiherrs. Most of them had been the scene of celebrated tournaments; several of them had witnessed the gorgeous marriages of Holy Roman Emperors; and every one of them was provided with some choice and selected first-class murders. Ghosts could be arranged for or not, as desired; and armorial bearings could be thrown in with the moat for a moderate extra remuneration.

The two we liked best of all these tempting piles were Schloss Planta and Schloss Lebenstein. We drove past both, and even I myself, I confess, was distinctly taken with them. (Besides, when a big purchase like this is on the stocks, a poor beggar of a secretary has always a chance of exerting his influence and earning for himself some modest commission.) Schloss Planta was the most striking externally, I should say, with its Rhine-like towers, and its great gnarled ivy-stems, that looked as if they antedated the House of Hapsburg; but Lebenstein was said to be better preserved within, and more fitted in every way for modern occupation. Its staircase has been photographed by 7000 amateurs.

We got tickets to view. The invaluable Césarine procured them for us. Armed with these, we drove off one fine afternoon, meaning to go to Planta, by Césarine's recommendation. Half-way there, however, we changed our minds, as it was such a lovely day, and went on up the long, slow hill to

Lebenstein. I must say the drive through the grounds was simply charming. The castle stands perched (say rather poised, like St. Michael the archangel in Italian pictures) on a solitary stack or crag of rock, looking down on every side upon its own rich vineyards. Chestnuts line the glens; the valley of the Etsch spreads below like a picture.

The vineyards alone make a splendid estate, by the way; they produce a delicious red wine, which is exported to Bordeaux, and there bottled and sold as a vintage claret under the name of Château Monnivet. Charles revelled in the idea of growing his own wines.

'Here we could sit,' he cried to Amelia, 'in the most literal sense, under our own vine and fig-tree. Delicious retirement! For my part, I'm sick and tired of the hubbub of Threadneedle Street.'

We knocked at the door—for there was really no bell, but a ponderous, old-fashioned, wrought-iron knocker. So deliciously mediæval! The late Graf Von Lebenstein had recently died, we knew; and his son, the present Count, a young man of means, having inherited from his mother's family a still more ancient and splendid schloss in the Salzburg district, desired to sell this outlying estate in order to afford himself a yacht, after the manner that is now becoming increasingly fashionable with the noblemen and gentlemen in Germany and Austria.

The door was opened for us by a high well-born menial, attired in a very ancient and honourable livery. Nice antique hall; suits of ancestral armour, trophies of Tyrolese hunters, coats of arms of ancient counts—the very thing to take Amelia's aristocratic and romantic fancy. The whole to be sold exactly as it stood; ancestors to be included at a valuation.

We went through the reception-rooms. They were lofty, charming, and with glorious views, all the more glorious for being framed by those graceful Romanesque windows, with their slender pillars and quaint, round-topped arches. Sir Charles had made his mind up. 'I must and will have it!' he cried. 'This is the place for me. Seldon! Pah, Seldon is a modern abomination.'

Could we see the high well-born Count? The liveried servant

(somewhat haughtily) would inquire of his Serenity. Sir Charles sent up his card, and also Lady Vandrift's. These foreigners know title spells money in England.

He was right in his surmise. Two minutes later the Count entered with our cards in his hands. A good-looking young man, with the characteristic Tyrolese long black moustache, dressed in a gentlemanly variant on the costume of the country. His air was a jäger's; the usual blackcock's plume stuck jauntily in the side of the conical hat (which he held in his hand), after the universal Austrian fashion.

He waved us to seats. We sat down. He spoke to us in French; his English, he remarked, with a pleasant smile, being a *négligeable* quantity. We might speak it, he went on; he could understand pretty well; but he preferred to answer, if we would allow him, in French or German.

'French,' Charles replied, and the negotiation continued thenceforth in that language, It is the only one, save English and his ancestral Dutch, with which my brother-in-law possesses even a nodding acquaintance.

We praised the beautiful scene. The Count's face lighted up with patriotic pride. Yes; it was beautiful, beautiful, his own green Tyrol. He was proud of it and attached to it. But he could endure to sell this place, the home of his fathers, because he had a finer in the Salzkammergut, and a *pied-à-terre* near Innsbruck. For Tyrol lacked just one joy—the sea. He was a passionate yachtsman. For that he had resolved to sell this estate; after all, three country houses, a ship, and a mansion in Vienna, are more than one man can comfortably inhabit.

'Exactly,' Charles answered. 'If I can come to terms with you about this charming estate I shall sell my own castle in the Scotch Highlands.' And he tried to look like a proud Scotch chief who harangues his clansmen.

Then they got to business. The Count was a delightful man to do business with. His manners were perfect. While we were talking to him, a surly person, a steward or bailiff, or something of the sort, came into the room unexpectedly and addressed him in German, which none of us understand. We were impressed by the singular urbanity and benignity of the nobleman's demeanour towards this sullen dependant. He evidently explained to the fellow what sort of people we were, and remonstrated with him in a very gentle way for interrupting us. The steward understood, and clearly regretted his insolent air; for after a few sentences he went out, and as he did so he bowed and made protestations of polite regard in his own language. The Count turned to us and smiled. 'Our people,' he said, 'are like your own Scotch peasants—kind-hearted, picturesque, free, musical, poetic, but wanting, *hélas*, in polish to strangers.' He was certainly an exception, if he described them aright; for he made us feel at home from the moment we entered.

He named his price in frank terms. His lawyers at Meran held the needful documents, and would arrange the negotiations in detail with us. It was a stiff sum, I must say—an extremely stiff sum; but no doubt he was charging us a fancy price for a fancy castle. 'He will come down in time,' Charles said. 'The sum first named in all these transactions is invariably a feeler. They know I'm a millionaire; and people always imagine millionaires are positively made of money.'

I may add that people always imagine it must be easier to squeeze money out of millionaires than out of other people— which is the reverse of the truth, or how could they ever have amassed their millions? Instead of oozing gold as a tree oozes gum, they mot it up like blotting-paper, and seldom give it out again.

We drove back from this first interview none the less very well satisfied. The price was too high; but preliminaries were arranged, and for the rest, the Count desired us to discuss all details with his lawyers in the chief street, Unter den Lauben. We inquired about these lawyers, and found they were most respectable and respected men; they had done the family business on either side for seven generations.

They showed us plans and title-deeds. Everything quite *en règle*. Till we came to the price there was no hitch of any sort.

As to price, however, the lawyers were obdurate. They stuck out for the Count's first sum to the uttermost florin. It was a very big estimate. We talked and shilly-shallied till Sir Charles grew angry. He lost his temper at last.

'They know I'm a millionaire, Sey,' he said, 'and they're playing the old game of trying to diddle me. But I won't be diddled. Except Colonel Clay, no man has ever yet succeeded in bleeding me. And shall I let myself be bled as if I were a chamois among these innocent mountains? Perish the thought!' Then he reflected a little in silence. 'Sey,' he mused on, at last, 'the question is, *are* they innocent? Do you know, I begin to believe there is no such thing left as pristine innocence anywhere. This Tyrolese Count knows the value of a pound as distinctly as if he hung out in Capel Court or Kimberley.'

Things dragged on in this way, inconclusively, for a week or two. *We* bid down; the lawyers stuck to it. Sir Charles grew half sick of the whole silly business. For my own part, I felt sure if the high well-born Count didn't quicken his pace, my respected relative would shortly have had enough of the Tyrol altogether, and be proof against the most lovely of crag-crowning castles. But the Count didn't see it. He came to call on us at our hotel—a rare honour for a stranger with these haughty and exclusive Tyrolese nobles—and even entered unannounced in the most friendly manner. But when it came to £ s. d., he was absolute adamant. Not one kreutzer would he abate from his original proposal.

'You misunderstand,' he said, with pride. 'We Tyrolese gentlemen are not shopkeepers or merchants, We do not higgle. If we say a thing we stick to it. Were you an Austrian, I should feel insulted by your ill-advised attempt to beat down my price. But as you belong to a great commerical nation——' he broke off with a snort and shrugged his shoulders compassionately.

We saw him several times driving in and out of the schloss, and every time he waved his hand at us gracefully. But when we tried to bargain, it was always the same thing: he retired behind the shelter of his Tyrolese nobility. We might take it or leave it. 'Twas still Schloss Lebenstein.

The lawyers were as bad. We tried all we knew, and got no forrarder.

At last Charles gave up the attempt in disgust. He was tiring, as I expected. 'It's the prettiest place I ever saw in my life,' he said; 'but, hang it all, Sey, I *won't* be imposed upon.'

So he made up his mind, it being now December, to return to London. We met the Count next day, and stopped his carriage, and told him so. Charles thought this would have the immediate effect of bringing the man to reason. But he only lifted his hat, with the blackcock's feather, and smiled a bland smile. 'The Archduke Karl is inquiring about it,' he answered, and drove on without parley.

Charles used some strong words, which I will not transcribe (I am a family man), and returned to England.

For the next two months we heard little from Amelia save her regret that the Count wouldn't sell us Schloss Lebenstein. Its pinnacles had fairly pierced her heart. Strange to say, she was absolutely infatuated about the castle. She rather wanted the place while she was there, and thought she could get it; now she thought she couldn't, her soul (if she has one) was wildly set upon it. Moreover, Césarine further inflamed her desire by gently hinting a fact which she had picked up at the courier's *table d'hôte* at the hotel—that the Count had been far from anxious to sell his ancestral and historical estate to a South African diamond king. He thought the honour of the family demanded, at least, that he should secure a wealthy buyer of good ancient lineage.

One morning in February, however, Amelia returned from the Row all smiles and tremors. (She had been ordered horse-exercise to correct the increasing excessiveness of her figure.)

'Who do you think I saw riding in the Park?' she inquired. 'Why, the Count of Lebenstein.'

'No!' Charles exclaimed, incredulous.

'Yes,' Amelia answered.

'Must be mistaken,' Charles cried.

But Amelia stuck to it. More than that, she sent out emissaries to inquire diligently from the London lawyers, whose name had been mentioned to us by the ancestral firm in Unter den Lauben as their English agents, as to the whereabouts of our friend; and her emissaries learned in effect that the Count was in town and stopping at Morley's.

'I see through it,' Charles exclaimed. 'He finds he's made a mistake; and now he's come over here to reopen negotiations.'

I was all for waiting prudently till the Count made the first move. 'Don't let him see your eagerness,' I said. But Amelia's ardour could not now be restrained. She insisted that Charles should call on the Graf as a mere return of his politeness in the Tyrol.

He was as charming as ever. He talked to us with delight about the quaintness of London. He would be ravished to dine next evening with Sir Charles. He desired his respectful salutations mean-while to Miladi Vandrift and Madame Ventvorth.

He dined with us, almost *en famille*. Amelia's cook did wonders. In the billiard-room, about midnight, Charles reopened the subject. The Count was really touched. It pleased him that still, amid the distractions of the City of Five Million Souls, we should remember with affection his beloved Lebenstein.

'Come to my lawyers,' he said, 'to-morrow, and I will talk it all over with you.'

We went—a most respectable firm in Southampton Row; old family solicitors. They had done business for years for the late Count, who had inherited from his grandmother estates in Ireland; and they were glad to be honoured with the confidence of his successor. Glad, too, to make the acquaintance of a prince of finance like Sir Charles Vandrift. Anxious (rubbing their hands) to arrange matters satisfactorily all round for everybody. (Two capital families with which to be mixed up, you see.)

Sir Charles named a price, and referred them to his solicitors. The Count named a higher, but still a little come-down, and left the matter to be settled between the lawyers. He was a soldier and a gentleman, he said, with a Tyrolese toss of his highborn head; he would abandon details to men of business.

As I was really anxious to oblige Amelia, I met the Count accidentally next day on the steps of Morley's. (Accidentally, that is to say, so far as he was concerned, though I had been hanging about in Trafalgar Square for half an hour to see him.) I explained, in guarded terms, that I had a great deal of influence in my way with Sir Charles; and that a word from me——I broke off. He stared at me blankly.

'Commission?' he inquired, at last, with a queer little smile.

'Well, not exactly commission,' I answered, wincing. 'Still, a friendly word, you know. One good turn deserves another.'

He looked at me from head to foot with a curious scrutiny. For one moment I feared the Tyrolese nobleman in him was going to raise its foot and take active measures. But the next, I saw that Sir Charles was right after all, and that pristine innocence has removed from this planet to other quarters.

He named his lowest price. 'M. Ventvorth,' he said, 'I am a Tyrolese *seigneur;* I do not dabble, myself, in commissions and percentages. But if your influence with Sir Charles—we understand each other, do we not?—as between gentlemen—a little friendly present—no money, of course—but the equivalent of say 5 per cent in jewellery, on whatever sum above his bid to-day you induce him to offer—eh?—*c'est convenu?'*

'Ten per cent is more usual,' I murmured.

He was the Austrian hussar again. 'Five, monsieur—or nothing!'

I bowed and withdrew. 'Well, five then,' I answered, 'just to oblige your Serenity.'

A secretary, after all, can do a great deal. When it came to the scratch, I had but little difficulty in persuading Sir Charles, with Amelia's aid, backed up on either side by Isabel and Césarine, to accede to the Count's more reasonable proposal. The Southampton Row people had possession of certain facts as to the value of the wines in the Bordeaux market which clinched the matter. In a week or two all was settled; Charles and I met the Count by appointment in Southampton Row, and saw him sign, seal, and deliver the title-deeds of Schloss Lebenstein. My brother-in-law paid the purchase-money into the Count's own hands, by cheque, crossed on a first-class London firm where the Count kept an account to his high well born order. Then he went away with the proud knowledge that he was owner of Schloss Lebenstein. And what to me was more important still, I received next morning by post a cheque for the five per cent, unfortunately drawn, by some misapprehension, to my order on the self-same bankers, and with the Count's signature. He explained in the accompanying note that the matter being now quite satisfactorily concluded, he saw no reason of delicacy why the amount he had promised should not be paid to me forthwith direct in money.

I cashed the cheque at once, and said nothing about the affair, not even to Isabel. My experience is that women are not to be trusted with intricate matters of commission and brokerage.

Though it was now late in March, and the House was sitting, Charles insisted that we must all run over at once to take possession of our magnificent Tyrolese castle. Amelia was almost equally burning with eagerness. She gave herself the airs of a Countess already. We took the Orient Express as far as Munich; then the Brenner to Meran, and put up for the night at the Erzherzog Johann. Though we had telegraphed our arrival, and expected some fuss, there was no demonstration. Next morning we drove out in state to the schloss, to enter into enjoyment of our vines and fig-trees.

We were met at the door by the surly steward. 'I shall dismiss that man,' Charles muttered, as Lord of Lebenstein. 'He's too sour-looking for my taste. Never saw such a brute. Not a smile of welcome!'

He mounted the steps. The surly man stepped forward and murmured a few morose words in German. Charles brushed him aside and strode on. Then there followed a curious scene of mutual misunderstanding. The surly man called lustily for his servants to eject us. It was some time before we began to catch at the truth. The surly man was the *real* Graf von Lebenstein.

And the Count with the moustache? It dawned upon us now. Colonel Clay again! More audacious than ever!

Bit by bit it all came out. He had ridden behind us the first day we viewed the place, and, giving himself out to the servants as one of our party, had joined us in the reception-room. We asked the real Count why he had spoken to the intruder. The Count explained in French that the man with the moustache had introduced my brother-in-law as the great South African millionaire, while he described himself as our courier and interpreter. As such he had had frequent interviews with the real Graf and his lawyers in Meran, and had driven almost daily across to the castle. The owner of the estate had named one price from the first, and had stuck to it manfully. He stuck to it still; and if Sir

Charles chose to buy Schloss Lebenstein over again he was welcome to have it. How the London lawyers had been duped the Count had not really the slightest idea. He regretted the incident, and (coldly) wished us a very good morning.

There was nothing for it but to return as best we might to the Erzherzog Johann, crestfallen, and telegraph particulars to the police in London.

Charles and I ran across post-haste to England to track down the villain. At Southampton Row we found the legal firm by no means penitent; on the contrary, they were indignant at the way we had deceived them. An impostor had written to them on Lebenstein paper from Meran to say that he was coming to London to negotiate the sale of the schloss and surrounding property with the famous millionaire, Sir Charles Vandrift; and Sir Charles had demonstratively recognised him at sight as the real Count von Lebenstein. The firm had never seen the present Graf at all, and had swallowed the impostor whole, so to speak, on the strength of Sir Charles's obvious recognition. He had brought over as documents some most excellent forgeries—facsimiles of the originals—which, as our courier and interpreter, he had every opportunity of examining and inspecting at the Meran lawyers.' It was a deeply-laid plot, and it had succeeded to a marvel. Yet, all of it depended upon the one small fact that we had accepted the man with the long moustache in the hall of the schloss as the Count von Lebenstein on his own representation.

He held our cards in his hands when he came in; and the servant had *not* given them to him, but to the genuine Count. That was the one unsolved mystery in the whole adventure.

By the evening's post two letters arrived for us at Sir Charles's house: one for myself, and one for my employer. Sir Charles's ran thus:—

'HIGH WELL-BORN INCOMPETENCE,—

'I only just pulled through! A very small slip nearly lost me everything. I believed you were going to Schloss Planta that day, not to Schloss Lebenstein. You changed your mind *en route*. That might have spoiled all. Happily I perceived it, rode up by the short cut, and arrived somewhat hurriedly and hotly at the gate before you. Then I introduced myself. I had one more bad moment when the rival claimant to my name and title intruded into the room. But fortune favours the brave: your utter ignorance of German saved me. The rest was pap. It went by itself almost.

'Allow me, now, as some small return for your various welcome cheques, to offer you a useful and valuable present—a German dictionary, grammar, and phrase-book!

'I kiss your hand.

'No longer

'VON LEBENSTEIN.'

The other note was to me. It was as follows:—

'DEAR GOOD MR. VENTVORTH,—

'Ha, ha, ha; just a *W* misplaced sufficed to take you in, then! And I risked the *TH*, though anybody with a head on his shoulders would surely have known our *TH* is by far more difficult than our *W* for foreigners! However, all's well that ends well; and now I've got you. The Lord has delivered you into my hands, dear friend—on your own initiative. I hold my cheque, endorsed by you, and cashed at my banker's, as a hostage, so to speak, for your future good behaviour. If ever you recognise me, and betray me to that solemn old ass, your employer, remember, I expose it, and you with it to him. So now we understand each other. I had not thought of this little dodge; it was you who suggested it. However, I jumped at it. Was it not well worth my while paying you that slight commission in return for a guarantee of your future silence? Your mouth is now closed. And cheap too at the price.— Yours, dear Comrade, in the great confraternity of rogues,

'CUTHBERT CLAY, *Colonel.*'

Charles laid his note down, and grizzled. 'What's yours, Sey?' he asked.

'From a lady,' I answered.

He gazed at me suspiciously. 'Oh, I thought it was the same hand,' he said. His eye looked through me.

'No,' I answered. 'Mrs. Mortimer's.' But I confess I trembled.

He paused a moment. 'You made all inquiries at this fellow's bank?' he went on, after a deep sigh.

'Oh, yes,' I put in quickly. (I had taken good care about that, you may be sure, lest he should spot the commission.) 'They say the self-styled Count von Lebenstein was introduced to them by the Southampton Row folks, and drew, as usual, on the Lebenstein account: so they were quite unsuspicious. A rascal who goes about the world on that scale, you know, and arrives with such credentials as theirs and yours, naturally imposes on anybody. The bank didn't even require to have him formally identified. The firm was enough. He came to pay money in, not to draw it out. And he withdrew his balance just two days later, saying he was in a hurry to get back to Vienna.'

Would he ask for items? I confess I felt it was an awkward moment. Charles, however, was too full of regrets to bother about the account. He leaned back in his easy chair, stuck his hands in his pockets, held his legs straight out on the fender before him, and looked the very picture of hopeless despondency.

'Sey,' he began, after a minute or two, poking the fire, reflectively, 'what a genius that man has! 'Pon my soul, I admire him. I sometimes wish——' He broke off and hesitated.

'Yes, Charles?' I answered.

'I sometimes wish . . . we had got him on the Board of the Cloetedorp Golcondas. Mag—nificent combinations he would make in the City!'

I rose from my seat and stared solemnly at my misguided brother-in-law.

'Charles,' I said, 'you are beside yourself. Too much Colonel Clay has told upon your clear and splendid intellect. There are certain remarks which, however true they may be, no self-respecting financier should permit himself to make, even in the privacy of his own room, to his most intimate friend and trusted adviser.'

Charles fairly broke down. 'You are right, Sey,' he sobbed out. 'Quite right. Forgive this outburst. At moments of emotion the truth will sometimes out, in spite of everything.'

I respected his feebleness. I did not even make it a fitting occasion to ask for a trifling increase of salary.

V

THE EPISODE OF THE
DRAWN GAME

The twelfth of August saw us, as usual, at Seldon Castle, Ross-shire. It is part of Charles's restless, roving temperament that, on the morning of the eleventh, wet or fine, he must set out from London, whether the House is sitting or not, in defiance of the most urgent three-line whips; and at dawn on the twelfth he must be at work on his moors, shooting down the young birds with might and main, at the earliest possible legal moment.

He goes on like Saul, slaying his thousands, or, like David, his tens of thousands, with all the guns in the house to help him, till the keepers warn him he has killed as many grouse as they consider desirable; and then, having done his duty, as he thinks, in this respect, he retires precipitately with flying colours to Brighton, Nice, Monte Carlo, or elsewhere. He must be always 'on the trek'; when he is buried, I believe he will not be able to rest quiet in his grave: his ghost will walk the world to terrify old ladies.

'At Seldon, at least,' he said to me, with a sigh, as he stepped into his Pullman, 'I shall be safe from that impostor!'

And indeed, as soon as he had begun to tire a little of counting up his hundreds of brace per *diem*, he found a trifling piece of financial work cut ready to his hand, which amply distracted his mind for the moment from Colonel Clay, his accomplices, and his villainies.

Sir Charles, I ought to say, had secured during that summer a very advantageous option in a part of Africa on the Transvaal frontier, rumoured to be auriferous. Now, whether it was auriferous or not before, the mere fact that Charles had secured some claim on it naturally made it so; for no man had ever the genuine Midas-touch to a greater degree than Charles Vandrift: whatever he handles turns at once to gold, if not to diamonds. Therefore, as soon as my brother-in-law had obtained this option from the native vendor (a most respected chief, by name Montsioa), and promoted a company of his own to develop it, his great rival in that region, Lord Craig-Ellachie (formerly Sir David Alexander Granton), immediately secured a similar option of an adjacent track, the larger part of which had pretty much the same geological conditions as that covered by Sir Charles's right of pre-emption.

We were not wholly disappointed, as it turned out, in the result. A month or two later, while we were still at Seldon, we received a long and encouraging letter from our prospectors on the spot, who had been hunting over the ground in search of gold-reefs. They reported that they had found a good aurif- erous vein in a corner of the tract, approachable by aditlevels; but, unfortunately, only a few yards of the lode lay within the limits of Sir Charles's area. The remainder ran on at once into what was locally known as Craig-Ellachie's section.

However, our prospectors had been canny, they said; though young Mr. Granton was prospecting at the same time, in the self-same ridge, not very far from them, his miners had failed to discover the auriferous quartz; so our men had held their tongues about it, wisely leaving it for Charles to govern him- self accordingly.

'Can you dispute the boundary?' I asked.

'Impossible,' Charles answered. 'You see, the limit is a meridian of longitude. There's no getting over that. Can't pre- tend to deny it. No buying over the sun! No bribing the instru- ments! Besides, we drew the line ourselves. We've only one way out of it, Sey. Amalgamate! Amalgamate!'

Charles is a marvellous man! The very voice in which he murmured that blessed word 'Amalgamate!' was in itself a poem.

'Capital!' I answered. 'Say nothing about it, and join forces with Craig-Ellachie.'

Charles closed one eye pensively.

That very same evening came a telegram in cipher from our

chief engineer on the territory of the option: 'Young Granton
has somehow given us the slip and gone home. We suspect he
knows all. But we have not divulged the secret to anybody.'

'Seymour,' my brother-in-law said impressively, 'there is no
time to be lost. I must write this evening to Sir David—I mean
to My Lord. Do you happen to know where he is stopping at
present?'

'The *Morning Post* announced two or three days ago that
he was at Glen-Ellachie,' I answered.

'Then I'll ask him to come over and thrash the matter out
with me,' my brother-in-law went on. 'A very rich reef, they
say. I must have my finger in it!'

We adjourned into the study, where Sir Charles drafted, I
must admit, a most judicious letter to the rival capitalist. He
pointed out that the mineral resources of the country were
probably great, but as yet uncertain. That the expense of
crushing and milling might be almost prohibitive. That access
to fuel was costly, and its conveyance difficult. That water was
scarce, and commanded by our section. That two rival companies, if they happened to hit upon ore, might cut one another's
throats by erecting two sets of furnaces or pumping plants,
and bringing two separate streams to the spot, where one
would answer. In short—to employ the golden word—that
amalgamation might prove better in the end than competition;
and that he advised, at least, a conference on the subject.

I wrote it out fair for him, and Sir Charles, with the air of a
Cromwell, signed it.

'This is important, Sey,' he said. 'It had better be registered,
for fear of falling into improper hands. Don't give it to Dob-
son; let Césarine take it over to Fowlis in the dog-cart.'

It is the drawback of Seldon that we are twelve miles from a
railway station, though we look out on one of the loveliest
firths in Scotland.

Césarine took it as directed—an invaluable servant, that
girl! Meanwhile, we learned from the *Morning Post* next day
that young Mr. Granton had stolen a march upon us. He had
arrived from Africa by the same mail with our agent's letter,
and had joined his father at once at Glen-Ellachie.

Two days later we received a most polite reply from the opposing interest. It ran after this fashion:—

'CRAIG-ELLACHIE LODGE,
'GLEN-ELLACHIE, INVERNESS-SHIRE.

'DEAR SIR CHARLES VANDRIFT—Thanks for yours of the 20th. In reply, I can only say I fully reciprocate your amiable desire that nothing adverse to either of our companies should happen in South Africa. With regard to your suggestion that we should meet in person, to discuss the basis of a possible amalgamation, I can only say my house is at present full of guests—as is doubtless your own—and I should therefore find it practically impossible to leave Glen-Ellachie. Fortunately, however, my son David is now at home on a brief holiday from Kimberley; and it will give him great pleasure to come over and hear what you have to say in favour of an arrangement which certainly, on some grounds, seems to me desirable in the interests of both our concessions alike. He will arrive tomorrow afternoon at Seldon, and he is authorised, in every respect, to negotiate with full powers on behalf of myself and the other directors. With kindest regards to your wife and sons, I remain, dear Sir Charles, yours faithfully,

'CRAIG-ELLACHIE.'

'Cunning old fox!' Sir Charles exclaimed, with a sniff. 'What's he up to now, I wonder? Seems almost as anxious to amalgamate as we ourselves are, Sey.' A sudden thought struck him. 'Do you know,' he cried, looking up, 'I really believe the same thing must have happened to *both* our exploring parties. *They* must have found a reef that goes under. *our* ground, and the wicked old rascal wants to cheat us out of it!'

'As we want to cheat him,' I ventured to interpose.

Charles looked at me fixedly. 'Well, if so, we're both in luck,' he murmured, after a pause; 'though *we* can only get to know the whereabouts of *their* find by joining hands with them and showing them ours. Still, it's good business either way. But I shall be cautious—cautious.'

'What a nuisance!' Amelia cried, when we told her of the

incident. 'I suppose I shall have to put the man up for the night—a nasty, raw-boned, half-baked Scotchman, you may be certain.'

On Wednesday afternoon, about three, young Granton arrived. He was a pleasant-featured, red haired, sandy-whiskered youth, not unlike his father; but, strange to say, he dropped in to call, instead of bringing his luggage.

'Why, you're not going back to Glen-Ellachie to-night, surely?' Charles exclaimed, in amazement. 'Lady Vandrift will be *so* disappointed! Besides, this business can't be arranged between two trains, do you think, Mr. Granton?'

Young Granton smiled. He had an agreeable smile—canny, yet open.

'Oh no,' he said frankly. 'I didn't mean to go back. I've put up at the inn. I have my wife with me, you know—and, I wasn't invited.'

Amelia was of opinion, when we told her this episode, that David Granton wouldn't stop at Seldon because he was an Honourable. Isabel was of opinion he wouldn't stop because he had married an unpresentable young woman somewhere out in South Africa. Charles was of opinion that, as representative of the hostile interest, he put up at the inn, because it might tie his hands in some way to be the guest of the chairman of the rival company. And *I* was of opinion that he had heard of the castle, and knew it well by report as the dullest country-house to stay at in Scotland.

However that may be, young Granton insisted on remaining at the Cromarty Arms, though he told us his wife would be delighted to receive a call from Lady Vandrift and Mrs. Wentworth. So we all returned with him to bring the Honourable Mrs. Granton up to tea at the Castle.

She was a nice little thing, very shy and timid, but by no means unpresentable, and an evident lady. She giggled at the end of every sentence; and she was endowed with a slight squint, which somehow seemed to point all her feeble sallies. She knew little outside South Africa; but of that she talked prettily; and she won all our hearts, in spite of the cast in her eye, by her unaffected simplicity.

Next morning Charles and I had a regular debate with young Granton about the rival options. Our talk was of cyanide processes, reverberatories, pennyweights, water-jackets. But it dawned upon us soon that, in spite of his red hair and his innocent manners, our friend, the Honourable David Granton, knew a thing or two. Gradually and gracefully he let us see that Lord Craig-Ellachie had sent him for the benefit of the company, but that *he* had come for the benefit of the Honourable David Granton.

'I'm a younger son, Sir Charles,' he said; 'and therefore I have to feather my nest for myself. I know the ground. My father will be guided implicitly by what I advise in the matter. We are men of the world. Now, let's be business-like. *You* want to amalgamate. You wouldn't do that, of course, if you didn't know of something to the advantage of my father's company—say, a lode on our land—which you hope to secure for yourself by amalgamation. Very well; *I* can make or mar your project. If you choose to render it worth my while, I'll induce my father and his directors to amalgamate. If you don't, I won't. That's the long and the short of it!'

Charles looked at him admiringly.

'Young man,' he said, 'you're deep, very deep—for your age. Is this candour—or deception? Do you mean what you say? Or do you know some reason why it suits your father's book to amalgamate as well as it suits mine? And are you trying to keep it from me?' He fingered his chin. 'If I only knew that,' he went on, 'I should know how to deal with you.'

Young Granton smiled again. 'You're a financier, Sir Charles,' he answered. 'I wonder, at your time of life, you should pause to ask another financier whether he's trying to fill his own pocket—or his father's. Whatever is my father's goes to his eldest son—and *I* am his youngest.'

'You are right as to general principles,' Sir Charles replied, quite affectionately. 'Most sound and sensible. But how do I know you haven't bargained already in the same way with your father? You may have settled with *him,* and be trying to diddle me.'

The young man assumed a most candid air. 'Look here,' he

said, leaning forward. 'I offer you this chance. Take it or leave
it. *Do* you wish to purchase my aid for this amalgamation by a
moderate commission on the net value of my father's option to
yourself—which I know approximately?'

'Say five per cent,' I suggested, in a tentative voice, just to
justify my presence.

He looked me through and through. '*Ten* is more usual,' he
answered, in a peculiar tone and with a peculiar glance.

Great heavens, how I winced! I knew what his words meant.
They were the very words I had said myself to Colonel Clay, as
the Count von Lebenstein, about the purchase-money of the
schloss—and in the very same accent. I saw through it all now.
That beastly cheque! This was Colonel Clay; and he was trying
to buy up my silence and assistance by the threat of exposure!

My blood ran cold. I didn't know how to answer him. What
happened at the rest of that interview I really couldn't tell you.
My brain reeled round. I heard just faint echoes of 'fuel' and
'reduction works.' What on earth was I to do? If I told Charles
my suspicion—for it was only a suspicion—the fellow might
turn upon me and disclose the cheque, which would suffice to
ruin me. If I didn't, I ran a risk of being considered by Charles
an accomplice and a confederate.

The interview was long. I hardly know how I struggled
through it. At the end young Granton went off, well satisfied,
if it was young Granton; and Amelia invited him and his wife
up to dinner at the castle.

Whatever else they were, they were capital company. They
stopped for three days more at the Cromarty Arms. And
Charles debated and discussed incessantly. He couldn't quite
make up his mind what to do in the affair; and *I* certainly
couldn't help him. I never was placed in such a fix in my life. I
did my best to preserve a strict neutrality.

Young Granton, it turned out, was a most agreeable person;
and so, in her way, was that timid, unpretending South African wife of his. She was naïvely surprised Amelia had never
met her mamma at Durban. They both talked delightfully,
and had lots of good stories—mostly with points that told
against the Craig-Ellachie people. Moreover, the Honourable

David was a splendid swimmer. He went out in a boat with us, and dived like a seal. He was burning to teach Charles and myself to swim, when we told him we could neither of us take a single stroke; he said it was an accomplishment incumbent upon every true Englishman. But Charles hates the water; while, as for myself, I detest every known form of muscular exercise.

However, we consented that he should row us on the Firth, and made an appointment one day with himself and his wife for four the next evening.

That night Charles came to me with a very grave face in my own bedroom. 'Sey,' he said, under his breath, 'have you observed? Have you watched? Have you any suspicions?'

I trembled violently. I felt all was up. 'Suspicions of whom?' I asked. 'Not surely of Simpson?' (he was Sir Charles's valet).

My respected brother-in-law looked at me contemptuously.

'Sey,' he said, 'are you trying to take me in? No, *not* of Simpson: of these two young folks. My own belief is—they're Colonel Clay and Madame Picardet.'

'Impossible!' I cried.

He nodded. 'I'm sure of it.'

'How do you know?'

'Instinctively.'

I seized his arm. 'Charles,' I said, imploring him, 'do nothing rash. Remember how you exposed yourself to the ridicule of fools over Dr. Polperro!'

'I've thought of that,' he answered, 'and I mean to ca' caller.' (When in Scotland as laird of Seldon, Charles loves both to dress and to speak the part thoroughly.) 'First thing to-morrow I shall telegraph over to inquire at Glen-Ellachie; I shall find out whether this is really young Granton or not; meanwhile, I shall keep my eye close upon the fellow.'

Early next morning, accordingly, a groom was dispatched with a telegram to Lord Craig-Ellachie. He was to ride over to Fowlis, send it off at once, and wait for the answer. At the same time, as it was probable Lord Craig-Ellachie would have started for the moors before the telegram reached the Lodge, I did not myself expect to see the reply arrive much before seven or eight that evening. Meanwhile, as it was far from certain we had not the real David Granton to deal with, it was necessary to be polite to our friendly rivals. Our experience in the Polperro incident had shown us both that too much zeal may be more dangerous than too little. Nevertheless, taught by previous misfortunes, we kept watching our man pretty close, determined that on this occasion, at least, he should neither do us nor yet escape us.

About four o'clock the red-haired young man and his pretty little wife came up to call for us. She looked so charming and squinted so enchantingly, one could hardly believe she was not as simple and innocent as she seemed to be. She tripped down to the Seldon boat-house, with Charles by her side, giggling and squinting her best, and then helped her husband to get the skiff ready. As she did so, Charles sidled up to me. 'Sey,' he whispered, 'I'm an old hand, and I'm not readily taken in. I've been talking to that girl, and upon my soul I think she's all right. She's a charming little lady. We may be mistaken after all, of course, about young Granton. In any case, it's well for the present to be courteous. A most important option! If it's really he, we must do nothing to annoy him or let him see we suspect him.'

I had noticed, indeed, that Mrs. Granton had made herself most agreeable to Charles from the very beginning. And as to one thing he was right. In her timid, shrinking way she was undeniably charming. That cast in her eye was all pure piquancy.

We rowed out on to the Firth, or, to be more strictly correct, the two Grantons rowed while Charles and I sat and leaned back in the stern on the luxurious cushions. They rowed fast and well. In a very few minutes they had rounded the point and got clear out of sight of the Cockneyfied towers and false battlements of Seldon.

Mrs. Granton pulled stroke. Even as she rowed she kept up a brisk undercurrent of timid chaff with Sir Charles, giggling all the while, half forward, half shy, like a school-girl who flirts with a man old enough to be her grandfather.

Sir Charles was flattered. He is susceptible to the pleasures of female attention, especially from the young, the simple, and the innocent. The wiles of women of the world he knows too well; but a pretty little *ingénue* can twist him round her finger. They rowed on and on, till they drew abreast of Seamew's island. It is a jagged stack or skerry, well out to sea, very wild and preciptious on the landward side, but shelving gently outward; perhaps an acre in extent, with steep gray cliffs, covered at that time with crimson masses of red valerian. Mrs. Granton rowed up close to it. 'Oh, what lovely flowers!' she cried, throwing her head back and gazing at them. 'I wish I could get some! Let's land here and pick them. Sir Charles, you shall gather me a nice bunch for my sitting-room.'

Charles rose to it innocently, like a trout to a fly.

'By all means, my dear child, I—I have a passion for flowers;' which was a flower of speech itself, but it served its purpose.

They rowed us round to the far side, where is the easiest landing-place. It struck me as odd at the moment that they seemed to know it. Then young Granton jumped lightly ashore; Mrs. Granton skipped after him. I confess it made me feel rather ashamed to see how clumsily Charles and I followed them, treading gingerly on the thwarts for fear of upsetting the boat, while the artless young thing just flew over the gunwale. So like White Heather! However, we got ashore at last in safety, and began to climb the rocks as well as we were able in search of the valerian.

Judge of our astonishment when next moment those two young people bounded back into the boat, pushed off with a peal of merry laughter, and left us there staring at them!

They rowed away, about twenty yards, into deep water. Then the man turned, and waved his hand at us gracefully. 'Good-bye!' he said, 'good-bye! Hope you'll pick a nice bunch! We're off to London!'

'Off!' Charles exclaimed, turning pale. 'Off! What do you mean? You don't surely mean to say you're going to leave us here?'

The young man raised his cap with perfect politeness, while Mrs. Granton smiled, nodded, and kissed her pretty hand to us. 'Yes,' he answered; 'for the present. We retire from the game. The fact of it is, it's a trifle too thin: this is a *coup manqué*.'

'A *what?*' Charles exclaimed, perspiring visibly.

'A *coup manqué,*' the young man replied, with a compassionate smile. 'A failure, don't you know; a bad shot; a fiasco. I learn from my scouts that you sent a telegram by special messenger to Lord Craig-Ellachie this morning. That shows you suspect me. Now, it is a principle of my system never to go on for one move with a game when I find myself suspected. The slightest symptom of distrust, and—I back out immediately. My plans can only be worked to satisfaction when there is perfect confidence on the part of my patient. It is a well-known rule of the medical profession. I *never* try to bleed a man who struggles. So now we're off. Ta-ta! Good luck to you!'

He was not much more than twenty yards away, and could talk to us quite easily. But the water was deep; the islet rose sheer from I'm sure I don't know how many fathoms of sea; and we could neither of us swim. Charles stretched out his arms imploringly. 'For Heaven's sake,' he cried, 'don't tell me you really mean to leave us here.'

He looked so comical in his distress and terror that Mrs. Granton—Madame Picardet—whatever I am to call her— laughed melodiously in her prettiest way at the sight of him. 'Dear Sir Charles,' she called out, 'pray don't be afraid! It's only a short and temporary imprisonment. We will send men to take you off. Dear David and I only need just time enough to get well ashore and make—oh!—a few slight alterations in our personal appearance.' And she indicated with her hand, laughing, dear David's red wig and false sandy whiskers, as we felt convinced they must be now. She looked at them and tittered. Her manner at this moment was anything but shy. In fact, I will venture to say, it was that of a bold and brazen-faced hoyden.

'Then you *are* Colonel Clay!' Sir Charles cried, mopping his brow with his handkerchief.

'If you choose to call me so,' the young man answered politely. 'I'm sure it's most kind of you to supply me with a commission in Her Majesty's service. However, time presses, and we want to push off. Don't alarm yourselves unnecessarily. I will send a boat to take you away from this rock at the earliest possible moment consistent with my personal safety and my dear companion's.' He laid his hand on his heart and struck a sentimental attitude. 'I have received too many unwilling kindnesses at your hands, Sir Charles,' he continued, 'not to feel how wrong it would be of me to inconvenience you for nothing. Rest assured that you shall be rescued by midnight at latest. Fortunately, the weather just at present is warm, and I see no chance of rain; so you will suffer, if at all, from nothing worse than the pangs of temporary hunger.'

Mrs. Granton, no longer squinting—'twas a mere trick she had assumed—rose up in the boat and stretched out a rug to us. 'Catch!' she cried, in a merry voice, and flung it at us, doubled. It fell at our feet; she was a capital thrower.

'Now, you dear Sir Charles,' she went on, 'take that to keep you warm! You know I am really quite fond of you. You're not half a bad old boy when one takes you the right way. You have a human side to you. Why, I often wear that sweetly pretty brooch you gave me at Nice, when I was Madame Picardet! And I'm sure your goodness to me at Lucerne, when I was the little curate's wife, is a thing to remember. 'We're so glad to have seen you in your lovely Scotch home you were always so proud of! *Don't* be frightened, please. We wouldn't hurt you for worlds. We *are* so sorry we have to take this inhospitable means of evading you. But dear David—I *must* call him dear David still—instinctively felt that you were beginning to suspect us; and he can't bear mistrust. He *is* so sensitive! The moment people mistrust him, he *must* break off with them at once. This was the only way to get you both off our hands while we make the needful little arrangements to depart; and we've been driven to avail ourselves of it. However, I will give you my word of honour, as a lady, you shall be fetched away to-night. If dear David doesn't do it, why, I'll do it myself.' And she blew another kiss to us.

Charles was half beside himself, divided between alternate terror and anger. 'Oh, we shall die here!' he exclaimed. 'Nobody'd ever dream of coming to this rock to search for me.'

'What a pity you didn't let me teach you to swim!' Colonel Clay interposed. 'It is a noble exercise, and very useful indeed

in such special emergencies! Well, ta-ta! I'm off! You nearly
scored one this time; but, by putting you here for the moment,
and keeping you till we're gone, I venture to say I've redressed
the board, and I think we may count it a drawn game, mayn't
we? The match stands at *three, love*—with some thousands in
pocket?'

'You're a murderer, sir!' Charles shrieked out. 'We shall
starve or die here!'

Colonel Clay on his side was all sweet reasonableness. 'Now,
my dear sir,' he expostulated, one hand held palm outward,
'*do* you think it probable I would kill the goose that lays the
golden eggs, with so little compunction? No, no, Sir Charles
Vandrift; I know too well how much you are worth to me. I
return you on my income-tax paper as five thousand a year,
clear profit of my profession. Suppose you were to die! I might
be compelled to find some new and far less lucrative source of
plunder. Your heirs, executors, or assignees might not suit my
purpose. The fact of it is, sir, your temperament and mine are
exactly adapted one to the other. *I* understand *you*; and *you*
do not understand *me*—which is often the basis of the firmest
friendships. I can catch you just where you are trying to catch
other people. Your very smartness assists me; for I admit you
are smart. As a regular financier, I allow, I couldn't hold a candle to you. But in my humbler walk of life I know just how to
utilise you. I lead you on, where you think you are going to
gain some advantage over others; and by dexterously playing
upon your love of a good bargain, your innate desire to best
somebody else—I succeed in besting you. There, sir, you have
the philosophy of our mutual relations.'

He bowed and raised his cap. Charles looked at him and
cowered. Yes, genius as he is, he positively cowered. 'And do
you mean to say,' he burst out, 'you intend to go on so bleeding me?'

The Colonel smiled a bland smile. 'Sir Charles Vandrift,' he
answered, 'I called you just now the goose that lays the golden
eggs. You may have thought the metaphor a rude one. But you
are a goose, you know, in certain relations. Smartest man on
the Stock Exchange, I readily admit; easiest fool to bamboozle

in the open country that ever I met with. You fail in one thing—the perspicacity of simplicity. For that reason, among others, I have chosen to fasten upon you. Regard me, my dear sir, as a microbe of millionaires, a parasite upon capitalists. You know the old rhyme:

> Great fleas have little fleas upon their backs to bite 'em,
> And these again have lesser fleas, and so *ad infinitum!*

Well, that's just how I view myself. *You* are a capitalist and a millionaire. In *your* large way you prey upon society. *You* deal in Corners, Options, Concessions, Syndicates. You drain the world dry of its blood and its money. You possess, like the mosquito, a beautiful instrument of suction—Founders' Shares—with which you absorb the surplus wealth of the community. In *my* smaller way, again, *I* relieve you in turn of a portion of the plunder. I am a Robin Hood of my age; and, looking upon *you* as an exceptionally bad form of millionaire—as well as an exceptionally easy form of pigeon for a man of my type and talents to pluck—I have, so to speak, taken up my abode upon you.'

Charles looked at him and groaned.

The young man continued, in a tone of gentle badinage. 'I love the plot-interest of the game,' he said, 'and so does dear Jessie here. We both of us adore it. As long as I find such good pickings upon you, I certainly am not going to turn away from so valuable a carcass, in order to batten myself, at considerable trouble, upon minor capitalists, out of whom it is difficult to extract a few hundreds. It may have puzzled you to guess why I fix upon you so persistently. Now you know, and understand. When a fluke finds a sheep that suits him, that fluke lives upon him. You are my host: I am your parasite. This *coup* has failed. But don't flatter yourself for a moment it will be the last one.'

'Why do you insult me by telling me all this?' Sir Charles cried, writhing.

The Colonel waved his hand. It was small and white. 'Because I *love* the game,' he answered, with a relish; 'and also, because the more prepared you are beforehand, the greater credit and amusement is there in besting you. Well, now, ta-ta once more! I am wasting valuable time. I might be cheating somebody. I must be off at once. . . . Take care of yourself, Wentworth. But I know you *will.* You always do. Ten per cent *is* more usual!'

He rowed away and left us. As the boat began to disappear round the corner of the island, White Heather—so she looked—stood up in the stern and shouted aloud through her pretty hands to us. 'By-bye, dear Sir Charles!' she cried. 'Do wrap the rug around you! I'll send the men to fetch you as soon as ever I possibly can. And thank you so much for those lovely flowers!'

The boat rounded the crags. We were alone on the island. Charles flung himself on the bare rock in a wild access of despondency. He is accustomed to luxury, and cannot get on without his padded cushions. As for myself, I climbed with some difficulty to the top of the cliff, landward, and tried to make signals of distress with my handkerchief to some passerby on the mainland. All in vain. Charles had dismissed the crofters on the estate; and, as the shooting-party that day was in an opposite direction, not a soul was near to whom we could call for succour.

I climbed down again to Charles. The evening came on slowly. Cries of sea-birds rang weird upon the water. Puffins and cormorants circled round our heads in the gray of twilight. Charles suggested that they might even swoop down upon us and bite us. They did not, however, but their flapping wings added none the less a painful touch of eeriness to our hunger and solitude. Charles was horribly depressed. For myself, I will confess I felt so much relieved at the fact that Colonel Clay had not openly betrayed me in the matter of the commission, as to be comparatively comfortable.

We crouched on the hard crag. About eleven o'clock we heard human voices. 'Boat ahoy!' I shouted. An answering shout aroused us to action. We rushed down to the landing-place and cooee'd for the men, to show them where we were. They came up at once in Sir Charles's own boat. They were fishermen from Niggarey, on the shore of the Firth opposite.

A lady and gentleman had sent them, they said, to return the boat and call for us on the island; their description corresponded to the two supposed Grantons. They rowed us home almost in silence to Seldon. It was half-past twelve by the gatehouse clock when we reached the castle. Men had been sent along the coast each way to seek us. Amelia had gone to bed, much alarmed for our safety. Isabel was sitting up. It was too late, of course, to do much that night in the way of apprehending the miscreants, though Charles insisted upon dispatching a groom, with a telegram for the police at Inverness, to Fowlis.

Nothing came of it all. A message awaited us from Lord Craig-Ellachie, to be sure, saying that his son had not left Glen-Ellachie Lodge; while research the next day and later showed that our correspondent had never even received our letter. An empty envelope alone had arrived at the house, and the postal authorities had been engaged meanwhile, with their usual lightning speed, in 'investigating the matter.' Césarine had posted the letter herself at Fowlis, and brought back the receipt; so the only conclusion we could draw was this— Colonel Clay must be in league with somebody at the post-office. As for Lord Craig-Ellachie's reply, that was a simple forgery; though, oddly enough, it was written on Glen-Ellachie paper.

However, by the time Charles had eaten a couple of grouse, and drunk a bottle of his excellent Rudesheimer, his spirits and valour revived exceedingly. Doubtless he inherits from his Boer ancestry a tendency towards courage of the Batavian description. He was in capital feather.

'After all, Sey,' he said, leaning back in his chair, 'this time we score one. He has *not* done us brown; we have at least detected him. To detect him in time is half-way to catching him. Only the remoteness of our position at Seldon Castle saved him from capture. Next set-to, I feel sure, we will not merely spot him, we will also nab him. I only wish he would try on such a rig in London.'

But the oddest part of it all was this, that from the moment those two people landed at Niggarey, and told the fishermen there were some gentlemen stranded on the Seamew's island, all trace of them vanished. At no station along the line could we gain any news of them. Their maid had left the inn the same morning with their luggage, and we tracked her to Inverness; but there the trail stopped short, no spoor lay farther. It was a most singular and insoluble mystery.

Charles lived in hopes of catching his man in London.

But for my part, I felt there was a show of reason in one last taunt which the rascal flung back at us as the boat receded: 'Sir Charles Vandrift, we are a pair of rogues. The law protects *you*. It persecutes *me*. That's all the difference.'

THE EPISODE OF THE
GERMAN PROFESSOR

That winter in town my respected brother-in-law had little time on his hands to bother himself about trifles like Colonel Clay. A thunderclap burst upon him. He saw his chief interest in South Africa threatened by a serious, an unexpected, and a crushing danger.

Charles does a little in gold, and a little in land; but his principal operations have always lain in the direction of diamonds. Only once in my life, indeed, have I seen him pay the slightest attention to poetry, and that was when I happened one day to recite the lines:—

> Full many a gem of purest ray serene
> The dark, unfathomed caves of ocean bear.

He rubbed his hands at once and murmured enthusiastically, 'I never thought of that. We might get up an Atlantic Exploration Syndicate, Limited.' So attached is he to diamonds. You may gather, therefore, what a shock it was to that gigantic brain to learn that science was rapidly reaching a point where his favourite gems might become all at once a mere drug in the market. Depreciation is the one bugbear that perpetually torments Sir Charles's soul, that winter he stood within measurable distance of so appalling a calamity.

It happened after this manner.

We were strolling along Piccadilly towards Charles's club one afternoon—he is a prominent member of the Crœsus, in Pall Mall—when, near Burlington House, whom should we happen to knock up against but Sir Adolphus Cordery, the

famous mineralogist, and leading spirit of the Royal Society!
He nodded to us pleasantly. 'Halloa, Vandrift,' he cried, in his
peculiarly loud and piercing voice; 'you're the very man I
wanted to meet to-day. Good morning, Wentworth. Well, how
about diamonds now, Sir Gorgius? You'll have to sing small.
It's all up with you Midases. Heard about this marvellous new
discovery of Schleiermacher's? It's calculated to make you diamond kings squirm like an eel in a frying-pan.'

I could see Charles wriggle inside his clothes. He was most
uncomfortable. That a man like Cordery should say such things,
in so loud a voice, on no matter how little foundation, openly in
Piccadilly, was enough in itself to make a sensitive barometer
such as Cloetedorp Golcondas go down a point or two.

'Hush, hush!' Charles said solemnly, in that awed tone of
voice which he always assumes when Money is blasphemed
against. '*Please* don't talk quite so loud! All London can hear
you.'

Sir Adolphus ran his arm through Charles's most amicably.
There's nothing Charles hates like having his arm taken.

'Come along with me to the Athenæum,' he went on, in the
same stentorian voice, 'and I'll tell you all about it. Most interesting discovery. Makes diamonds cheap as dirt. Calculated to
supersede South Africa altogether.'

Charles allowed himself to be dragged along. There was
nothing else possible. Sir Adolphus continued, in a somewhat
lower key, induced upon him by Charles's mute look of protest. It was a disquieting story. He told it with gleeful unction.
It seems that Professor Schleiermacher, of Jena, 'the greatest
living authority on the chemistry of gems,' he said, had lately
invented, or claimed to have invented, a system for artificially
producing diamonds, which had yielded most surprising and
unexceptionable results.

Charles's lip curled slightly. 'Oh, I know the sort of thing,'
he said. 'I've heard of it before. Very inferior stones, quite
small and worthless, produced at immense cost, and even then
not worth looking at. I'm an old bird, you know, Cordery; not
to be caught with chaff. Tell me a better one!'

Sir Adolphus produced a small cut gem from his pocket.

'How's that for the first water?' he inquired, passing it across, with a broad smile, to the sceptic. 'Made under my own eyes— and quite inexpensively!'

Charles examined it close, stopping short against the railings in St. Jámes's Square to look at it with his pocket-lens. There was no denying the truth. It was a capital small gem of the finest quality.

'Made under your own eyes?' he exclaimed, still incredulous. 'Where, my dear sir?—at Jena?'

The answer was a thunderbolt from a blue sky. 'No, here in London; last night as ever was; before myself and Dr. Gray; and about to be exhibited by the President himself at a meeting of Fellows of the Royal Society.'

Charles drew a long breath. 'This nonsense must be stopped,' he said firmly—'it must be nipped in the bud. It won't do, my dear friend; we can't have such tampering with important Interests.'

'How do you mean?' Cordery asked, astonished.

Charles gazed at him steadily. I could see by the furtive gleam in my brother-in-law's eye he was distinctly frightened. 'Where *is* the fellow?' he asked. 'Did he come himself, or send over a deputy?'

'Here in London,' Sir Adolphus replied. 'He's staying at my house; and he says he'll be glad to show his experiments to anybody scientifically interested in diamonds. We propose to have a demonstration of the process to-night at Lancaster Gate. Will you drop in and see it?'

Would he 'drop in' and see it? 'Drop in' at such a function! Could he possibly stop away? Charles clutched the enemy's arm with a nervous grip. 'Look here, Cordery,' he said, quivering; 'this is a question affecting very important Interests. Don't do anything rash. Don't do anything foolish. Remember that Shares may rise or fall on this.' He said 'Shares' in a tone of profound respect that I can hardly even indicate. It was the crucial word in the creed of his religion.

'I should think it very probable,' Sir Adolphus replied, with the callous indifference of the mere man of science to financial suffering.

Sir Charles was bland, but peremptory. 'Now, observe,' he said, 'a grave responsibility rests on your shoulders. The Market depends upon you. You must not ask in any number of outsiders to witness these experiments. Have a few mineralogists and experts, if you like; but also take care to invite representatives of the menaced Interests. I will come myself—I'm engaged to dine out, but I can contract an indisposition; and I should advise you to ask Mosenheimer, and, say, young Phipson. They would stand for the mines, as you and the mineralogists would stand for science. Above all, don't blab; for Heaven's sake, let there be no premature gossip. Tell Schleiermacher not to go gassing and boasting of his success all over London.'

'We are keeping the matter a profound secret, at Schleiermacher's own request,' Cordery answered, more seriously.

'Which is why,' Charles said, in his severest tone, 'you bawled it out at the very top of your voice in Piccadilly!'

However, before nightfall, everything was arranged to Charles's satisfaction; and off we went to Lancaster Gate, with a profound expectation that the German professor would do nothing worth seeing.

He was a remarkable-looking man, once tall, I should say, from his long, thin build, but now bowed and bent with long devotion to study and leaning over a crucible. His hair, prematurely white, hung down upon his forehead, but his eye was keen and his mouth sagacious. He shook hands cordially with the men of science, whom he seemed to know of old, whilst he bowed somewhat distantly to the South African interest. Then he began to talk, in very German-English, helping out the sense now and again, where his vocabulary failed him, by waving his rather dirty and chemical-stained hands demonstratively about him. His nails were a sight, but his fingers, I must say, had the delicate shape of a man's accustomed to minute manipulation. He plunged at once into the thick of the matter, telling us briefly in his equally thick accent that he 'now brobosed by his new brocess to make for us some goot and sadisfactory tiamonds.'

He brought out his apparatus, and explained—or, as he

said, 'eggsblained'—his novel method. 'Tiamonds,' he said, 'were nozzing but pure crystalline carbon. He knew how to crystallise it—zat was all ze secret.' The men of science examined the pots and pans carefully. Then he put in a certain number of raw materials, and went to work with ostentatious openness. There were three distinct processes, and he made two stones by each simultaneously. The remarkable part of his methods, he said, was their rapidity and their cheapness. In three-quarters of an hour (and he smiled sardonically) he could produce a diamond worth at current prices two hundred pounds sterling. 'As you shall now see me berform,' he remarked, 'viz zis simple abbaradus.'

The materials fizzed and fumed. The Professor stirred them. An unpleasant smell like burnt feathers pervaded the room. The scientific men craned their necks in their eagerness, and looked over one another; Vane-Vivian, in particular, was all attention. After three-quarters of an hour, the Professor, still smiling, began to empty the apparatus. He removed a large quantity of dust or powder, which he succinctly described as 'by-broducts,' and then took between finger and thumb from the midst of each pan a small white pebble, not water-worn apparently, but slightly rough and wart-like on the surface.

From one pair of the pannikins he produced two such stones, and held them up before us triumphantly. 'Zese,' he said, 'are genuine tiamonds, manufactured at a gost of fourteen shillings and siggspence abiece!' Then he tried the second pair. 'Zese,' he said, still more gleefully, 'are broduced at a gost of eleffen and ninebence!' Finally, he came to the third pair, which he positively brandished before our astonished eyes. 'And zese,' he cried, transported, 'haff gost me no more zan tree and eightbence!'

They were handed round for inspection. Rough and uncut as they stood, it was, of course, impossible to judge of their value. But one thing was certain. The men of science had been watching close at the first, and were sure Herr Schleiermacher had not put the stones in; they were keen at the withdrawal, and were equally sure he had taken them honestly out of the pannikins.

'I vill now disdribute zem,' the Professor remarked in a casual tone, as if diamonds were peas, looking round at the company. And he singled out my brother-in-law. 'One to Sir Charles!' he said, handing it; 'one to Mr. Mosenheimer; one to Mr. Phibson—as representing the tiamond interest. Zen, one each to Sir Atolphus, to Dr. Gray, to Mr. Fane-Fiffian, as representing science. You will haff zem cut and rebort upon zem in due gourse. We meet again at zis blace ze day afder do-morrow.'

Charles gazed at him reproachfully. The profoundest chords of his moral nature were stirred. 'Professor,' he said, in a voice of solemn warning, '*are* you aware that, *if* you have succeeded, you have destroyed the value of thousands of pounds' worth of precious property?'

The Professor shrugged his shoulders. 'Fot is dat to me?' he inquired, with a curious glance of contempt. 'I am not a financier! I am a man of science. I seek to know; I do not seek to make a fortune.'

'Shocking!' Charles exclaimed. 'Shocking! I never before in my life beheld so strange an instance of complete insensibility to the claims of others!'

We separated early. The men of science were coarsely jubilant. The diamond interest exhibited a corresponding depression. If this news were true, they foresaw a slump. Every eye grew dim. It was a terrible business.

Charles walked homeward with the Professor. He sounded him gently as to the sum required, should need arise, to purchase his secrecy. Already Sir Adolphus had bound us all down to temporary silence—as if that were necessary; but Charles wished to know how much Schleiermacher would take to suppress his discovery. The German was immovable.

'No, no!' he replied, with positive petulance. 'You do not unterstant. I do not buy and sell. Zis is a chemical fact. We must bublish it for the sake off its seoretical falue. I do not care for wealse. I haff no time to waste in making money.'

'What an awful picture of a misspent life!' Charles observed to me afterwards.

And, indeed, the man seemed to care for nothing on earth but the abstract question—not whether he could make good diamonds or not, but whether he could or could not produce a crystalline form of pure carbon!

On the appointed night Charles went back to Lancaster Gate, as I could not fail to remark, with a strange air of complete and painful preoccupation. Never before in his life had I seen him so anxious.

The diamonds were produced, with one surface of each slightly scored by the cutters, so as to show the water. Then a curious result disclosed itself. Strange to say, each of the three diamonds given to the three diamond kings turned out to be a most inferior and valueless stone; while each of the three intrusted to the care of the scientific investigators turned out to be a fine gem of the purest quality.

I confess it was a sufficiently suspicious conjunction. The three representatives of the diamond interest gazed at each other with inquiring sideglances. Then their eyes fell suddenly: they avoided one another. Had each independently substituted a weak and inferior natural stone for Professor Schleiermacher's manufactured pebbles? It almost seemed so. For a moment, I admit, I was half inclined to suppose it. But next second I changed my mind. Could a man of Sir Charles Vandrift's integrity and high principle stoop for lucre's sake to so mean an expedient?—not to mention the fact that, even if he did, and if Mosenheimer did likewise, the stones submitted to the scientific men would have amply sufficed to establish the reality and success of the experiments!

Still, I must say, Charles looked guiltily across at Mosenheimer, and Mosenheimer at Phipson, while three more uncomfortable or unhappy-faced men could hardly have been found at that precise minute in the City of Westminster.

Then Sir Adolphus spoke—or, rather, he orated. He said, in his loud and grating voice, we had that evening, and on a previous evening, been present at the conception and birth of an Epoch in the History of Science. Professor Schleiermacher was one of those men of whom his native Saxony might well be proud; while as a Briton he must say he regretted somewhat that this discovery, like so many others, should have been 'Made in Germany.' However, Professor Schleiermacher was a

specimen of that noble type of scientific men to whom gold
was merely the rare metal Au, and diamonds merely the element C in the scarcest of its manifold allotropic embodiments.
The Professor did not seek to make money out of his discovery. He rose above the sordid greed of capitalists. Content
with the glory of having traced the element C to its crystalline
origin, he asked no more than the approval of science. However, out of deference to the wishes of those financial gentlemen who were oddly concerned in maintaining the present
price of C in its crystalline form—in other words, the diamond interest—they had arranged that the secret should be
strictly guarded and kept for the present; not one of the few
persons admitted to the experiments would publicly divulge
the truth about them. This secrecy would be maintained till he
himself, and a small committee of the Royal Society, should
have time to investigate and verify for themselves the Professor's beautiful and ingemous processes—an investigation and
verification which the learned Professor himself both desired
and suggested. (Schleiermacher nodded approval.) When that
was done, if the process stood the test, further concealment
would be absolutely futile. The price of diamonds must fall at
once below that of paste, and any protest on the part of the
financial world would, of course, be useless. The laws of
Nature were superior to millionaires. Meanwhile, in deference
to the opinion of Sir Charles Vandrift, whose acquaintance
with that fascinating side of the subject nobody could deny,
they had consented to send no notices to the Press, and to
abstain from saying anything about this beautiful and simple
process in public. He dwelt with horrid gusto on that epithet
'beautiful.' And now, in the name of British mineralogy, he
must congratulate Professor Schleiermacher, our distinguished
guest, on his truly brilliant and crystalline contribution to our
knowledge of brilliants and of crystalline science.

Everybody applauded. It was an awkward moment. Sir
Charles bit his lip. Mosenheimer looked glum. Young Phipson
dropped an expression which I will not transcribe. (I understand this work may circulate among families.) And after a
solemn promise of death-like secrecy, the meeting separated.

I noticed that my brother-in-law somewhat ostentatiously avoided Mosenheimer at the door; and that Phipson jumped quickly into his own carriage. 'Home!' Charles cried gloomily to the coachman as we took our seats in the brougham. And all the way to Mayfair he leaned back in his seat, with close-set lips, never uttering a syllable.

Before he retired to rest, however, in the privacy of the billiard-room, I ventured to ask him: 'Charles, will you unload Golcondas to-morrow?' Which, I need hardly explain, is the slang of the Stock Exchange for getting rid of undesirable securities. It struck me as probable that, in the event of the invention turning out a reality, Cloetedorp A's might become unsaleable within the next few weeks or so.

He eyed me sternly. 'Wentworth,' he said, 'you're a fool!' (Except on occasions when he is *very* angry, my respected connection *never* calls me 'Wentworth'; the familiar abbreviation, 'Sey'—derived from Seymour—is his usual mode of address to me in private.) '*Is* it likely I would unload, and wreck the confidence of the public in the Cloetedorp Company at such a moment? As a director—as Chairman—would it be just or right of me? I ask you, sir, *could* I reconcile it to my conscience?'

'Charles,' I answered, 'you are right. Your conduct is noble. You will not save your own personal interests at the expense of those who have put their trust in you. Such probity is, alas! very rare in finance!' And I sighed involuntarily; for I had lost in Liberators.

At the same time I thought to myself, '*I* am not a director. No trust is reposed in *me. I* have to think first of dear Isabel and the baby. Before the crash comes *I* will sell out to-morrow the few shares I hold, through Charles's kindness, in the Cloetedorp Golcondas.'

With his marvellous business instinct, Charles seemed to divine my thought, for he turned round to me sharply. 'Look here, Sey,' he remarked, in an acidulous tone, 'recollect, you're my brother-in-law. You are also my secretary. The eyes of London will be upon us to-morrow. If *you* were to sell out, and operators got to know of it, they'd suspect there was something up, and the company would suffer for it. Of course, you can do what you like with your own property. I can't interfere with *that*. I do not dictate to you. But as Chairman of the Golcondas, I am bound to see that the interests of widows and orphans whose All is invested with me should not suffer at this crisis.' His voice seemed to falter. 'Therefore, though I don't like to threaten,' he went on, 'I am bound to give you warning: *if* you sell out those shares of yours, openly or secretly, you are no longer my secretary; you receive forthwith six months' salary in lieu of notice, and—you leave me instantly.'

'Very well, Charles,' I answered, in a submissive voice; though I debated with myself for a moment whether it would be best to stick to the ready money and quit the sinking ship, or to hold fast by my friend, and back Charles's luck against the Professor's science. After a short, sharp struggle within my own mind, I am proud to say, friendship and gratitude won. I felt sure that, whether diamonds went up or down, Charles Vandrift was the sort of man who would come to the top in the end in spite of everything. And I decided to stand by him!

I slept little that night, however. My mind was a whirlwind. At breakfast Charles also looked haggard and moody. He ordered the carriage early, and drove straight into the City.

There was a block in Cheapside. Charles, impatient and nervous, jumped out and walked. I walked beside him. Near Wood Street a man we knew casually stopped us.

'I think I ought to mention to you,' he said, confidentially, 'that I have it on the very best authority that Schleiermacher, of Jena——'

'Thank you,' Charles said, crustily, 'I know that tale, and—there's not a word of truth in it.'

He brushed on in haste. A yard or two farther a broker paused in front of us.

'Halloa, Sir Charles!' he called out, in a bantering tone. 'What's all this about diamonds? Where are Cloetedorps today? Is it Golconda, or Queer Street?'

Charles drew himself up very stiff. 'I fail to understand you,' he answered, with dignity.

'Why, you were there yourself,' the man cried. 'Last night at

Sir Adolphus's! Oh yes, it's all over the place; Schleiermacher of Jena has succeeded in making the most perfect diamonds—for sixpence apiece—as good as real—and South Africa's ancient history. In less than six weeks Kimberley, they say, will be a howling desert. Every costermonger in Whitechapel will wear genuine Koh-i-noors for buttons on his coat; every girl in Bermondsey will sport a *rivière* like Lady Vandrift's to her favourite music-hall. There's a slump in Golcondas. Sly, sly, I can see; but *we* know all about it!'

Charles moved on, disgusted. The man's manners were atrocious. Near the Bank we ran up against a most respectable jobber.

'Ah, Sir Charles,' he said; 'you here? Well, this is strange news, isn't it? For my part, I advise you not to take it too seriously. Your stock will go down, of course, like lead this morning. But it'll rise to-morrow, mark my words, and fluctuate every hour till the discovery's proved or disproved for certain. There's a fine time coming for operators, I feel sure. Reports this way and that. Rumours, rumours, rumours. And nobody will know which way to believe till Sir Adolphus has tested it.'

We moved on towards the House. Black care was seated on Sir Charles's shoulders. As we drew nearer and nearer, everybody was discussing the one fact of the moment. The seal of secrecy had proved more potent than publication on the house-tops. Some people told us of the exciting news in confidential whispers; some proclaimed it aloud in vulgar exultation. The general opinion was that Cloetedorps were doomed, and that the sooner a man cleared out the less was he likely to lose by it.

Charles strode on like a general; but it was a Napoleon brazening out his retreat from Moscow. His mien was resolute. He disappeared at last into the precincts of an office, waving me back, not to follow. After a long consultation he came out and rejoined me.

All day long the City rang with Golcondas, Golcondas. Everybody murmured, 'Slump, slump in Golcondas.' The brokers had more business to do than they could manage; though, to be sure, almost every one was a seller and no one a buyer. But Charles stood firm as a rock, and so did his brokers. 'I don't want to sell,' he said, doggedly. 'The whole thing is trumped up. It's a mere piece of jugglery. For my own part, I believe Professor Schleiermacher is deceived, or else is deceiving us. In another week the bubble will have burst, and prices will restore themselves.' His brokers, Finglemores, had only one answer to all inquiries: 'Sir Charles has every confidence in the stability of Golcondas, and doesn't wish to sell or to increase the panic.'

All the world said he was splendid, splendid! There he stationed himself on 'Change like some granite stack against which the waves roll and break themselves in vain. He took no notice of the slump, but ostentatiously bought up a few shares here and there so as to restore public confidence.

'I would buy more,' he said, freely, 'and make my fortune; only, as I was one of those who happened to spend last night at Sir Adolphus's, people might think I had helped to spread the rumour and produce the slump, in order to buy in at panic rates for my own advantage. A chairman, like Cæsar's wife, should be above suspicion. So I shall only buy up just enough, now and again, to let people see I, at least, have no doubt as to the firm future of Cloetedorps.'

He went home that night, more harassed and ill than I have ever seen him. Next day was as bad. The slump continued, with varying episodes. Now, a rumour would surge up that Sir Adolphus had declared the whole affair a sham, and prices would steady a little; now, another would break out that the diamonds were actually being put upon the market in Berlin by the cart-load, and timid old ladies would wire down to their brokers to realise off-hand at whatever hazard. It was an awful day. I shall never forget it.

The morning after, as if by miracle, things righted themselves of a sudden. While we were wondering what it meant, Charles received a telegram from Sir Adolphus Cordery:—

'The man is a fraud. Not Schleiermacher at all. Just had a wire from Jena saying the Professor knows nothing about him. Sorry unintentionally to have caused you trouble. Come round and see me.'

'Sorry unintentionally to have caused you trouble.' Charles

was beside himself with anger. Sir Adolphus had upset the share-market for forty-eight mortal hours, half-ruined a round dozen of wealthy operators, convulsed the City, upheaved the House, and now—he apologised for it as one might apologise for being late ten minutes for dinner! Charles jumped into a hansom and rushed round to see him. How had he dared to introduce the impostor to solid men as Professor Schleiermacher? Sir Adolphus shrugged his shoulders. The fellow had come and introduced himself as the great Jena chemist; he had long white hair, and a stoop in the shoulders. What reason had *he* for doubting his word? (I reflected to myself that on much the same grounds Charles in turn had accepted the Honourable David Granton and Graf von Lebenstein.) Besides, what object could the creature have for this extraordinary deception? Charles knew only too well. It was clear it was done to disturb the diamond market, and we realised, too late, that the man who had done it was—Colonel Clay, in 'another of his manifold allotropic embodiments!' Charles had had his wish, and had met his enemy once more in London!

We could see the whole plot. Colonel Clay was polymorphic, like the element carbon! Doubtless, with his extraordinary sleight of hand, he had substituted real diamonds for the shapeless mass that came out of the apparatus, in the interval between handing the pebbles round for inspection, and distributing them piecemeal to the men of science and representatives of the diamond interest. We all watched him closely, of course, when he opened the crucibles; but when once we had satisfied ourselves that *something* came out, our doubts were set at rest, and we forgot to watch whether he distributed those somethings or not to the recipients. Conjurers always depend upon such momentary distractions or lapses of attention. As usual, too, the Professor had disappeared into space the moment his trick was once well performed. He vanished like smoke, as the Count and Seer had vanished before, and was never again heard of.

Charles went home more angry than I have ever beheld him. I couldn't imagine why. He seemed as deeply hipped as if he had lost his thousands. I endeavoured to console him. 'After all,' I said, 'though Golcondas have suffered a temporary loss, it's a comfort to think that you should have stood so firm, and not only stemmed the tide, but also prevented yourself from losing anything at all of your own through panic. I'm sorry, of course, for the widows and orphans; but if Colonel Clay has rigged the market, at least it isn't *you* who lose by it this time.'

Charles withered me with a fierce scowl of undisguised contempt. 'Wentworth,' he said once more, 'you are a fool!' Then he relapsed into silence.

'But you declined to sell out,' I said.

He gazed at me fixedly. 'Is it likely,' he asked at last, 'I would tell *you* if I meant to sell out? or that I'd sell out openly through Finglemore, my usual broker? Why, all the world would have known, and Golcondas would have been finished. As it is, I don't desire to tell an ass like you exactly how much I've lost. But I *did* sell out, and some unknown operator bought in at once, and closed for ready money, and has sold again this morning; and after all that has happened, it will be impossible to track him. He didn't wait for the account: he settled up instantly. And he sold in like manner. I know now what has been done, and how cleverly it has all been disguised and covered; but the most I'm going to tell you to-day is just this— it's by far the biggest haul Colonel Clay has made out of me. He could retire on it if he liked. My one hope is, it may satisfy him for life; but, then, no man has ever had enough of making money.'

'*You* sold out!' I exclaimed. '*You*, the Chairman of the company! *You* deserted the ship! And how about your trust? How about the widows and orphans confided to you?'

Charles rose and faced me. 'Seymour Wentworth,' he said, in his most solemn voice, 'you have lived with me for years and had every advantage. You have seen high finance. Yet you ask me that question! It's my belief you will never, never understand business!'

VII

THE EPISODE OF THE ARREST OF THE COLONEL

How much precisely Charles dropped over the slump in Cloete-dorps I never quite knew. But the incident left him dejected, limp, and dispirited.

'Hang it all, Sey,' he said to me in the smoking-room, a few evenings later. 'This Colonel Clay is enough to vex the patience of Job—and Job had large losses, too, if I recollect aright, from the Chaldeans and other big operators of the period.'

'Three thousand camels,' I murmured, recalling my dear mother's lessons; 'all at one fell swoop; not to mention five hundred yoke of oxen, carried off by the Sabeans, then a leading firm of speculative cattle-dealers!'

'Ah, well,' Charles meditated aloud, shaking the ash from his cheroot into a Japanese tray—fine antique bronze-work. 'There were big transactions in live-stock even then! Still, Job or no Job, the man is too much for me.'

'The difficulty is,' I assented, 'you never know where to have him.'

'Yes,' Charles mused; 'if he were always the same, like Horniman's tea or a good brand of whisky, it would be easier, of course; you'd stand some chance of spotting him. But when a man turns up smiling every time in a different disguise, which fits him like a skin, and always apparently with the best credentials, why, hang it all, Sey, there's no wrestling with him anyhow.'

'Who could have come to us, for example, better vouched,' I acquiesced, 'than the Honourable David?'

'Exactly so,' Charles murmured. 'I invited him myself, for my own advantage. And he arrived with all the prestige of the Glen-Ellachie connection.'

'Or the Professor?' I went on. 'Introduced to us by the leading mineralogist of England.'

I had touched a sore point. Charles winced and remained
silent.

'Then, women again,' he resumed, after a painful pause. 'I
must meet in society many charming women. I can't everywhere and always be on my guard against every dear soul of
them. Yet the moment I relax my attention for one day—or
even when I don't relax it—I am bamboozled and led a dance
by that arch Mme. Picardet, or that transparently simple little
minx, Mrs. Granton. She's the cleverest girl I ever met in my
life, that hussy, whatever we're to call her. She's a different
person each time; and each time, hang it all, I lose my heart
afresh to that different person.'

I glanced round to make sure Amelia was well out of earshot.

'No, Sey,' my respected connection went on, after another
long pause, sipping his coffee pensively, 'I feel I must be aided
in this superhuman task by a professional unraveller of cunning disguises. I shall go to Marvillier's to-morrow—fortunate
man, Marvillier—and ask him to supply me with a really good
'tec, who will stop in the house and keep an eye upon every
living soul that comes near me. He shall scan each nose, each
eye, each wig, each whisker. He shall be my watchful half, my
unsleeping self; it shall be his business to suspect all living
men, all breathing women. The Archbishop of Canterbury
shall not escape for a moment his watchful regard; he will take
care that royal princesses don't collar the spoons or walk off
with the jewel-cases. He must see possible Colonel Clays in the
guard of every train and the parson of every parish; he must
detect the off-chance of a Mme. Picardet in every young girl
that takes tea with Amelia, every fat old lady that comes to
call upon Isabel. Yes, I have made my mind up. I shall go to-
morrow and secure such a man at once at Marvillier's.'

'If you please, Sir Charles,' Césarine interposed, pushing her
head through the portière, 'her ladyship says, will you and Mr.
Wentworth remember that she goes out with you both this
evening to Lady Carisbrooke's?'

'Bless my soul,' Charles cried, 'so she does! And it's now

past ten! The carriage will be at the door for us in another five minutes!'

Next morning, accordingly, Charles drove round to Marvillier's. The famous detective listened to his story with glistening eyes; then he rubbed his hands and purred. 'Colonel Clay!' he said; 'Colonel Clay! That's a very tough customer! The police of Europe are on the look-out for Colonel Clay. He is wanted in London, in Paris, in Berlin. It is *le Colonel Caoutchouc* here, *le Colonel Caoutchouc* there; till one begins to ask, at last, *is* there *any* Colonel Caoutchouc, or is it a convenient class name invented by the Force to cover a gang of undiscovered sharpers? However, Sir Charles, we will do our best. I will set on the track without delay the best and cleverest detective in England.'

'The very man I want,' Charles said. 'What name, Marvillier?'

The principal smiled. 'Whatever name you like,' he said. 'He isn't particular. Medhurst he's called at home. *We* call him Joe. I'll send him round to your house this afternoon for certain.'

'Oh no,' Charles said promptly, 'you won't; or Colonel Clay himself will come instead of him. I've been sold too often. No casual strangers! I'll wait here and see him.'

'But he isn't in,' Marvillier objected.

Charles was firm as a rock. 'Then send and fetch him.'

In half an hour, sure enough, the detective arrived. He was an odd-looking small man, with hair cut short and standing straight up all over his head, like a Parisian waiter. He had quick, sharp eyes, very much like a ferret's; his nose was depressed, his lips thin and bloodless. A scar marked his left cheek—made by a sword-cut, he said, when engaged one day in arresting a desperate French smuggler, disguised as an officer of Chasseurs d'Afrique. His mien was resolute. Altogether, a quainter or 'cuter little man it has never yet been my lot to set eyes on. He walked in with a brisk step, eyed Charles up and down, and then, without much formality, asked for what he was wanted.

'This is Sir Charles Vandrift, the great diamond king,' Marvillier said, introducing us.

'So I see,' the man answered.

'Then you know me?' Charles asked.

'I wouldn't be worth much,' the detective replied, 'if I didn't
know everybody. And *you're* easy enough to know; why, every
boy in the street knows you.'

'Plain spoken!' Charles remarked.

'As you like it, sir,' the man answered in a respectful tone. 'I
endeavour to suit my dress and behaviour on every occasion to
the taste of my employers.'

'Your name?' Charles asked, smiling.

'Joseph Medhurst, at your service. What sort of work?
Stolen diamonds? Illicit diamond-buying?'

'No,' Charles answered, fixing him with his eye. 'Quite
another kind of job. You've heard of Colonel Clay?'

Medhurst nodded. 'Why, certainly,' he said; and, for the
first time, I detected a lingering trace of American accent. 'It's
my business to know about him.'

'Well, I want you to catch him,' Charles went on.

Medhurst drew a long breath. 'Isn't that rather a large order?'
he murmured, surprised.

Charles explained to him exactly the sort of services he
required. Medhurst promised to comply. 'If the man comes
near you, I'll spot him,' he said, after a moment's pause. 'I can
promise you that much. I'll pierce any disguise. I should know
in a minute whether he's got up or not. I'm death on wigs, false
moustaches, artificial complexions. I'll engage to bring the
rogue to book if I see him. You may set your mind at rest, that,
while *I'm* about you, Colonel Clay can do nothing without my
instantly spotting him.'

'He'll do it,' Marvillier put in. 'He'll do it, if he says it. He's
my very best hand. Never knew any man like him for unravel-
ling and unmasking the cleverest disguises.'

'Then he'll suit me,' Charles answered, 'for *I* never knew any
man like Colonel Clay for assuming and maintaining them.'

It was arranged accordingly that Medhurst should take up his
residence in the house for the present, and should be described to
the servants as assistant secretary. He came that very day, with a
marvellously small portmanteau. But from the moment he
arrived, we noticed that Césarine took a violent dislike to him.

Medhurst was a most efficient detective. Charles and I told him all we knew about the various shapes in which Colonel Clay had 'materialised,' and he gave us in turn many valuable criticisms and suggestions. Why, when we began to suspect the Honourable David Granton, had we not, as if by accident, tried to knock his red wig off? Why, when the Reverend Richard Peploe Brabazon first discussed the question of the paste diamonds, had we not looked to see if any of Amelia's unique gems were missing? Why, when Professor Schleiermacher made his bow to assembled science at Lancaster Gate, had we not strictly inquired how far he was personally known beforehand to Sir Adolphus Cordery and the other mineralogists? He supplied us also with several good hints about false hair and make-up; such as that Schleiermacher was probably much shorter than he looked, but by imitating a stoop with padding at his back he had produced the illusion of a tall bent man, though in reality no bigger than the little curate or the Graf von Lebenstein. High heels did the rest; while the scientific keenness we noted in his face was doubtless brought about by a trifle of wax at the end of the nose, giving a peculiar tilt that is extremely effective. In short, I must frankly admit, Medhurst made us feel ashamed of ourselves. Sharp as Charles is, we realised at once he was nowhere in observation beside the trained and experienced senses of this professional detective.

The worst of it all was, while Medhurst was with us, by some curious fatality, Colonel Clay stopped away from us. Now and again, to be sure, we ran up against somebody whom Medhurst suspected; but after a short investigation (conducted, I may say, with admirable cleverness), the spy always showed us the doubtful person was really some innocent and well-known character, whose antecedents and surroundings he elucidated most wonderfully. He was a perfect marvel, too, in his faculty of suspicion. He suspected everybody. If an old friend dropped in to talk business with Charles, we found out afterwards that Medhurst had lain concealed all the time behind the curtain, and had taken short-hand notes of the whole conversation, as well as snap-shot photographs of the supposed sharper, by means of a kodak. If a fat old lady came to call upon

Amelia, Medhurst was sure to be lurking under the ottoman in the drawing-room, and carefully observing, with all his eyes, whether or not she was really Mme. Picardet, padded. When Lady Tresco brought her four plain daughters to an 'At Home' one night, Medhurst, in evening dress, disguised as a waiter, followed them each round the room with obtrusive ices, to satisfy himself just how much of their complexion was real, and how much was patent rouge and Bloom of Ninon. He doubted whether Simpson, Sir Charles's valet, was not Colonel Clay in plain clothes; and he had half an idea that Césarine herself was our saucy White Heather in an alternative avatar. We pointed out to him in vain that Simpson had often been present in the very same room with David Granton, and that Césarine had dressed Mrs. Brabazon's hair at Lucerne: this partially satisfied him, but only partially. He remarked that Simpson might double both parts with somebody else unknown; and that as for Césarine, she might well have a twin sister who took her place when she was Mme. Picardet.

Still, in spite of all his care—or because of all his care—Colonel Clay stopped away for whole weeks together. An explanation occurred to us. Was it possible he knew we were guarded and watched? Was he afraid of measuring swords with this trained detective?

If so, how had he found it out? I had an inkling, myself—but, under all the circumstances, I did not mention it to Charles. It was clear that Césarine intensely disliked this new addition to the Vandrift household. She would not stop in the room where the detective was, or show him common politeness. She spoke of him always as 'that odious man, Medhurst.' Could she have guessed, what none of the other servants knew, that the man was a spy in search of the Colonel? I was inclined to believe it. And then it dawned upon me that Césarine had known all about the diamonds and their story; that it was Césarine who took us to see Schloss Lebenstein; that it was Césarine who posted the letter to Lord Craig-Ellachie! If Césarine was in league with Colonel Clay, as I was half inclined to surmise, what more natural than her obvious dislike to the detective who was there to catch her principal? What more simple for her than to warn her fellow-conspirator of the danger that awaited him if he approached this man Medhurst?

However, I was too much frightened by the episode of the cheque to say anything of my nascent suspicions to Charles. I waited rather to see how events would shape themselves.

After a while Medhurst's vigilance grew positively annoying. More than once he came to Charles with reports and short-hand notes distinctly distasteful to my excellent brother-in-law. 'The fellow is getting to know too much about us,' Charles said to me one day. 'Why, Sey, he spies out everything. Would you believe it, when I had that confidential interview with Brook-field the other day, about the new issue of Golcondas, the man was under the easy-chair, though I searched the room before-hand to make sure he wasn't there; and he came to me after-wards with full notes of the conversation, to assure me he thought Brookfield—whom I've known for ten years—was too tall by half an inch to be one of Colonel Clay's impersonations.'

'Oh, but, Sir Charles,' Medhurst cried, emerging suddenly from the bookcase, 'you must never look upon *any one* as above suspicion merely because you've known him for ten years or thereabouts. Colonel Clay may have approached you at various times under many disguises. He may have built up this thing gradually. Besides, as to my knowing too much, why, of course, a detective always learns many things about his employer's fam-ily which he is not supposed to know; but professional honour and professional etiquette, as with doctors and lawyers, compel him to lock them up as absolute secrets in his own bosom. You need never be afraid I will divulge one jot of them. If I did, my occupation would be gone, and my reputation shattered.'

Charles looked at him, appalled. 'Do you dare to say,' he burst out, 'you've been listening to my talk with my brother-in-law and secretary?'

'Why, of course,' Medhurst answered. 'It's my business to listen, and to suspect everybody. If you push me to say so, how do I know Colonel Clay is not—Mr. Wentworth?'

Charles withered him with a look. 'In future, Medhurst,' he said, 'you must never conceal yourself in a room where I am without my leave and knowledge.'

Medhurst bowed politely. 'Oh, as you will, Sir Charles,' he answered; 'that's *quite* at your own wish. Though how can I act as an efficient detective, any way, if you insist upon tying my hands like that, beforehand?'

Again I detected a faint American flavour.

After that rebuff, however, Medhurst seemed put upon his mettle. He redoubled his vigilance in every direction. 'It's not my fault,' he said plaintively, one day, 'if my reputation's so good that, while I'm near you, this rogue won't approach you. If I can't *catch* him, at least I keep him away from coming near you!'

A few days later, however, he brought Charles some photographs. These he produced with evident pride. The first he showed us was a vignette of a little parson. 'Who's that, then?' he inquired, much pleased.

We gazed at it, open-eyed. One word rose to our lips simultaneously: 'Brabazon!'

'And how's this for high?' he asked again, producing another— the photograph of a gay young dog in a Tyrolese costume.

We murmured, 'Von Lebenstein!'

'*And* this?' he continued, showing us the portrait of a lady with a most fetching squint.

We answered with one voice, 'Little Mrs. Granton!'

Medhurst was naturally proud of this excellent exploit. He replaced them in his pocket-book with an air of just triumph.

'How did you get them?' Charles asked.

Medhurst's look was mysterious. 'Sir Charles,' he answered, drawing himself up, 'I must ask you to trust me awhile in this matter. Remember, there are people whom you decline to suspect. *I* have learned that it is always those very people who are most dangerous to capitalists. If I were to give you the names now, you would refuse to believe me. Therefore, I hold them over discreetly for the moment. One thing, however, I say. I *know* to a certainty where Colonel Clay is at this present speaking. But I will lay my plans deep, and I hope before long to secure him. You shall be present when I do so; and I shall make him confess his personality openly. More than that you cannot reasonably ask. I shall leave it to *you*, then, whether or not you wish to arrest him.'

Charles was considerably puzzled, not to say piqued, by this curious reticence; he begged hard for names; but Medhurst was adamant. 'No, no,' he replied; 'we detectives have our own just pride in our profession. If I told you now, you would probably spoil all by some premature action. You are too open and impulsive! I will mention this alone: Colonel Clay will be shortly in Paris, and before long will begin from that city a fresh attempt at defrauding you, which he is now hatching. Mark my words, and see whether or not I have been kept well informed of the fellow's movements!'

He was perfectly correct. Two days later, as it turned out, Charles received a 'confidential' letter from Paris, purporting to come from the head of a second-rate financial house with which he had had dealings over the Craig-Ellachie Amalgamation—by this time, I ought to have said, an accomplished union. It was a letter of small importance in itself—a mere matter of detail; but it paved the way, so Medhurst thought, to some later development of more serious character. Here once more the man's singular foresight was justified. For, in another week, we received a second communication, containing other proposals of a delicate financial character, which would have involved the transference of some two thousand pounds to the head of the Parisian firm at an address given. Both these letters Medhurst cleverly compared with those written to Charles before, in the names of Colonel Clay and of Graf von Lebenstein. At first sight, it is true, the differences between the two seemed quite enormous: the Paris hand was broad and black, large and bold; while the earlier manuscript was small, neat, thin, and gentlemanly. Still, when Medhurst pointed out to us certain persistent twists in the formation of his capitals, and certain curious peculiarities in the relative length of his *t*'s, his *l*'s, his *b*'s, and his *h*'s, we could see for ourselves he was right; both were the work of one hand, writing in the one case with a sharp-pointed nib, very small, and in the other with a quill, very large and freely.

This discovery was *most* important. We stood now within measurable distance of catching Colonel Clay, and bringing forgery and fraud home to him without hope of evasion.

To make all sure, however, Medhurst communicated with

the Paris police, and showed us their answers. Meanwhile, Charles continued to write to the head of the firm, who had given a private address in the Rue Jean Jacques, alleging, I must say, a most clever reason why the negotiations at this stage should be confidentially conducted. But one never expected from Colonel Clay anything less than consummate cleverness. In the end, it was arranged that we three were to go over to Paris together, that Medhurst was to undertake, under the guise of being Sir Charles, to pay the two thousand pounds to the pretended financier, and that Charles and I, waiting with the police outside the door, should, at a given signal, rush in with our forces and secure the criminal.

We went over accordingly, and spent the night at the Grand, as is Charles's custom. The Bristol, which I prefer, he finds too quiet. Early next morning we took a *fiacre* and drove to the Rue Jean Jacques. Medhurst had arranged everything in advance with the Paris police, three of whom, in plain clothes, were waiting at the foot of the staircase to assist us. Charles had further provided himself with two thousand pounds, in notes of the Bank of France, in order that the payment might be duly made, and no doubt arise as to the crime having been perpetrated as well as meditated—in the former case, the penalty would be fifteen years; in the latter, three only. He was in very high spirits. The fact that we had tracked the rascal to earth at last, and were within an hour of apprehending him, was in itself enough to raise his courage greatly. We found, as we expected, that the number given in the Rue Jean Jacques was that of an hotel, not a private residence. Medhurst went in first, and inquired of the landlord whether our man was at home, at the same time informing him of the nature of our errand, and giving him to understand that if we effected the capture by his friendly aid, Sir Charles would see that the expenses incurred on the swindler's bill were met in full, as the price of his assistance. The landlord bowed; he expressed his deep regret, as M. le Colonel—so we heard him call him—was a most amiable person, much liked by the household; but justice, of course, must have its way; and, with a regretful sigh, he undertook to assist us.

The police remained below, but Charles and Medhurst were

each provided with a pair of handcuffs. Remembering the Polperro case, however, we determined to use them with the greatest caution. We would only put them on in case of violent resistance. We crept up to the door where the miscreant was housed. Charles handed the notes in an open envelope to Medhurst, who seized them hastily and held them in his hands in readiness for action. We had a sign concerted. Whenever he sneezed—which he could do in the most natural manner—we were to open the door, rush in, and secure the criminal!

He was gone for some minutes. Charles and I waited outside in breathless expectation. Then Medhurst sneezed. We flung the door open at once, and burst in upon the creature.

Medhurst rose as we did so. He pointed with his finger. '*This* is Colonel Clay!' he said; 'keep him well in charge while I go down to the door for the police to arrest him!'

A gentlemanly man, about middle height, with a grizzled beard and a well-assumed military aspect, rose at the same moment. The envelope in which Charles had placed the notes lay on the table before him. He clutched it nervously. 'I am at a loss, gentlemen,' he said, in an excited voice, 'to account for this interruption.' He spoke with a tremor, yet with all the politeness to which we were accustomed in the little curate and the Honourable David.

'No nonsense!' Charles exclaimed, in his authoritative way. 'We know who you are. We have found you out this time. You are Colonel Clay. If you attempt to resist—take care—I will handcuff you!'

The military gentleman gave a start. 'Yes, I *am* Colonel Clay,' he answered. 'On what charge do you arrest me?'

Charles was bursting with wrath. The fellow's coolness seemed never to desert him. 'You *are* Colonel Clay!' he muttered. 'You have the unspeakable effrontery to stand there and admit it?'

'Certainly,' the Colonel answered, growing hot in turn. 'I have done nothing to be ashamed of. What do you mean by this conduct? How dare you talk of arresting me?'

Charles laid his hand on the man's shoulder. 'Come, come, my friend,' he said. 'That sort of bluff won't go down with us.

You know very well on what charge I arrest you; and here are the police to give effect to it.'

He called out 'Entrez!' The police entered the room. Charles explained as well as he could in most doubtful Parisian what they were next to do. The Colonel drew himself up in an indignant attitude. He turned and addressed them in excellent French.

'I am an officer in the service of her Britannic Majesty,' he said. 'On what ground do you venture to interfere with me, messieurs?'

The chief policeman explained. The Colonel turned to Charles. '*Your* name, sir?' he inquired.

'You know it very well,' Charles answered. 'I am Sir Charles Vandrift; and, in spite of your clever disguise, I can instantly recognise you. I know your eyes and ears. I can see the same man who cheated me at Nice, and who insulted me on the island.'

'*You* Sir Charles Vandrift!' the rogue cried. 'No, no, sir, you are a madman!' He looked round at the police. 'Take care what you do!' he cried. 'This is a raving maniac. I had business just now with Sir Charles Vandrift, who quitted the room as these gentlemen entered. This person is mad, and you, monsieur, I doubt not,' bowing to me, 'you are, of course, his keeper.'

'Do not let him deceive you,' I cried to the police, beginning to fear that with his usual incredible cleverness the fellow would even now manage to slip through our fingers. 'Arrest him, as you are told. *We* will take the responsibility.' Though I trembled when I thought of that cheque he held of mine.

The chief of our three policemen came forward and laid his hand on the culprit's shoulder. 'I advise you, M. le Colonel,' he said, in an official voice, 'to come with us quietly for the present. Before the *juge d'instruction* we can enter at length into all these questions.'

The Colonel, very indignant still—and acting the part marvellously—yielded and went along with them.

'Where's Medhurst?' Charles inquired, glancing round as we reached the door. 'I wish he had stopped with us.'

'You are looking for monsieur your friend?' the landlord inquired, with a side bow to the Colonel. 'He has gone away in a *fiacre*. He asked me to give this note to you.'

He handed us a twisted note. Charles opened and read it. 'Invaluable man!' he cried. 'Just hear what he says, Sey: "Having secured Colonel Clay, I am off now again on the track of Mme. Picardet. She was lodging in the same house. She has just driven away; I know to what place; and I am after her to arrest her. In blind haste, MEDHURST." That's smartness, *if* you like. Though poor little woman, I think he might have left her.'

'Does a Mme. Picardet stop here?' I inquired of the landlord, thinking it possible she might have assumed again the same old alias.

He nodded assent. '*Oui, oui, oui,*' he answered. 'She has just driven off, and monsieur your friend has gone posting after her.'

'Splendid man!' Charles cried. 'Marvillier was quite right. He is the prince of detectives!'

We hailed a couple of *fiacres*, and drove off, in two detachments, to the *juge d'instruction*. There Colonel Clay continued to brazen it out, and asserted that he was an officer in the Indian Army, home on six months' leave, and spending some weeks in Paris. He even declared he was known at the Embassy, where he had a cousin an *attaché;* and he asked that this gentleman should be sent for at once from our Ambassador's to identify him. The *juge d'instruction* insisted that this must be done; and Charles waited in very bad humour for the foolish formality. It really seemed as if, after all, when we had actually caught and arrested our man, he was going by some cunning device to escape us.

After a delay of more than an hour, during which Colonel Clay fretted and fumed quite as much as we did, the *attaché* arrived. To our horror and astonishment, he proceeded to salute the prisoner most affectionately.

'Halloa, Algy!' he cried, grasping his hand; 'what's up? What do these ruffians want with you?'

It began to dawn upon us, then, what Medhurst had meant by 'suspecting everybody': the real Colonel Clay was no common adventurer, but a gentleman of birth and high connections!

The Colonel glared at us. 'This fellow declares he's Sir Charles Vandrift,' he said sulkily. 'Though, in fact, there are two of them. And he accuses me of forgery, fraud, and theft, Bertie.'

The *attaché* stared hard at us. 'This *is* Sir Charles Vandrift,' he replied, after a moment. 'I remember hearing him make a speech once at a City dinner. And what charge have you to prefer, Sir Charles, against my cousin?'

'Your cousin?' Charles cried. 'This is Colonel Clay, the notorious sharper!'

The *attaché* smiled a gentlemanly and superior smile. 'This is Colonel Clay,' he answered, 'of the Bengal Staff Corps.'

It began to strike us there was something wrong somewhere.

'But he has cheated me, all the same,' Charles said—'at Nice two years ago, and many times since; and this very day he has tricked me out of two thousand pounds in French bank-notes, which he has now about him!'

The Colonel was speechless. But the *attaché* laughed. 'What he has done to-day I don't know,' he said; 'but if it's as apocryphal as what you say he did two years ago, you've a thundering bad case, sir; for he was then in India, and I was out there, visiting him.'

'Where are the two thousand pounds?' Charles cried. 'Why, you've got them in your hand! You're holding the envelope!'

The Colonel produced it. 'This envelope,' he said, 'was left with me by the man with short stiff hair, who came just before you, and who announced himself as Sir Charles Vandrift. He said he was interested in tea in Assam, and wanted me to join the board of directors of some bogus company. These are his papers, I believe,' and he handed them to his cousin.

'Well, I'm glad the notes are safe, anyhow,' Charles murmured, in a tone of relief, beginning to smell a rat. 'Will you kindly return them to me?'

The *attaché* turned out the contents of the envelope. They proved to be prospectuses of bubble companies of the moment, of no importance.

'Medhurst must have put them there,' I cried, 'and decamped with the cash.'

Charles gave a groan of horror. 'And Medhurst is Colonel Clay!' he exclaimed, clapping his hand to his forehead.

'I beg your pardon, sir,' the Colonel interposed. 'I have but one personality, and no aliases.'

It took quite half an hour to explain this imbroglio. But as soon as all was explained, in French and English, to the satisfaction of ourselves and the *juge d'instruction*, the real Colonel shook hands with us in a most forgiving way, and informed us that he had more than once wondered, when he gave his name at shops in Paris, why it was often received with such grave suspicion. We instructed the police that the true culprit was Medhurst, whom they had seen with their own eyes, and whom we urged them to pursue with all expedition. Meanwhile, Charles and I, accompanied by the Colonel and the *attaché*—'to see the fun out,' as they said—called at the Bank of France for the purpose of stopping the notes immediately. It was too late, however. They had been presented at once, and cashed in gold, by a pleasant little lady in an American costume, who was afterwards identified by the hotel-keeper (from our description) as his lodger, Mme. Picardet. It was clear she had taken rooms in the same hotel, to be near the Indian Colonel; and it was *she* who had received and sent the letters. As for our foe, he had vanished into space, as always.

Two days later we received the usual insulting communication on a sheet of Charles's own dainty note. Last time he wrote it was on Craig-Ellachie paper: this time, like the wanton lapwing, he had got himself another crest.

'MOST PERSPICACIOUS OF MILLIONAIRES!—Said I not well, as Medhurst, that you must distrust everybody? And the one man you never dreamt of distrusting was—Medhurst. Yet see how truthful I was! I told you I knew where Colonel Clay was living—and I *did* know, exactly. I promised to take you to Colonel Clay's rooms, and to get him arrested for you—and I kept my promise. I even exceeded your expectations; for I gave you *two* Colonel Clays instead of one—and you took the wrong man—that is to say, the real one. This was a neat little trick; but it cost me some trouble.

'First, I found out there *was* a real Colonel Clay, in the Indian Army. I also found out he chanced to be coming home on leave this season. I might have made more out of him, no doubt; but I disliked annoying him, and preferred to give myself the fun of this peculiar mystification. I therefore waited for him to reach Paris, where the police arrangements suited me better than in London. While I was looking about, and delaying operations for his return, I happened to hear you wanted a detective. So I offered myself as out of work to my old employer, Marvillier, from whom I have had many good jobs in the past; and there you get, in short, the kernel of the Colonel.

'Naturally, after this, I can never go back as a detective to Marvillier's. But, on the large scale on which I have learned to work since I first had the pleasure of making your delightful acquaintance, this matters little. To say the truth, I begin to feel detective work a cut or two below me. I am now a gentleman of means and leisure. Besides, the extra knowledge of your movements which I have acquired in your house has helped still further to give me various holds upon you. So the fluke will be true to his own pet lamb. To vary the metaphor, you are not fully shorn yet.

'Remember me most kindly to your charming family, give Wentworth my love, and tell Mlle. Césarine I owe her a grudge which I shall never forget. She clearly suspected me. You are much too rich, dear Charles; I relieve your plethora. I bleed you financially. Therefore I consider myself—Your sincerest friend,

                                        'CLAY-BRABAZON-MEDHURST,
                        'Fellow of the Royal College of Surgeons.'

Charles was threatened with apoplexy. This blow was severe. 'Whom can I trust,' he asked, plaintively, 'when the detectives themselves, whom I employ to guard me, turn out to be swindlers? Don't you remember that line in the Latin grammar—something about, "Who shall watch the watchers?" I think it used to run, "Quis custodes custodiet ipsos?"'

But I felt this episode had at least disproved my suspicions of poor Césarine.

VIII

THE EPISODE OF THE SELDON GOLD-MINE

On our return to London, Charles and Marvillier had a difference of opinion on the subject of Medhurst.

Charles maintained that Marvillier ought to have known the man with the cropped hair was Colonel Clay, and ought never to have recommended him. Marvillier maintained that Charles had *seen* Colonel Clay half-a-dozen times, at least, to his own never; and that my respected brother-in-law had therefore nobody on earth but himself to blame if the rogue imposed upon him. The head detective had known Medhurst for ten years, he said, as a most respectable man, and even a ratepayer; he had always found him the cleverest of spies, as well he might be, indeed, on the familiar set-a-thief-to-catch-a-thief principle. However, the upshot of it all was, as usual—nothing. Marvillier was sorry to lose the services of so excellent a hand; but he had done the very best he could for Sir Charles, he declared; and if Sir Charles was not satisfied, why, he might catch his Colonel Clays for himself in future.

'So I will, Sey,' Charles remarked to me, as we walked back from the office in the Strand by Piccadilly. 'I won't trust any more to these private detectives. It's my belief they're a pack of thieves themselves, in league with the rascals they're set to catch, and with no more sense of honour than a Zulu diamond-hand.'

'Better try the police,' I suggested, by way of being helpful. One must assume an interest in one's employer's business.

But Charles shook his head. 'No, no,' he said; 'I'm sick of all these fellows. I shall trust in future to my own sagacity. We learn by experience, Sey—and I've learned a thing or two.

One of them is this: It's not enough to suspect everybody; you must have no preconceptions. Divest yourself entirely of every fixed idea if you wish to cope with a rascal of this calibre. Don't jump at conclusions. We should disbelieve everything, as well as distrust everybody. That's the road to success; and I mean to pursue it.'

So, by way of pursuing it, Charles retired to Seldon.

'The longer the man goes on, the worse he grows,' he said to me one morning. 'He's just like a tiger that has tasted blood. Every successful haul seems only to make him more eager for another. I fully expect now before long we shall see him down here.'

About three weeks later, sure enough, my respected connection received a communication from the abandoned swindler, with an Austrian stamp and a Vienna post-mark.

'MY DEAR VANDRIFT.—(After so long and so varied an acquaintance we may surely drop the absurd formalities of "Sir Charles" and "Colonel.") I write to ask you a delicate question. Can you kindly tell me exactly how much I have received from your various generous acts during the last three years? I have mislaid my account-book, and as this is the season for making the income tax return, I am anxious, as an honest and conscientious citizen, to set down my average profits out of you for the triennial period. For reasons which you will amply understand, I do not this time give my private address, in Paris or elsewhere; but if you will kindly advertise the total amount, above the signature "Peter Simple," in the Agony Column of the *Times*, you will confer a great favour upon the Revenue Commissioners, and also upon your constant friend and companion,

CUTHBERT CLAY,
'*Practical Socialist.*'

'Mark my word, Sey,' Charles said, laying the letter down, 'in a week or less the man himself will follow. This is his cunning way of trying to make me think he's well out of the country and far away from Seldon. That means he's meditating another descent. But he told us too much last time, when he was Medhurst the detective. He gave us some hints about disguises and their unmasking that I shall not forget. This turn I shall be even with him.'

On Saturday of that week, in effect, we were walking along the road that leads into the village, when we met a gentlemanly-looking man, in a rough and rather happy-go-lucky brown tweed suit, who had the air of a tourist. He was middle-aged, and of middle height; he wore a small leather wallet suspended round his shoulder; and he was peering about at the rocks in a suspicious manner. Something in his gait attracted our attention.

'Good-morning,' he said, looking up as we passed; and Charles muttered a somewhat surly inarticulate, 'Good-morning.'

We went on without saying more. 'Well, *that's* not Colonel Clay, anyhow,' I said, as we got out of earshot. 'For he accosted us first; and you may remember it's one of the Colonel's most marked peculiarities that, like the model child, he never speaks till he's spoken to—never begins an acquaintance. He always waits till we make the first advance; he doesn't go out of his way to cheat us; he loiters about till we ask him to do it.'

'Seymour,' my brother-in-law responded, in a severe tone, 'there you are, now, doing the very thing I warned you not to do! You're succumbing to a preconception. Avoid fixed ideas. The probability is this man *is* Colonel Clay. Strangers are generally scarce at Seldon. If he isn't Colonel Clay, what's he here for, I'd like to know? What money is there to be made here in any other way? I shall inquire about him.'

We dropped in at the Cromarty Arms, and asked good Mrs. M'Lachlan if she could tell us anything about the gentlemanly stranger. Mrs. M'Lachlan replied that he was from London, she believed, a pleasant gentleman enough; and he had his wife with him.

'Ha! Young? Pretty?' Charles inquired, with a speaking glance at me.

'Weel, Sir Charles, she'll no be exactly what you'd be ca'ing a bonny lass,' Mrs. M'Lachlan replied; 'but she's a guid body for a' that, an' a fine braw woman.'

'Just what I should expect,' Charles murmured, 'He varies

the programme. The fellow has tried White Heather as the parson's wife, and as Madame Picardet, and as squinting little Mrs. Granton, and as Medhurst's accomplice; and now, he has almost exhausted the possibilities of a disguise for a really young and pretty woman; so he's playing her off at last as the riper product—a handsome matron. Clever, extremely clever; but—we begin to see through him.' And he chuckled to himself quietly.

Next day, on the hillside, we came upon our stranger again, occupied as before in peering into the rocks, and sounding them with a hammer. Charles nudged me and whispered, 'I have it this time. He's posing as a geologist.'

I took a good look at the man. By now, of course, we had some experience of Colonel Clay in his various disguises; and I could observe that while the nose, the hair, and the beard were varied, the eyes and the build remained the same as ever. He was a trifle stouter, of course, being got up as a man of between forty and fifty; and his forehead was lined in a way which a less consummate artist than Colonel Clay could easily have imitated. But I felt we had at least some grounds for our identification; it would not do to dismiss the suggestion of Clayhood at once as a flight of fancy.

His wife was sitting near, upon a bare boss of rock, reading a volume of poems. Capital variant, that, a volume of poems! Exactly suited the selected type of a cultivated family. White Heather and Mrs. Granton never used to read poems. But that was characteristic of all Colonel Clay's impersonations, and Mrs. Clay's too—for I suppose I must call her so. They were not mere outer disguises; they were finished pieces of dramatic study. Those two people were an actor and actress, as well as a pair of rogues; and in both their *rôles* they were simply inimitable.

As a rule, Charles is by no means polite to casual trespassers on the Seldon estate; they get short shrift and a summary ejection. But on this occasion he had a reason for being courteous, and he approached the lady with a bow of recognition. 'Lovely day,' he said, 'isn't it? Such belts on the sea, and the heather smells sweet. You are stopping at the inn, I fancy?'

'Yes,' the lady answered, looking up at him with a charming smile. ('I know that smile,' Charles whispered to me. 'I have succumbed to it too often.') 'We're stopping at the inn, and my husband is doing a little geology on the hill here. I hope Sir Charles Vandrift won't come and catch us. He's so down upon trespassers. They tell us at the inn he's a regular Tartar.'

('Saucy minx as ever,' Charles murmured to me. 'She said it on purpose.') 'No, my dear madam,' he continued, aloud; 'you have been quite misinformed. *I* am Sir Charles Vandrift; and I am *not* a Tartar. If your husband is a man of science I respect and admire him. It is geology that has made me what I am to-day.' And he drew himself up proudly. 'We owe to it the present development of South African mining.'

The lady blushed as one seldom sees a mature woman blush—but exactly as I had seen Madame Picardet and White Heather. 'Oh, I'm so sorry,' she said, in a confused way that recalled Mrs. Granton. 'Forgive my hasty speech. I—I didn't know you.'

('She did,' Charles whispered. 'But let that pass.') 'Oh, don't think of it again; so many people disturb the birds, don't you know, that we're obliged in self-defence to warn trespassers sometimes off our lovely mountains. But I do it with regret—with profound regret. I admire the—er—the beauties of Nature myself; and, therefore, I desire that all others should have the freest possible access to them—possible, that is to say, consistently with the superior claims of Property.'

'I see,' the lady replied, looking up at him quaintly. 'I admire your wish, though not your reservation. I've just been reading those sweet lines of Wordsworth's—

> And O, ye fountains, meadows, hills, and groves,
> Forebode not any severing of our loves.

I suppose you know them?' And she beamed on him pleasantly.

'Know them?' Charles answered. 'Know them! Oh, of course, I know them. They're old favourites of mine—in fact, I adore Wordsworth.' (I doubt whether Charles has ever in his life read

a line of poetry, except Doss Chiderdoss in the *Sporting Times*.)
He took the book and glanced at them. 'Ah, charming, charming!' he said, in his most ecstatic tone. But his eyes were on the
lady, and not on the poet.

I saw in a moment how things stood. No matter under what
disguise that woman appeared to him, and whether he recognised her or not, Charles couldn't help falling a victim to Madame Picardet's attractions. Here he actually suspected her;
yet, like a moth round a candle, he was trying his hardest to
get his wings singed! I almost despised him with his gigantic
intellect! The greatest men are the greatest fools, I verily
believe, when there's a woman in question.

The husband strolled up by this time, and entered into conversation with us. According to his own account, his name was
Forbes-Gaskell, and he was a Professor of Geology in one of
those new-fangled northern colleges. He had come to Seldon
rock-spying, he said, and found much to interest him. He was
fond of fossils, but his special hobby was rocks and minerals.
He knew a vast deal about cairngorms and agates and such-like
pretty things, and showed Charles quartz and felspar and red
cornelian, and I don't know what else, in the crags on the hillside. Charles pretended to listen to him with the deepest interest
and even respect, never for a moment letting him guess he knew
for what purpose this show of knowledge had been recently
acquired. If we were ever to catch the man, we must not allow
him to see we suspected him. So Charles played a dark game.
He swallowed the geologist whole without question.

Most of that morning we spent with them on the hillside.
Charles took them everywhere and showed them everything.
He pretended to be polite to the scientific man, and he was
really polite, most polite, to the poetical lady. Before lunch
time we had become quite friends.

The Clays were always easy people to get on with; and, bar
their roguery, we could not deny they were delightful compan-
ions. Charles asked them in to lunch. They accepted willingly. He
introduced them to Amelia with sundry raisings of his eyebrows and contortions of his mouth. 'Professor and Mrs. Forbes-
Gaskell,' he said, half-dislocating his jaw with his violent efforts.

'They're stopping at the inn, dear. I've been showing them over the place, and they're good enough to say they'll drop in and take a share in our cold roast mutton;' which was a frequent form of Charles's pleasantry.

Amelia sent them upstairs to wash their hands—which, in the Professor's case, was certainly desirable, for his fingers were grimed with earth and dust from the rocks he had been investigating. As soon as we were left alone Charles drew me into the library.

'Seymour,' he said, 'more than ever there is a need for us strictly to avoid preconceptions. We must not make up our minds that this man is Colonel Clay—nor, again, that he isn't. We must remember that we have been mistaken in *both* ways in the past, and must avoid our old errors. I shall hold myself in readiness for either event—and a policeman in readiness to arrest them, if necessary!'

'A capital plan,' I murmured. 'Still, if I may venture a suggestion, in what way are these two people endeavouring to entrap us? They have no scheme on hand—no schloss, no amalgamation.'

'Seymour,' my brother-in-law answered in his board-room style, 'you are a great deal too previous, as Medhurst used to say—I mean, Colonel Clay in his character as Medhurst. In the first place, these are early days; our friends have not yet developed their intentions. We may find before long they have a property to sell, or a company to promote, or a concession to exploit in South Africa or elsewhere. Then again, in the second place, we don't always spot the exact nature of their plan until it has burst in our hands, so to speak, and revealed its true character. What could have seemed more transparent than Medhurst, the detective, till he ran away with our notes in the very moment of triumph? What more innocent than White Heather and the little curate, till they landed us with a couple of Amelia's own gems as a splendid bargain? I will not take it for granted *any* man is not Colonel Clay, merely because I don't happen to spot the particular scheme he is trying to work against me. The rogue has so many schemes, and some of them so well concealed, that up to the moment of the actual explosion you fail to detect the presence of moral dynamite. Therefore, I shall proceed as if there were dynamite everywhere. But in the third place—and this is *very* important—you mark my words, I believe I detect already the lines he will work upon. He's a geologist, he says, with a taste for minerals. Very good. You see if he doesn't try to persuade me before long he has found a coal mine, whose locality he will disclose for a trifling consideration; or else he will salt the Long Mountain with emeralds, and claim a big share for helping to discover them; or else he will try something in the mineralogical line to *do* me somehow. I see it in the very transparency of the fellow's face; and I'm determined this time neither to pay him one farthing on any pretext, nor to let him escape me!'

We went in to lunch. The Professor and Mrs. Forbes-Gaskell, all smiles, accompanied us. I don't know whether it was Charles's warning to take nothing for granted that made me do so—but I kept a close eye upon the suspected man all the time we were at table. It struck me there was something very odd about his hair. It didn't seem quite the same colour all over. The locks that hung down behind, over the collar of his coat, were a trifle lighter and a trifle grayer than the black mass that covered the greater part of his head. I examined it carefully. The more I did so, the more the conviction grew upon me: he was wearing a wig. There was no denying it!

A trifle less artistic, perhaps, than most of Colonel Clay's get-ups; but then, I reflected (on Charles's principle of taking nothing for granted), we had never before suspected Colonel Clay himself, except in the one case of the Honourable David, whose red hair and whiskers even Madame Picardet had admitted to be absurdly false by her action of pointing at them and tittering irrepressibly. It was possible that in every case, if we had scrutinised our man closely, we should have found that the disguise betrayed itself at once (as Medhurst had suggested) to an acute observer.

The detective, in fact, had told us too much. I remembered what he said to us about knocking off David Granton's red wig the moment we doubted him; and I positively tried to help myself awkwardly to potato-chips, when the footman offered them, so as to hit the supposed wig with an apparently careless brush of my elbow. But it was of no avail. The fellow seemed to anticipate or suspect my intention, and dodged aside carefully, like one well accustomed to saving his disguise from all chance of such real or seeming accidents.

I was so full of my discovery that immediately after lunch I induced Isabel to take our new friends round the home garden and show them Charles's famous prize dahlias, while I proceeded myself to narrate to Charles and Amelia my observations and my frustrated experiment.

'It *is* a wig,' Amelia assented. '*I* spotted it at once. A very good wig, too, and most artistically planted. Men don't notice these things, though women do. It is creditable to you, Seymour, to have succeeded in detecting it.'

Charles was less complimentary. 'You fool,' he answered, with that unpleasant frankness which is much too common with him. 'Supposing it *is*, why on earth should you try to knock it off and disclose him? What good would it have done? If it *is* a wig, and we spot it, that's all that we need. We are put on our guard; we know with whom we have now to deal. But you can't take a man up on a charge of wig-wearing. The law doesn't interfere with it. Most respectable men may sometimes wear wigs. Why, I knew a promoter who did, and also the director of fourteen companies! What we have to do next is, wait till he tries to cheat us, and then—pounce down upon him. Sooner or later, you may be sure, his plans will reveal themselves.'

So we concocted an excellent scheme to keep them under constant observation, lest they should slip away again, as they did from the island. First of all, Amelia was to ask them to come and stop at the castle, on the ground that the rooms at the inn were uncomfortably small. We felt sure, however, that, as on a previous occasion, they would refuse the invitation, in order to be able to slink off unperceived, in case they should find themselves apparently suspected. Should they decline, it was arranged that Césarine should take a room at the Cromarty Arms as long as they stopped there, and report upon their movements; while, during the day, we would have the house watched by the head gillie's son, a most intelligent young man, who could be trusted, with true Scotch canniness, to say nothing to anybody.

To our immense surprise, Mrs. Forbes-Gaskell accepted the invitation with the utmost alacrity. She was profuse in her thanks, indeed; for she told us the Arms was an ill-kept house, and the cookery by no means agreed with her husband's liver. It was sweet of us to invite them; such kindness to perfect strangers was quite unexpected. She should always say that nowhere on earth had she met with so cordial or friendly a reception as at Seldon Castle. But—she accepted, unreservedly.

'It *can't* be Colonel Clay,' I remarked to Charles. 'He would never have come here. Even as David Granton, with far more reason for coming, he wouldn't put himself in our power: he preferred the security and freedom of the Cromarty Arms.'

'Sey,' my brother-in-law said sententiously, 'you're incorrigible. You *will* persist in being the slave of prepossessions. He may have some good reason of his own for accepting. Wait till he shows his hand—and then, we shall understand everything.'

So for the next three weeks the Forbes-Gaskells formed part of the house-party at Seldon. I must say, Charles paid them most assiduous attention. He positively neglected his other guests in order to keep close to the two new-comers. Mrs. Forbes-Gaskell noticed the fact, and commented on it. 'You are really too good to us, Sir Charles,' she said. 'I'm afraid you allow us quite to monopolise you!'

But Charles, gallant as ever, replied with a smile, 'We have you with us for so short a time, you know!' Which made Mrs. Forbes-Gaskell blush again that delicious blush of hers.

During all this time the Professor went on calmly and persistently mineralogising. 'Wonderful character!' Charles said to me. 'He works out his parts so well! Could anything exceed the picture he gives one of scientific ardour?' And, indeed, he was at it, morning, noon, and night. 'Sooner or later,' Charles observed, 'something practical must come of it.'

Twice, meanwhile, little episodes occurred which are well worth notice. One day I was out with the Professor on the

Long Mountain, watching him hammer at the rocks, and a little bored by his performance, when, to pass the time, I asked him what a particular small water-worn stone was. He looked at it and smiled. 'If there were a little more mica in it,' he said, 'it would be the characteristic gneiss of ice-borne boulders, hereabouts. But there isn't *quite* enough.' And he gazed at it curiously.

'Indeed,' I answered, 'it doesn't come up to sample, doesn't it?'

He gave me a meaning look. 'Ten per cent,' he murmured in a slow, strange voice; 'ten per cent is more usual.'

I trembled violently. Was he bent, then, upon ruining me? 'If you betray me——' I cried, and broke off.

'I beg your pardon,' he said. He was all pure innocence.

I reflected on what Charles had said about taking nothing for granted, and held my tongue prudently.

The other incident was this. Charles picked a sprig of white heather on the hill one afternoon, after a picnic lunch, I regret to say, when he had taken perhaps a glass more champagne than was strictly good for him. He was not exactly the worse for it, but he was excited, good-humoured, reckless, and lively. He brought the sprig to Mrs. Forbes-Gaskell, and handed it to her, ogling a little. 'Sweets to the sweet,' he murmured, and looked at her meaningly. 'White heather to White Heather.' Then he saw what he had done, and checked himself instantly.

Mrs. Forbes-Gaskell coloured up in the usual manner. 'I—I don't quite understand,' she faltered.

Charles scrambled out of it somehow. 'White heather for luck,' he said, 'and—the man who is privileged to give a piece of it to you is surely lucky.'

She smiled, none too well pleased. I somehow felt she suspected us of suspecting her.

However, as it turned out, nothing came, after all, of the untoward incident.

Next day Charles burst upon me, triumphant. 'Well, he has shown his hand!' he cried. 'I knew he would. He has come to me to-day with—what do you think?—a fragment of gold, in quartz, from the Long Mountain.'

'No!' I exclaimed.

'Yes,' Charles answered. 'He says there's a vein there with distinct specks of gold in it, which might be worth mining. When a man begins *that* way you know what he's driving at! And what's more, he's got up the subject beforehand; for he began saying to me there had long been gold in Sutherlandshire— why not therefore in Ross-shire? And then he went at full into the comparative geology of the two regions.'

'This is serious,' I said. 'What will you do?'

'Wait and watch,' Charles answered; 'and the moment he develops a proposal for shares in the syndicate to work the mine, or a sum of money down as the price of his discovery— get in the police, and arrest him.'

For the next few days the Professor was more active and ardent than ever. He went peering about the rocks on every side with his hammer. He kept on bringing in little pieces of stone, with gold specks stuck in them, and talking learnedly of the 'probable cost of crushing and milling.' Charles had heard all that before; in point of fact, he had assisted at the drafting of some dozens of prospectuses. So he took no notice, and waited for the man with the wig to develop his proposals. He knew they would come soon; and he watched and waited. But, of course, to draw him on he pretended to be interested.

While we were all in this attitude of mind, attending on Providence and Colonel Clay, we happened to walk down by the shore one day, in the opposite direction from the Seamew's island. Suddenly we came upon the Professor linked arm-in-arm with—Sir Adolphus Cordery! They were wrapped in deep talk, and appeared to be most amicable.

Now, naturally, relations had been a trifle strained between Sir Adolphus and the house of Vandrift since the incident of the Slump; but under the present circumstances, and with such a matter at stake as the capture of Colonel Clay, it was necessary to overlook all such minor differences. So Charles managed to disengage the Professor from his friend, sent Amelia on with Forbes-Gaskell towards the castle, and stopped behind, himself, with Sir Adolphus and me, to clear up the question.

'Do you know this man, Cordery?' he asked, with some little suspicion.

'Know him? Why, of course I do,' Sir Adolphus answered. 'He's Marmaduke Forbes-Gaskell, of the Yorkshire College, a very distinguished man of science. First-rate mineralogist—perhaps the best (*but* one) in England.' Modesty forbade him to name the exception.

'But are you sure it's he?' Charles inquired, with growing doubt. 'Have you known him before? This isn't a second case of Schleiermachering me, is it?'

'Sure it's he?' Sir Adolphus echoed. 'Am I sure of myself? Why, I've known Marmy Gaskell ever since we were at Trinity together. Knew him before he married Miss Forbes of Glenluce, my wife's second cousin, and hyphened his name with hers, to keep the property in the family. Know them both most intimately. Came down here to the inn because I heard that Marmy was on the prowl among these hills, and I thought he had probably something good to prowl after—in the way of fossils.'

'But the man wears a wig!' Charles expostulated.

'Of course,' Cordery answered. 'He's as bald as a bat—in front at least—and he wears a wig to cover his baldness.'

'It's disgraceful,' Charles exclaimed; 'disgraceful—taking us in like that.' And he grew red as a turkey-cock.

Sir Adolphus has no delicacy. He burst out laughing.

'Oh, I see,' he cried out, simply bursting with amusement. 'You thought Forbes-Gaskell was Colonel Clay in disguise! Oh, my stars, what a lovely one!'

'*You*, at least, have no right to laugh,' Charles responded, drawing himself up and growing still redder. 'You led me once into a similar scrape, and then backed out of it in a way unbecoming a gentleman. Besides,' he went on, getting angrier at each word, 'this fellow, whoever he is, has been trying to cheat me on his own account. Colonel Clay or no Colonel Clay, he's been salting my rocks with gold-bearing quartz, and trying to lead me on into an absurd speculation!'

Sir Adolphus exploded. 'Oh, this is too good,' he cried. 'I must go and tell Marmy!' And he rushed off to where Forbes-Gaskell was seated on a corner of rock with Amelia.

As for Charles and myself, we returned to the house. Half an hour later Forbes-Gaskell came back, too, in a towering temper.

'What is the meaning of this, sir?' he shouted out, as soon as he caught sight of Charles. 'I'm told you've invited my wife and myself here to your house in order to spy upon us, under the impression that I was Clay, the notorious swindler!'

'I thought you were,' Charles answered, equally angry. 'Perhaps you may be still! Anyhow, you're a rogue, and you tried to bamboozle me!'

Forbes-Gaskell, white with rage, turned to his trembling wife. 'Gertrude,' he said, 'pack up your box and come away from these people instantly. Their pretended hospitality has been a studied insult. They've put you and me in a most ridiculous position. We were told before we came here—and no doubt with truth—that Sir Charles Vandrift was the most close-fisted and tyrannical old curmudgeon in Scotland. We've been writing to all our friends to say ecstatically that he was, on the contrary, a most hospitable, generous, and large-hearted gentleman. And now we find out he's a disgusting cad, who asks strangers to his house from the meanest motives, and then insults his guests with gratuitous vituperation. It is well such people should hear the plain truth now and again in their lives; and it therefore gives me the greatest pleasure to tell Sir Charles Vandrift that he's a vulgar bounder of the first water. Go and pack your box, Gertrude! I'll run down to the Cromarty Arms, and order a cab to carry us away at once from this inhospitable sham castle.'

'You wear a wig, sir; you wear a wig,' Charles exclaimed, half-choking with passion. For, indeed, as Forbes-Gaskell spoke, and tossed his head angrily, the nature of his hair-covering grew painfully apparent. It was quite one-sided.

'I do, sir, that I may be able to shake it in the face of a cad!' the Professor responded, tearing it off to readjust it; and, suiting the action to the word, he brandished it thrice in Charles's eyes; after which he darted from the room, speechless with indignation.

As soon as they were gone, and Charles had recovered breath sufficiently to listen to rational conversation, I ventured to observe, 'This comes of being too sure! We made one mistake. We took it for granted that because a man wears a wig, he *must* be an impostor—which does not necessarily follow. We forgot that not Colonel Clays alone have false coverings to their heads, and that wigs may sometimes be worn from motives of pure personal vanity. In fact, we were again the slaves of preconceptions.'

I looked at him pointedly. Charles rose before he replied. 'Seymour Wentworth,' he said at last, gazing down upon me with lofty scorn, 'your moralising is ill-timed. It appears to me you entirely misunderstand the position and duties of a private secretary!

The oddest part of it all, however, was this—that Charles, being convinced Forbes-Gaskell, though he wasn't Colonel Clay, had been fraudulently salting the rocks with gold, with intent to deceive, took no further notice of the alleged discoveries. The consequence was that Forbes-Gaskell and Sir Adolphus went elsewhere with the secret; and it was not till after Charles had sold the Seldon Castle estate (which he did shortly afterward, the place having somehow grown strangely distasteful to him) that the present 'Seldon Eldorados, Limited,' were put upon the market by Lord Craig-Ellachie, who purchased the place from him. Forbes-Gaskell, as it happened, had reported to Craig-Ellachie that he had found a lode of high-grade ore on an estate unnamed, which he would particularise on promise of certain contingent claims to founder's shares; and the old lord jumped at it. Charles sold at grouse-moor prices; and the consequence is that the capital of the Eldorados is yielding at present very fair returns, even after allowing for expenses of promotion—while Charles has been done out of a good thing in gold-mines!

But, remembering 'the position and duties of a private secretary,' I refrained from pointing out to him at the time that this loss was due to a fixed idea—though as a matter of fact it depended upon Charles's strange preconception that the man with the wig, whoever he might be, was trying to diddle him.

IX

THE EPISODE OF THE JAPANNED DISPATCH-BOX

'Sey,' my brother-in-law said next spring, 'I'm sick and tired of London! Let's shoulder our wallets at once, and I will to some distant land, where no man doth me know.'

'Mars or Mercury?' I inquired; 'for, in our own particular planet, I'm afraid you'll find it just a trifle difficult for Sir Charles Vandrift to hide his light under a bushel.'

'Oh, I'll manage it,' Charles answered. 'What's the good of being a millionaire, I should like to know, if you're always obliged to "behave as sich"? I shall travel *incog*. I'm dog-tired of being dogged by these endless impostors.'

And, indeed, we had passed through a most painful winter. Colonel Clay had stopped away for some months, it is true, and for my own part, I will confess, since it wasn't *my* place to pay the piper, I rather missed the wonted excitement than otherwise. But Charles had grown horribly and morbidly suspicious. He carried out his principle of 'distrusting everybody and disbelieving everything,' till life was a burden to him. He spotted impossible Colonel Clays under a thousand disguises; he was quite convinced he had frightened his enemy away at least a dozen times over, beneath the varying garb of a fat club waiter, a tall policeman, a washer-woman's boy, a solicitor's clerk, the Bank of England beadle, and the collector of water-rates. He saw him as constantly, and in as changeful forms, as mediæval saints used to see the devil. Amelia and I really began to fear for the stability of that splendid intellect; we foresaw that unless the Colonel Clay nuisance could be abated somehow, Charles might sink by degrees to the mental level of a common or ordinary Stock-Exchange plunger.

So, when my brother-in-law announced his intention of going away *incog.* to parts unknown, on the succeeding Saturday, Amelia and I felt a flush of relief from long-continued tension. Especially Amelia—who was *not* going with him.

'For rest and quiet,' he said to us at breakfast, laying down the *Morning Post*, 'give *me* the deck of an Atlantic liner! No letters; no telegrams. No stocks; no shares. No *Times;* no *Saturday*. I'm sick of these papers!'

'The *World* is too much with us,' I assented cheerfully. I regret to say, nobody appreciated the point of my quotation.

Charles took infinite pains, I must admit, to ensure perfect secrecy. He made me write and secure the best state-rooms—main deck, amidships—under my own name, without mentioning his, in the *Etruria*, for New York, on her very next voyage. He spoke of his destination to nobody but Amelia; and Amelia warned Césarine, under pains and penalties, on no account to betray it to the other servants. Further to secure his *incog.*, Charles assumed the style and title of Mr. Peter Porter, and booked as such in the *Etruria* at Liverpool.

The day before starting, however, he went down with me to the City for an interview with his brokers in Adam's Court, Old Broad Street. Finglemore, the senior partner, hastened, of course, to receive us. As we entered his private room a good-looking young man rose and lounged out. 'Halloa, Finglemore,' Charles said, 'that's that scamp of a brother of yours! I thought you had shipped him off years and years ago to China?'

'So I did, Sir Charles,' Finglemore answered, rubbing his hands somewhat nervously. 'But he never went there. Being an idle young dog, with a taste for amusement, he got for the time no further than Paris. Since then, he's hung about a bit, here, there, and everywhere, and done no particular good for himself or his family. But about three or four years ago he somehow "struck ile": he went to South Africa, poaching on your preserves; and now he's back again—rich, married, and respectable. His wife, a nice little woman, has reformed him. Well, what can I do for you this morning?'

Charles has large interests in America, in Santa Fé and

Topekas, and other big concerns; and he insisted on taking out
several documents and vouchers connected in various ways
with his widespread ventures there. He meant to go, he said,
for complete rest and change, on a general tour of private
inquiry—New York, Chicago, Colorado, the mining districts.
It was a millionaire's holiday. So he took all these valuables in
a black japanned dispatch-box, which he guarded like a child
with absurd precautions. He never allowed that box out of his
sight one moment; and he gave me no peace as to its safety and
integrity. It was a perfect fetish. 'We must be cautious,' he
said, 'Sey, cautious! Especially in travelling. Recollect how
that little curate spirited the diamonds out of Amelia's jewel-
case! I shall not let this box out of my sight. I shall stick to it
myself, if we go to the bottom.'

We did *not* go to the bottom. It is the proud boast of the
Cunard Company that it has 'never lost a passenger's life'; and
the captain would not consent to send the *Etruria* to Davy
Jones's locker, merely in order to give Charles a chance of
sticking to his dispatch-box under trying circumstances. On
the contrary, we had a delightful and uneventful passage; and
we found our fellow-passengers most agreeable people. Charles,
as Mr. Peter Porter, being freed for the moment from his terror
of Colonel Clay, would have felt really happy, I believe—had it
not been for the dispatch-box. He made friends from the first
hour (quite after the fearless old fashion of the days before
Colonel Clay had begun to embitter life for him) with a nice
American doctor and his charming wife, on their way back to
Kentucky. Dr. Elihu Quackenboss—that was his characteristi-
cally American name—had been studying medicine for a year
in Vienna, and was now returning to his native State with a
brain close crammed with all the latest bacteriological and
antiseptic discoveries. His wife, a pretty and piquant little
American, with a tip-tilted nose and the quaint sharpness of
her countrywomen, amused Charles not a little. The funny
way in which she would make room for him by her side on the
bench on deck, and say, with a sweet smile, 'You sit right here,
Mr. Porter; the sun's just elegant,' delighted and flattered him.
He was proud to find out that female attention was not always

due to his wealth and title; and that plain Mr. Porter could command on his merits the same amount of blandishments as Sir Charles Vandrift, the famous millionaire, on his South African celebrity.

During the whole of that voyage, it was Mrs. Quackenboss here, and Mrs. Quackenboss there, and Mrs. Quackenboss the other place, till, for Amelia's sake, I was glad she was not on board to witness it. Long before we sighted Sandy Hook, I will admit, I was fairly sick of Charles's two-stringed harp—Mrs. Quackenboss and the dispatch-box.

Mrs. Quackenboss, it turned out, was an amateur artist, and she painted Sir Charles, on calm days on deck, in all possible attitudes. She seemed to find him a most attractive model.

The doctor, too, was a precious clever fellow. He knew something of chemistry—and of most other subjects, including, as I gathered, the human character. For he talked to Charles about various ideas of his, with which he wished to 'liven up folks in Kentucky a bit,' on his return, till Charles conceived the highest possible regard for his intelligence and enterprise. 'That's a go-ahead fellow, Sey!' he remarked to me one day. 'Has the right sort of grit in him! Those Americans are the men. Wish I had a round hundred of them on my works in South Africa!'

That idea seemed to grow upon him. He was immensely taken with it. He had lately dismissed one of his chief superintendents at the Cloetedorp mine, and he seriously debated whether or not he should offer the post to the smart Kentuckian. For my own part, I am inclined to connect this fact with his expressed determination to visit his South African undertakings for three months yearly in future; and I am driven to suspect he felt life at Cloetedorp would be rendered much more tolerable by the agreeable society of a quaint and amusing American lady.

'If you offer it to him,' I said, 'remember, you must disclose your personality.'

'Not at all,' Charles answered. 'I can keep it dark for the present, till all is arranged for. I need only say I have interests in South Africa.'

So, one morning on deck, as we were approaching the Banks, he broached his scheme gently to the doctor and Mrs. Quackenboss. He remarked that he was connected with one of the biggest financial concerns in the Southern hemisphere; and that he would pay Elihu fifteen hundred a year to represent him at the diggings.

'What, dollars?' the lady said, smiling and accentuating the tip-tilted nose a little more. 'Oh, Mr. Porter, it ain't good enough!'

'No, pounds, my dear madam,' Charles responded. 'Pounds sterling, you know. In United States currency, seven thousand five hundred.'

'I guess Elihu would just jump at it,' Mrs. Quackenboss replied, looking at him quizzically.

The doctor laughed. 'You make a good bid, sir,' he said, in his slow American way, emphasising all the most unimportant words: '*but* you overlook one element. I *am* a man of science, not a speculator. I *have* trained myself for medical work, *at* considerable cost, *in* the best schools of Europe, *and* I do not propose *to* fling away the results *of* much arduous labour *by* throwing myself out elastically *into* a new line of work *for* which my faculties *may* not perhaps equally adapt me.'

('How thoroughly American!' I murmured, in the background.)

Charles insisted; all in vain. Mrs. Quackenboss was impressed; but the doctor smiled always a sphinx-like smile, and reiterated his belief in the unfitness of mid-stream as an ideal place for swopping horses. The more he declined, and the better he talked, the more eager Charles became each day to secure him. And, as if on purpose to draw him on, the doctor each day gave more and more surprising proofs of his practical abilities. 'I *am* not a specialist,' he said. 'I just ketch the drift, appropriate the kernel, *and* let the rest slide.'

He could do anything, it really seemed, from shoeing a mule to conducting a camp-meeting; he was a capital chemist, a very sound surgeon, a fair judge of horseflesh, a first class euchre player, and a pleasing baritone. When occasion demanded he could occupy a pulpit. He had invented a corkscrew which brought him in a small revenue; and he was now engaged in the translation of a Polish work on the 'Application of Hydrocyanic Acid to the Cure of Leprosy.'

Still, we reached New York without having got any nearer our goal, as regarded Dr. Quackenboss. He came to bid us good-bye at the quay, with that sphinx-like smile still playing upon his features. Charles clutched the dispatch-box with one hand, and Mrs. Quackenboss's little palm with the other.

'*Don't* tell us,' he said, 'this is good-bye—for ever!' And his voice quite faltered.

'I guess so, Mr. Porter,' the pretty American replied, with a telling glance. 'What hotel do you patronise?'

'The Murray Hill,' Charles responded.

'Oh my, ain't that odd?' Mrs. Quackenboss echoed. 'The Murray Hill! Why, that's just where we're going too, Elihu!'

The upshot of which was that Charles persuaded them, before returning to Kentucky, to diverge for a few days with us to Lake George and Lake Champlain, where he hoped to over-persuade the recalcitrant doctor.

To Lake George therefore we went, and stopped at the excellent hotel at the terminus of the railway. We spent a good deal of our time on the light little steamers that ply between that point and the road to Ticonderoga. Somehow, the mountains mirrored in the deep green water reminded me of Lucerne; and Lucerne reminded me of the little curate. For the first time since we left England a vague terror seized me. *Could* Elihu Quackenboss be Colonel Clay again, still dogging our steps through the opposite continent?

I could not help mentioning my suspicion to Charles—who, strange to say, pooh-poohed it. He had been paying great court to Mrs. Quackenboss that day, and was absurdly elated because the little American had rapped his knuckles with her fan and called him 'a real silly.'

Next day, however, an odd thing occurred. We strolled out together, all four of us, along the banks of the lake, among woods just carpeted with strange, triangular flowers—trilliums, Mrs. Quackenboss called them—and lined with delicate ferns in the first green of springtide.

I began to grow poetical. (I wrote verses in my youth before I went to South Africa.) We threw ourselves on the grass, near a small mountain stream that descended among moss-clad boulders from the steep woods above us. The Kentuckian flung himself at full length on the sward, just in front of Charles. He had a strange head of hair, very thick and shaggy. I don't know why, but, of a sudden, it reminded me of the Mexican Seer, whom we had learned to remember as Colonel Clay's first embodiment. At the same moment the same thought seemed to run through Charles's head; for, strange to say, with a quick impulse he leant forward and examined it. I saw Mrs. Quackenboss draw back in wonder. The hair looked too thick and close for nature. It ended abruptly, I now remembered, with a sharp line on the forehead. Could this, too, be a wig? It seemed very probable.

Even as I thought that thought, Charles appeared to form a sudden and resolute determination. With one lightning swoop he seized the doctor's hair in his powerful hand, and tried to lift it off bodily. He had made a bad guess. Next instant the doctor uttered a loud and terrified howl of pain, while several of his hairs, root and all, came out of his scalp in Charles's hand, leaving a few drops of blood on the skin of the head in the place they were torn from. There was no doubt at all it was not a wig, but the Kentuckian's natural hirsute covering.

The scene that ensued I am powerless to describe. My pen is unequal to it. The doctor arose, not so much angry as astonished, white and incredulous. 'What did you do that for, any way?' he asked, glaring fiercely at my brother-in-law. Charles was all abject apology. He began by profusely expressing his regret, and offering to make any suitable reparation, monetary or otherwise. Then he revealed his whole hand. He admitted that he was Sir Charles Vandrift, the famous millionaire, and that he had suffered egregiously from the endless machinations of a certain Colonel Clay, a machiavellian rogue, who had hounded him relentlessly round the capitals of Europe. He described in graphic detail how the impostor got himself up with wigs and wax, so as to deceive even those who knew him intimately; and then he threw himself on Dr. Quackenboss's mercy, as a man who had been cruelly taken in so often that he could not help suspecting the best of men falsely. Mrs. Quackenboss admitted it was natural to have suspicions—'Especially,' she said, with candour, 'as you're not the first to observe the notable way Elihu's hair seems to originate from his forehead,' and she pulled it up to show us. But Elihu himself sulked on in the dumps: his dignity was offended. '*If* you wanted to know,' he said, 'you might as well have asked me. Assault *and* battery *is* not the right way to test whether *a* citizen's hair is primitive or acquired.'

'It was an impulse,' Charles pleaded; 'an instinctive impulse!'

'Civilised man restrains his impulses,' the doctor answered. 'You *have* lived too long *in* South Africa, Mr. Porter—I mean, Sir Charles Vandrift, if that's the right way *to* address such a gentleman. You appear to *have* imbibed the habits *and* manners of the Kaffirs you lived among.'

For the next two days, I will really admit, Charles seemed more wretched than I could have believed it possible for him to be on somebody else's account. He positively grovelled. The fact was, he saw he had hurt Dr. Quackenboss's feelings, and—much to my surprise—he seemed truly grieved at it. If the doctor would have accepted a thousand pounds down to shake hands at once and forget the incident—in my opinion Charles would have gladly paid it. Indeed, he said as much in other words to the pretty American—for he could not insult her by offering her money. Mrs. Quackenboss did her best to make it up, for she was a kindly little creature, in spite of her roguishness; but Elihu stood aloof. Charles urged him still to go out to South Africa, increasing his bait to two thousand a year; yet the doctor was immovable. 'No, no,' he said; 'I had half decided *to* accept your offer—*till* that unfortunate impulse; but that settled the question. *As* an American citizen, I decline *to* become the representative *of* a British nobleman who takes such means *of* investigating questions which affect the hair and happiness *of* his fellow-creatures.'

I don't know whether Charles was most disappointed at missing the chance of so clever a superintendent for the mine at Cloetedorp, or elated at the novel description of himself as

'a British nobleman;' which is not precisely our English idea of
a colonial knighthood.

Three days later, accordingly, the Quackenbosses left the
Lakeside Hotel. We were bound on an expedition up the lake
ourselves, when the pretty little woman burst in with a dash to
tell us they were leaving. She was charmingly got up in the
neatest and completest of American travelling-dresses. Charles
held her hand affectionately. 'I'm sorry it's good-bye,' he said.
'I have done my best to secure your husband.'

'You couldn't have tried harder than I did,' the little woman
answered, and the tip-tilted nose looked quite pathetic; 'for I
just hate to be buried right down there in Kentucky! However,
Elihu is the sort of man a woman can neither drive nor lead; so
we've got to put up with him.' And she smiled upon us sweetly,
and disappeared for ever.

Charles was disconsolate all that day. Next morning he
rose, and announced his intention of setting out for the West
on his tour of inspection. He would recreate by revelling in
Colorado silver lodes.

We packed our own portmanteaus, for Charles had not
brought even Simpson with him, and then we prepared to set
out by the morning train for Saratoga.

Up till almost the last moment Charles nursed his dispatch-
box. But as the 'baggage-smashers' were taking down our luggage, and a chambermaid was lounging officiously about in
search of a tip, he laid it down for a second or two on the
centre table while he collected his other immediate impedi-
menta. He couldn't find his cigarette-case, and went back to
the bedroom for it. I helped him hunt, but it had disappeared
mysteriously. That moment lost him. When we had found the
cigarette-case, and returned to the sitting-room—lo, and
behold! the dispatch-box was missing! Charles questioned the
servants, but none of them had noticed it. He searched round
the room—not a trace of it anywhere.

'Why, I laid it down here just two minutes ago!' he cried.
But it was not forthcoming.

'It'll turn up in time,' I said. 'Everything turns up in the
end—including Mrs. Quackenboss's nose.'

'Seymour,' said my brother-in-law, 'your hilarity is inopportune.'

To say the truth, Charles was beside himself with anger. He took the elevator down to the 'Bureau,' as they call it, and complained to the manager. The manager, a sharp-faced New Yorker, smiled as he remarked in a nonchalant way that guests with valuables were required to leave them in charge of the management, in which case they were locked up in the safe and duly returned to the depositor on leaving. Charles declared somewhat excitedly that he had been robbed, and demanded that nobody should be allowed to leave the hotel till the dispatch-box was discovered. The manager, quite cool, and obtrusively picking his teeth, responded that such tactics might be possible in an hotel of the European size, putting up a couple of hundred guests or so; but that an American house, with over a thousand visitors—many of whom came and went daily—could not undertake such a quixotic quest on behalf of a single foreign complainant.

That epithet, 'foreign,' stung Charles to the quick. No Englishman can admit that he is anywhere a foreigner. 'Do you know who I am, sir?' he asked, angrily. 'I am Sir Charles Vandrift, of London—a member of the English Parliament.'

'You may be the Prince of Wales,' the man answered, 'for all I care. You'll get the same treatment as anyone else, in America. But if you're Sir Charles Vandrift,' he went on, examining his books, 'how does it come you've registered as Mr. Peter Porter?'

Charles grew red with embarrassment. The difficulty deepened.

The dispatch-box, always covered with a leather case, bore on its inner lid the name 'Sir Charles Vandrift, K.C.M.G.,' distinctly painted in the orthodox white letters. This was a painful *contretemps:* he had lost his precious documents; he had given a false name; and he had rendered the manager supremely careless whether or not he recovered his stolen property. Indeed, seeing he had registered as Porter, and now 'claimed' as Vandrift, the manager hinted in pretty plain language he very much doubted whether there had ever been a dispatch-box in the matter at all, or whether, if there were one, it had ever contained any valuable documents.

We spent a wretched morning. Charles went round the hotel, questioning everybody as to whether they had seen his dispatch-box. Most of the visitors resented the question as a personal imputation; one fiery Virginian, indeed, wanted to settle the point then and there with a six-shooter. Charles telegraphed to New York to prevent the shares and coupons from being negotiated; but his brokers telegraphed back that, though they had stopped the numbers as far as possible, they did so with reluctance, as they were not aware of Sir Charles Vandrift being now in the country. Charles declared he wouldn't leave the hotel till he recovered his property; and for myself, I was inclined to suppose we would have to remain there accordingly for the term of our natural lives—and longer.

That night again we spent at the Lakeside Hotel. In the small hours of the morning, as I lay awake and meditated, a thought broke across me. I was so excited by it that I rose and rushed into my brother-in-law's bedroom. 'Charles, Charles!' I exclaimed, 'we have taken too much for granted once more. Perhaps Elihu Quackenboss carried off your dispatch-box!'

'You fool,' Charles answered, in his most unamiable manner (he applies that word to me with increasing frequency); 'is *that* what you've waked me up for? Why, the Quackenbosses left Lake George on Tuesday morning, and I had the dispatch-box in my own hands on Wednesday.'

'We have only their word for it,' I cried. 'Perhaps they stopped on—and walked off with it afterwards!'

'We will inquire to-morrow,' Charles answered. 'But I confess I don't think it was worth waking me up for. I could stake my life on that little woman's integrity.'

We *did* inquire next morning—with this curious result: it turned out that, though the Quackenbosses had left the Lakeside Hotel on Tuesday, it was only for the neighbouring Washington House, which they quitted on Wednesday morning, taking the same train for Saratoga which Charles and I had intended to go by. Mrs. Quackenboss carried a small brown paper parcel in her hands—in which, under the circumstances, we had little difficulty in recognising Charles's dispatch-box, loosely enveloped.

Then I knew how it was done. The chambermaid, loitering about the room for a tip, was—Mrs. Quackenboss! It needed but an apron to transform her pretty travelling-dress into a chambermaid's costume; and in any of those huge American hotels one chambermaid more or less would pass in the crowd without fear of challenge.

'We will follow them on to Saratoga,' Charles cried. 'Pay the bill at once, Seymour.'

'Certainly,' I answered. 'Will you give me some money?'

Charles clapped his hand to his pockets. 'All, all in the dispatch-box,' he murmured.

That tied us up another day, till we could get some ready cash from our agents in New York; for the manager, already most suspicious at the change of name and the accusation of theft, peremptorily refused to accept Charles's cheque, or anything else, as he phrased it, except 'hard money.' So we lingered on perforce at Lake George in ignoble inaction.

'Of course,' I observed to my brother-in-law that evening, 'Elihu Quackenboss was Colonel Clay.'

'I suppose so,' Charles murmured resignedly. 'Everybody I meet seems to be Colonel Clay nowadays—except when I believe they *are*, in which case they turn out to be harmless nobodies. But who would have thought it was he after I pulled his hair out? Or after he persisted in his trick, even when I suspected him— which, he told us at Seldon, was against his first principles?'

A light dawned upon me again. But, warned by previous ebullitions, I expressed myself this time with becoming timidity. 'Charles,' I suggested, 'may we not here again have been the slaves of a preconception? We thought Forbes-Gaskell was Colonel 'Clay for no better reason than because he wore a wig. We thought Elihu Quackenboss wasn't Colonel Clay—for no better reason than because he didn't wear one. But how do we know he *ever* wears wigs? Isn't it possible, after all, that those hints he gave us about make-up, when he was Medhurst the detective, were framed on purpose, so as to mislead and deceive us? And isn't it possible what he said of his methods at the Seamew's island that day was similarly designed in order to hoodwink us?'

'That is so obvious, Sey,' my brother-in-law observed, in a most aggrieved tone, 'that I should have thought any secretary worth his salt would have arrived at it instantly.'

I abstained from remarking that Charles himself had not arrived at it even now, until I told him. I thought that to say so would serve no good purpose. So I merely went on: 'Well, it seems to me likely that when he came as Medhurst, with his hair cut short, he was really wearing his own natural crop, in its simplest form and of its native hue. By now it has had time to grow long and bushy. When he was David Granton, no doubt, he clipped it to an intermediate length, trimmed his beard and moustache, and dyed them all red, to a fine Scotch colour. As the Seer, again, he wore his hair much the same as Elihu's; only, to suit the character, more combed and fluffy. As the little curate, he darkened it and plastered it down. As Von Lebenstein, he shaved close, but cultivated his moustache to its utmost dimensions, and dyed it black after the Tyrolese fashion. He need never have had a wig; his own natural hair would throughout have been sufficient, allowing for intervals.'

'You're right, Sey,' my brother-in-law said, growing almost friendly. 'I will do you the justice to admit that's the nearest thing we have yet struck out to an idea for tracking him.'

On the Saturday morning a letter arrived which relieved us a little from our momentary tension. It was from our enemy himself—but most different in tone from his previous bantering communications:—

'Saratoga, Friday.

'SIR CHARLES VANDRIFT—Herewith I return your dispatch-box, intact, with the papers untouched. As you will readily observe, it has not even been opened.

'You will ask me the reason for this strange conduct. Let me be serious for once, and tell you truthfully.

'White Heather and I (for I will stick to Mr. Wentworth's judicious *sobriquet*) came over on the *Etruria* with you, intending, as usual, to make something out of you. We followed you to

Lake George—for I had "forced a card," after my habitual plan, by inducing you to invite us, with the fixed intention of playing a particular trick upon you. It formed no part of our original game to steal your dispatch-box; that I consider a simple and elementary trick unworthy the skill of a practised operator. We persisted in the preparations for our *coup*, till you pulled my hair out. Then, to my great surprise, I saw you exhibited a degree of regret and genuine compunction with which, till that moment, I could never have credited you. You thought you had hurt my feelings; and you behaved more like a gentleman than I had previously known you to do. You not only apologised, but you also endeavoured voluntarily to make reparation. That produced an effect upon me. You may not believe it, but I desisted accordingly from the trick I had prepared for you.

'I might also have accepted your offer to go to South Africa, where I could soon have cleared out, having embezzled thousands. But, then, I should have been in a position of trust and responsibility—and I am not *quite* rogue enough to rob you under those conditions.

'Whatever else I am, however, I am not a hypocrite. I do not pretend to be anything more than a common swindler. If I return you your papers intact, it is only on the same principle as that of the Australian bushranger, who made a lady *a present* of her own watch because she had sung to him and reminded him of England. In other words, he did not take it from her. In like manner, when I found you had behaved, for once, like a gentleman, contrary to my expectation, I declined to go on with the trick I then meditated. Which does not mean to say I may not hereafter play you some other. *That* will depend upon your future good behaviour.

'Why, then, did I get White Heather to purloin your dispatch-box, with intent to return it? Out of pure lightness of heart? Not so; but in order to let you see I really meant it. If I had gone off with no swag, and then written you this letter, you would not have believed me. You would have thought it was merely another of my failures. But when I have actually got all your papers into my hands, and give them up again of my own free will, you must see that I mean it.

'I will end, as I began, seriously. My trade has not quite crushed out of me all germs or relics of better feeling; and when I see a millionaire behave like a man, I feel ashamed to take advantage of that gleam of manliness.

'Yours, with a tinge of penitence, but still a rogue,

CUTHBERT CLAY.'

The first thing Charles did on receiving this strange communication was to bolt downstairs and inquire for the dispatch-box. It had just arrived by Eagle Express Company. Charles rushed up to our rooms again, opened it feverishly, and counted his documents. When he found them all safe, he turned to me with a hard smile. 'This letter,' he said, with quivering lips, 'I consider still more insulting than all his previous ones.'

But, for myself, I really thought there was a ring of truth about it. Colonel Clay was a rogue, no doubt—a most unblushing rogue; but even a rogue, I believe, has his better moments.

And the phrase about the 'position of trust and responsibility' touched Charles to the quick, I suppose, *in re* the Slump in Cloetedorp Golcondas. Though, to be sure, it was a hit at me as well, over the ten per cent commission.

X

THE EPISODE OF
THE GAME OF POKER

'Seymour,' my brother-in-law said, with a deep-drawn sigh, as we left Lake George next day by the Rennselaer and Saratoga Railroad, 'no more Peter Porter for me, *if* you please! I'm sick of disguises. Now that we know Colonel Clay is here in America, they serve no good purpose; so I may as well receive the social consideration and proper respect to which my rank and position naturally entitle me.'

'And which they secure for the most part (except from hotel clerks), even in this republican land,' I answered briskly.

For in my humble opinion, for sound copper-bottomed snobbery, registered AI at Lloyd's, give *me* the free-born American citizen.

We travelled through the States, accordingly, for the next four months, from Maine to California, and from Oregon to Florida, under our own true names, 'Confirming the churches,' as Charles facetiously put it—or in other words, looking into the management and control of railways, syndicates, mines, and cattle-ranches. We inquired about everything. And the result of our investigations appeared to be, as Charles further remarked, that the Sabeans who so troubled the sons of Job seemed to have migrated in a body to Kansas and Nebraska, and that several thousand head of cattle seemed mysteriously to vanish, *à la* Colonel Clay, into the pure air of the prairies just before each branding.

However, we were fortunate in avoiding the incursions of the Colonel himself, who must have migrated meanwhile on some enchanted carpet to other happy hunting-grounds.

It was chill October before we found ourselves safe back in

New York, *en route* for England. So long a term of freedom from the Colonel's depredations (as Charles fondly imagined—but I will not anticipate) had done my brother-in-law's health and spirits a world of good; he was so lively and cheerful that he began to fancy his tormentor must have succumbed to yellow fever, then raging in New Orleans, or eaten himself ill, as we nearly did ourselves, on a generous mixture of clam-chowder, terrapin, soft-shelled crabs, Jersey peaches, canvas-backed ducks, Catawba wine, winter cherries, brandy cocktails, strawberry-shortcake, ice-creams, corn-dodger, and a judicious brew commonly known as a Colorado corpse-reviver. However that may be, Charles returned to New York in excellent trim; and, dreading in that great city the wiles of his antagonist, he cheerfully accepted the invitation of his brother millionaire, Senator Wrengold of Nevada, to spend a few days before sailing in the Senator's magnificent and newly-finished palace at the upper end of Fifth Avenue.

'There, at least, I shall be safe, Sey,' he said to me plaintively, with a weary smile. 'Wrengold, at any rate, won't try to take me in—except, of course, in the regular way of business.'

Boss-Nugget Hall (as it is popularly christened) is perhaps the handsomest brown stone mansion in the Richardsonian style on all Fifth Avenue. We spent a delightful week there. The lines had fallen to us in pleasant places. On the night we arrived Wrengold gave a small bachelor party in our honour. He knew Sir Charles was travelling without Lady Vandrift, and rightly judged he would prefer on his first night an informal party, with cards and cigars, instead of being bothered with the charming, but still somewhat hampering addition of female society.

The guests that evening were no more than seven, all told, ourselves included—making up, Wrengold said, that perfect number, an octave. He was a *nouveau riche* himself—the newest of the new—commonly known in exclusive old-fashioned New York society as the Gilded Squatter; for he 'struck his reef' no more than ten years ago; and he was therefore doubly anxious, after the American style, to be 'just dizzy with culture.' In his capacity of Mæcenas, he had invited amongst others the latest of English literary arrivals in New York—Mr. Algernon Coleyard, the famous poet, and leader of the Briar-rose school of West-country fiction.

'You know him in London, of course?' he observed to Charles, with a smile, as we waited dinner for our guests.

'No,' Charles answered stolidly. 'I have not had that honour. We move, you see, in different circles.'

I observed by a curious shade which passed over Senator Wrengold's face that he quite misapprehended my brother-in-law's meaning. Charles wished to convey, of course, that Mr. Coleyard belonged to a mere literary and Bohemian set in London, while he himself moved on a more exalted plane of peers and politicians. But the Senator, better accustomed to the new-rich point of view, understood Charles to mean that *he* had not the entrée of that distinguished coterie in which Mr. Coleyard posed as a shining luminary. Which naturally made him rate even higher than before his literary acquisition.

At two minutes past the hour the poet entered. Even if we had not been already familiar with his portrait at all ages in *The Strand Magazine*, we should have recognised him at once for a genuine bard by his impassioned eyes, his delicate mouth, the artistic twirl of one gray lock upon his expansive brow, the grizzled moustache that gave point and force to the genial smile, and the two white rows of perfect teeth behind it. Most of our fellow-guests had met Coleyard before at a reception given by the Lotus Club that afternoon, for the bard had reached New York but the previous evening; so Charles and I were the only visitors who remained to be introduced to him. The lion of the hour was attired in ordinary evening dress, with no foppery of any kind, but he wore in his buttonhole a dainty blue flower whose name I do not know; and as he bowed distantly to Charles, whom he surveyed through his eyeglass, the gleam of a big diamond in the middle of his shirt-front betrayed the fact that the Briar-rose school, as it was called (from his famous epic), had at least succeeded in making money out of poetry. He explained to us a little later, in fact, that he was over in New York to look after his royalties. 'The beggars,' he said, 'only gave me eight hundred pounds on my last volume. I couldn't stand *that*, you know; for a modern bard, moving with the age, can only sing when duly wound up; so I've run across to investigate. Put a penny in the slot, don't you see, and the poet will pipe for you.'

'Exactly like myself,' Charles said, finding a point in common. '*I'm* interested in mines; and I, too, have come over to look after my royalties.'

The poet placed his eyeglass in his eye once more, and surveyed Charles deliberately from head to foot. 'Oh,' he murmured slowly. He said not a word more; but somehow, everybody felt that Charles was demolished. I saw that Wrengold, when we went in to dinner, hastily altered the cards that marked their places. He had evidently put Charles at first to sit next the poet; he varied that arrangement now, setting Algernon Coleyard between a railway king and a magazine editor. I have seldom seen my respected brother-in-law so completely silenced.

The poet's conduct during dinner was most peculiar. He kept quoting poetry at inopportune moments.

'Roast lamb or boiled turkey, sir?' said the footman.

'Mary had a little lamb,' said the poet. 'I shall imitate Mary.'

Charles and the Senator thought the remark undignified.

After dinner, however, under the mellowing influence of some excellent Roederer, Charles began to expand again, and grew lively and anecdotal. The poet had made us all laugh not a little with various capital stories of London literary society—at least two of them, I think, new ones; and Charles was moved by generous emulation to contribute his own share to the amusement of the company. He was in excellent cue. He is not often brilliant; but when he chooses, he has a certain dry vein of caustic humour which is decidedly funny, though not perhaps strictly without being vulgar. On this particular night, then, warmed with the admirable Wrengold champagne—the best made in America—he launched out into a full and embroidered description of the various ways in which Colonel Clay had deceived him. I will not say that he narrated them in full with the same frankness and accuracy that I have shown in these pages; he suppressed not a few of the most amusing details—on no other ground, apparently, than because they happened to tell against himself; and he enlarged a good deal on the surprising cleverness with which several times he had nearly secured his man; but still, making all allowances for native vanity in concealment and addition, he was distinctly funny—he represented the matter for once in its ludicrous rather than in its disastrous aspect. He observed also, looking around the table, that after all he had lost less by Colonel Clay in four years of persecution than he often lost by one injudicious move in a single day on the London Stock Exchange; while he seemed to imply to the solid men of New York, that he would cheerfully sacrifice such a fleabite as that, in return for the amusement and excitement of the chase which the Colonel had afforded him.

The poet was pleased. 'You are a man of spirit, Sir Charles,' he said. 'I love to see this fine old English admiration of pluck and adventure! The fellow must really have some good in him, after all. I should like to take notes of a few of those stories; they would supply nice material for basing a romance upon.'

'I hardly know whether I'm exactly the man to make the hero of a novel,' Charles murmured, with complacence. And he certainly didn't look it.

'*I* was thinking rather of Colonel Clay as the hero,' the poet responded coldly.

'Ah, that's the way with you men of letters,' Charles answered, growing warm. 'You always have a sneaking sympathy with the rascals.'

'That may be better,' Coleyard retorted, in an icy voice, 'than sympathy with the worst forms of Stock Exchange speculation.'

The company smiled uneasily. The railway king wriggled. Wrengold tried to change the subject hastily. But Charles would not be put down.

'You must hear the end, though,' he said. 'That's not quite the worst. The meanest thing about the man is that he's also a hypocrite. He wrote me *such* a letter at the end of his last trick—here, positively here, in America.' And he proceeded to give his own version of the Quackenboss incident, enlivened with sundry imaginative bursts of pure Vandrift fancy.

When Charles spoke of Mrs. Quackenboss the poet smiled. 'The worst of married women,' he said, 'is—that you can't marry them; the worst of unmarried women is—that they want to marry you.' But when it came to the letter, the poet's eye was upon my brother-in-law. Charles, I must fain admit, garbled the document sadly. Still, even so, some gleam of good feeling remained in its sentences. But Charles ended all by saying, 'So, to crown his misdemeanours, the rascal shows himself a whining cur and a disgusting Pharisee.'

'Don't you think,' the poet interposed, in his cultivated drawl, 'he may have really meant it? Why should not some grain of compunction have stirred his soul still?—some remnant of conscience made him shrink from betraying a man who confided in him? I have an idea, myself, that even the worst of rogues have always some good in them. I notice they often succeed to the end in retaining the affection and fidelity of women.'

'Oh, I said so!' Charles sneered. 'I told you you literary men have always an underhand regard for a scoundrel.'

'Perhaps so,' the poet answered. 'For we are all of us human. Let him that is without sin among us cast the first stone.' And then he relapsed into moody silence.

We rose from table. Cigars went round. We adjourned to the smoking-room. It was a Moorish marvel, with Oriental hangings. There, Senator Wrengold and Charles exchanged reminiscences of bonanzas and ranches and other exciting postprandial topics; while the magazine editor cut in now and again with a pertinent inquiry or a quaint and sarcastic parallel instance. It was clear he had an eye to future copy. Only Algernon Coleyard sat brooding and silent, with his chin on one hand, and his brow intent, musing and gazing at the embers in the fireplace. The hand, by the way, was remarkable for a curious, antique-looking ring, apparently of Egyptian or Etruscan workmanship, with a projecting gem of several large facets. Once only, in the midst of a game of whist, he broke out with a single comment.

'Hawkins was made an earl,' said Charles, speaking of some London acquaintance.

'What for?' asked the Senator.

'Successful adulteration,' said the poet tartly.

'Honours are easy,' the magazine editor put in.

'And two by tricks to Sir Charles,' the poet added.

Towards the close of the evening, however—the poet still remaining moody, not to say positively grumpy—Senator Wrengold proposed a friendly game of Swedish poker. It was the latest fashionable variant in Western society on the old gambling round, and few of us knew it, save the omniscient poet and the magazine editor. It turned out afterwards that Wrengold proposed that particular game because he had heard Coleyard observe at the Lotus Club the same afternoon that it was a favourite amusement of his. Now, however, for a while he objected to playing. He was a poor man, he said, and the rest were all rich; why should he throw away the value of a dozen golden sonnets just to add one more pinnacle to the gilded roofs of a millionaire's palace? Besides, he was half-way through with an ode he was inditing to Republican simplicity. The pristine austerity of a democratic senatorial cottage had naturally inspired him with memories of Dentatus, the Fabii, Camillus. But Wrengold, dimly aware he was being made fun of somehow, insisted that the poet must take a hand with the financiers. 'You can pass, you know,' he said, 'as often as you like; and you can stake low, or go it blind, according as you're inclined to. It's a democratic game; every man decides for himself how high he will play, except the banker; and you needn't take bank unless you want it.'

'Oh, if you insist upon it,' Coleyard drawled out, with languid reluctance, 'I'll play, of course. I won't spoil your evening. But remember, I'm a poet; I have strange inspirations.'

The cards were 'squeezers'—that is to say, had the suit and the number of pips in each printed small in the corner, as well as over the face, for ease of reference. We played low at first. The poet seldom staked; and when he did—a few pounds—he lost, with singular persistence. He wanted to play for doubloons or sequins, and could with difficulty be induced to condescend to dollars. Charles looked across at him at last; the stakes by that time were fast rising higher, and we played for ready money. Notes lay thick on the green cloth. 'Well,' he murmured provokingly, 'how about your inspiration? Has Apollo deserted you?'

It was an unwonted flight of classical allusion for Charles, and I confess it astonished me. (I discovered afterwards he had cribbed it from a review in that evening's *Critic*.) But the poet smiled.

'No,' he answered calmly, 'I am waiting for one now. When it comes, you may be sure you shall have the benefit of it.'

Next round, Charles dealing and banking, the poet staked on his card, unseen as usual. He staked like a gentleman. To our immense astonishment he pulled out a roll of notes, and remarked, in a quiet tone, 'I have an inspiration now. *Half-hearted* will do. I go five thousand.' That was dollars, of course; but it amounted to a thousand pounds in English money—high play for an author.

Charles smiled and turned his card. The poet turned his— and won a thousand.

'Good shot!' Charles murmured, pretending not to mind, though he detests losing.

'Inspiration!' the poet mused, and looked once more abstracted.

Charles dealt again. The poet watched the deal with boiled-fishy eyes. His thoughts were far away. His lips moved audibly. '*Myrtle*, and *kirtle*, and *hurtle*,' he muttered. 'They'll do for three. Then there's *turtle*, meaning dove; and that finishes the possible. *Laurel* and *coral* make a very bad rhyme. Try *myrtle*; don't you think so?'

'Do you stake?' Charles asked, severely, interrupting his reverie.

The poet started. 'No, pass,' he replied, looking down at his card, and subsided into muttering. We caught a tremor of his lips again, and heard something like this: 'Not less but more republican than thou, Half-hearted watcher by the Western sea, After long years I come to visit thee, And test thy fealty to that maiden vow, That bound thee in thy budding prime For Freedom's bride——'

'Stake?' Charles interrupted, inquiringly, again.

'Yes, five thousand,' the poet answered dreamily, pushing forward his pile of notes, and never ceasing from his murmur: 'For Freedom's bride to all succeeding time. *Succeeding; succeeding;* weak word, *succeeding*. Couldn't go five dollars on it.'

Charles turned his card once more. The poet had won again. Charles passed over his notes. The poet raked them in with a far-away air, as one who looks at infinity, and asked if he could borrow a pencil and paper. He had a few priceless lines to set down which might otherwise escape him.

'This is play,' Charles said pointedly. '*Will* you kindly attend to one thing or the other?'

The poet glanced at him with a compassionate smile. 'I told you I had inspirations,' he said. 'They always come together. I can't win your money as fast as I would like, unless at the same time I am making verses. Whenever I hit upon a good epithet, I back my luck, don't you see? I won a thousand on *Halfhearted*, and a thousand on *budding;* if I were to back *succeeding*, I should lose, to a certainty. You understand my system?'

'I call it pure rubbish,' Charles answered. 'However, continue. Systems were made for fools—and to suit wise men. Sooner or later you *must* lose at such a stupid fancy.'

The poet continued. 'For Freedom's bride to all *ensuing* time.'

'Stake!' Charles cried sharply. We each of us staked.

'*Ensuing*,' the poet murmured. 'To all *ensuing* time. First-rate epithet that. I go ten thousand, Sir Charles, on *ensuing*.'

We all turned up. Some of us lost, some won; but the poet had secured his two thousand sterling.

'I haven't that amount about me,' Charles said, in that austerely nettled voice which he always assumes when he loses at cards; 'but—I'll settle it with you to-morrow.'

'Another round?' the host asked, beaming.

'No, thank you,' Charles answered; 'Mr. Coleyard's inspirations come too pat for my taste. His luck beats mine. I retire from the game, Senator.'

Just at that moment a servant entered, bearing a salver, with a small note in an envelope. 'For Mr. Coleyard,' he observed; 'and the messenger said, *urgent*.'

Coleyard tore it open hurriedly. I could see he was agitated. His face grew white at once.

'I—I beg your pardon,' he said. 'I—I must go back instantly. My wife is dangerously ill—quite a sudden attack. Forgive me, Senator. Sir Charles, you shall have your revenge to-morrow.'

It was clear that his voice faltered. We felt at least he was a man of feeling. He was obviously frightened. His coolness forsook him. He shook hands as in a dream, and rushed downstairs for his dust-coat. Almost as he closed the front door, a new guest entered, just missing him in the vestibule.

'Halloa, you men,' he said, 'we've been taken in, do you know? It's all over the Lotus. The man we made an honorary member of the club to-day is *not* Algernon Coleyard. He's a blatant impostor. There's a telegram come in on the tape to-night saying Algernon Coleyard is dangerously ill at his home in England.'

Charles gasped a violent gasp. 'Colonel Clay!' he shouted, aloud. 'And once more he's done me. There's not a moment to lose. After him, gentlemen! after him!'

Never before in our lives had we had such a close shave of catching and fixing the redoubtable swindler. We burst down the stairs in a body, and rushed out into Fifth Avenue. The pretended poet had only a hundred yards' start of us, and he saw he was discovered. But he was an excellent runner. So was I, weight for age; and I dashed wildly after him. He turned round a corner; it proved to lead nowhere, and lost him time. He darted back again, madly. Delighted with the idea that I was capturing so famous a criminal, I redoubled my efforts—and came up with him, panting. He was wearing a light dust-coat. I seized it in my hands. 'I've got you at last!' I cried; 'Colonel Clay, I've got you!'

He turned and looked at me. 'Ha, old Ten Per Cent!' he called out, struggling. 'It's you, then, is it? Never, never to *you*, sir!' And as he spoke, he somehow flung his arms straight out behind him, and let the dust-coat slip off, which it easily did, the sleeves being new and smoothly silk-lined. The suddenness of the movement threw me completely off my guard, and off my legs as well. I was clinging to the coat and holding him. As the support gave way I rolled over backward, in the mud of the street, and hurt my back seriously. As for Colonel Clay, with a nervous laugh, he bolted off at full speed in his evening coat, and vanished round a corner.

It was some seconds before I had sufficiently recovered my breath to pick myself up again, and examine my bruises. By this time Charles and the other pursuers had come up, and I explained my condition to them. Instead of commending me for my zeal in his cause—which had cost me a barked arm and a good evening suit—my brother-in-law remarked, with an unfeeling sneer, that when I had so nearly caught my man I might as well have held him.

'I have his coat, at least,' I said. 'That may afford us a clue.' And I limped back with it in my hands, feeling horribly bruised and a good deal shaken.

When we came to examine the coat, however, it bore no maker's name; the strap at the back, where the tailor proclaims with pride his handicraft, had been carefully ripped off, and its place was taken by a tag of plain black tape without inscription of any sort. We searched the breast-pocket. A handkerchief, similarly nameless, but of finest cambric. The side-pockets—ha, what was this? I drew a piece of paper out in triumph. It was a note—a real find—the one which the servant had handed to our friend just before at the Senator's.

We read it through breathlessly:—

'DARLING PAUL,—I *told* you it was too dangerous. You should have listened to me. You ought *never* to have imitated any real person. I happened to glance at the hotel tape just now, to see the quotations for Cloetedorps to-day, and what do you think I read as part of the latest telegram from England? "Mr. Algernon Coleyard, the famous poet, is lying on his death-bed at his home in Devonshire." By this time all New York knows. Don't stop one minute. Say I'm dangerously ill, and come away at once. Don't return to the hotel. I am removing our things. Meet me at Mary's. Your devoted,

MARGOT.'

'This is *very* important,' Charles said. 'This *does* give us a clue. We know two things now: his real name is Paul—whatever else it may be, and Madame Picardet's is Margot.'

I searched the pocket again, and pulled out a ring. Evidently he had thrust these two things there when he saw me pursuing him, and had forgotten or neglected them in the heat of the *mêlée*.

I looked at it close. It was the very ring I had noticed on his finger while he was playing Swedish poker. It had a large compound gem in the centre, set with many facets, and rising like a pyramid to a point in the middle. There were eight faces in all, some of them composed of emerald, amethyst, or turquoise. But *one* face—the one that turned at a direct angle towards the wearer's eye—was *not* a gem at all, but an extremely tiny convex mirror. In a moment I spotted the trick. He held this hand carelessly on the table while my brother-in-law dealt; and when he saw that the suit and number of his own card mirrored in it by means of the squeezers were better than Charles's, he had 'an inspiration,' and backed his luck—or rather his knowledge—with perfect confidence. I did not doubt, either, that his odd-looking eyeglass was a powerful magnifier which helped him in the trick. Still, we tried another deal, by way of experiment—I wearing the ring; and even with the naked eye I was able to distinguish in every case the suit and pips of the card that was dealt me.

'Why, that was almost dishonest,' the Senator said, drawing back. He wished to show us that even far-Western speculators drew a line somewhere.

'Yes,' the magazine editor echoed. 'To back your skill is legal; to back your luck is foolish; to back your knowledge is——'

'Immoral,' I suggested.

'Very good business,' said the magazine editor.

'It's a simple trick,' Charles interposed. 'I should have spotted it if it had been done by any other fellow. But his patter about inspiration put me clean off the track. That's the rascal's dodge. He plays the regular conjurer's game of distracting your attention from the real point at issue—so well that you never find out what he's really about till he's sold you irretrievably.'

We set the New York police upon the trail of the Colonel; but of course he had vanished at once, as usual, into the thin smoke of Manhattan. Not a sign could we find of him. 'Mary's,' we found an insufficient address.

We waited on in New York for a whole fortnight. Nothing came of it. We never found 'Mary's.' The only token of Colonel Clay's presence vouchsafed us in the city was one of his customary insulting notes. It was conceived as follows:—

'O ETERNAL GULLIBLE!—Since I saw you on Lake George, I have run back to London, and promptly come out again. I had business to transact there, indeed, which I have now completed; the excessive attentions of the English police sent me once more, like great Orion, 'sloping slowly to the west.' I returned to America in order to see whether or not you were still impenitent. On the day of my arrival I happened to meet Senator Wrengold, and accepted his kind invitation solely that I might see how far my last communication had had a proper effect upon you. As I found you quite obdurate, and as you furthermore persisted in misunderstanding my motives, I determined to read you one more small lesson. It nearly failed; and I confess the accident has affected my nerves a little. I am now about to retire from business altogether, and settle down for life at my place in Surrey. I mean to try just one more small *coup;* and, when that is finished, Colonel Clay will hang up his sword, like Cincinnatus, and take to farming. You need no longer fear me. I have realised enough to secure me for life a modest competence; and as I am not possessed like yourself with an immoderate greed of gain, I recognise that good citizenship demands of me now an early retirement in favour of some younger and more deserving rascal. I shall always look back with pleasure upon our agreeable adventures together; and as you hold my dust-coat, together with a ring and letter to which I attach importance, I consider we are quits, and I shall withdraw with dignity. Your sincere well-wisher,

CUTHBERT CLAY, *Poet.*'

'Just like him!' Charles said, 'to hold this one last *coup* over my head *in terrorem*. Though even when he has played it, why should I trust his word? A scamp like that may say it, of course, on purpose to disarm me.'

For my own part, I quite agreed with 'Margot.' When the Colonel was reduced to dressing the part of a known personage I felt he had reached almost his last card, and would be well advised to retire into Surrey.

But the magazine editor summed up all in a word. 'Don't believe that nonsense about fortunes being made by industry and ability,' he said. 'In life, as at cards, two things go to produce success—the first is chance; the second is cheating.'

THE EPISODE OF THE
BERTILLON METHOD

We had a terrible passage home from New York. The Captain told us he 'knew every drop of water in the Atlantic personally'; and he had never seen them so uniformly obstreperous. The ship rolled in the trough; Charles rolled in his cabin, and would not be comforted. As we approached the Irish coast, I scrambled up on deck in a violent gale, and retired again somewhat precipitately to announce to my brother-in-law that we had just come in sight of the Fastnet Rock Lighthouse. Charles merely turned over in his berth and groaned. 'I don't believe it,' he answered. 'I expect it is probably Colonel Clay in another of his manifold disguises!'

At Liverpool, however, the Adelphi consoled him. We dined luxuriously in the Louis Quinze restaurant, as only millionaires can dine, and proceeded next day by Pullman car to London.

We found Amelia dissolved in tears at a domestic cataclysm. It seemed that Césarine had given notice.

Charles was scarcely home again when he began to bethink him of the least among his investments. Like many other wealthy men, my respected connection is troubled more or less, in the background of his consciousness, by a pervading dread that he will die a beggar. To guard against this misfortune—which I am bound to admit nobody else fears for him—he invested, several years ago, a sum of two hundred thousand pounds in Consols, to serve as a nest-egg in case of the collapse of Golcondas and South Africa generally. It is part of the same amiable mania, too, that he will not allow the dividend-warrants on this sum to be sent to him by post, but insists, after the fashion of old ladies and country parsons, upon calling personally at the Bank of England four times a year to claim his interest. He is well known by sight to not a few of the clerks; and his appearance in Threadneedle Street is looked forward to with great regularity within a few weeks of each lawful quarter-day.

So, on the morning after our arrival in town, Charles observed to me, cheerfully, 'Sey, I must run into the City to-day to claim my dividends. There are two quarters owing.'

I accompanied him in to the Bank. Even that mighty official, the beadle at the door, unfastened the handle of the millionaire's carriage. The clerk who received us smiled and nodded. 'How much?' he asked, after the stereotyped fashion.

'Two hundred thousand,' Charles answered, looking affable.

The clerk turned up the books. 'Paid!' he said, with decision. 'What's your game, sir, if I may ask you?'

'Paid!' Charles echoed, drawing back.

The clerk gazed across at him. 'Yes, Sir Charles,' he answered, in a somewhat severe tone. 'You must remember you drew a quarter's dividend from myself—last week—at this very counter.'

Charles stared at him fixedly. 'Show me the signature,' he said at last, in a slow, dazed fashion. I suspected mischief.

The clerk pushed the book across to him. Charles examined the name close.

'Colonel Clay again!' he cried, turning to me with a despondent air. 'He must have dressed the part. I shall die in the workhouse, Sey! That man has stolen away even my nest-egg from me.'

I saw it at a glance. 'Mrs. Quackenboss!' I put in. 'Those portraits on the *Etruria!* It was to help him in his make-up! You recollect, she sketched your face and figure at all possible angles.'

'And last quarter's?' Charles inquired, staggering.

The clerk turned up the entry. 'Drawn on the 10th of July,' he answered, carelessly, as if it mattered nothing.

Then I knew why the Colonel had run across to England.

Charles positively reeled. 'Take me home, Sey,' he cried. 'I am ruined, ruined! He will leave me with not half a million in the world. My poor, poor boys will beg their bread, unheeded, through the streets of London!'

(As Amelia has landed estate settled upon her worth a hundred and fifty thousand pounds, this last contingency affected me less to tears than Charles seemed to think necessary.)

We made all needful inquiries, and put the police upon the quest at once, as always. But no redress was forthcoming. The money, once paid, could not be recovered. It is a playful little privilege of Consols that the Government declines under any circumstances to pay twice over. Charles drove back to Mayfair a crushed and broken man. I think if Colonel Clay himself could have seen him just then, he would have pitied that vast intellect in its grief and bewilderment.

After lunch, however, my brother-in-law's natural buoyancy reasserted itself by degrees. He rallied a little. 'Seymour,' he said to me, 'you've heard, of course, of the Bertillon system of measuring and registering criminals.'

'I have,' I answered. 'And it's excellent as far as it goes. But, like Mrs. Glasse's jugged hare, it all depends upon the initial step. "First catch your criminal." Now, we have never caught Colonel Clay——'

'Or, rather,' Charles interposed unkindly, 'when you *did* catch him, you didn't hold him.'

I ignored the unkindly suggestion, and continued in the same voice, 'We have never secured Colonel Clay; and until we secure him, we cannot register him by the Bertillon method. Besides, even if we had once caught him and duly noted the shape of his nose, his chin, his ears, his forehead, of what use would that be against a man who turns up with a fresh face each time, and can mould his features into what form he likes, to deceive and foil us?'

'Never mind, Sey,' my brother-in-law said. 'I was told in New York that Dr. Frank Beddersley, of London, was the best exponent of the Bertillon system now living in England; and to Beddersley I shall go. Or, rather, I'll invite him here to lunch to-morrow.'

'Who told you of him?' I inquired. '*Not* Dr. Quackenboss, I hope; nor yet Mr. Algernon Coleyard?'

Charles paused and reflected. 'No, neither of them,' he answered, after a short internal deliberation. 'It was that magazine editor chap we met at Wrengold's.'

'*He's* all right,' I said; 'or, at least, I think so.'

So we wrote a polite invitation to Dr. Beddersley, who pursued the method professionally, asking him to come and lunch with us at Mayfair at two next day.

Dr. Beddersley came—a dapper little man, with pent-house eyebrows, and keen, small eyes, whom I suspected at sight of being Colonel Clay himself in another of his clever polymorphic embodiments. He was clear and concise. His manner was scientific. He told us at once that though the Bertillon method was of little use till the expert had seen the criminal once, yet if we had consulted him earlier he might probably have saved us some serious disasters. 'A man so ingenious as this,' he said, 'would no doubt have studied Bertillon's principles himself, and would take every possible means to prevent recognition by them. Therefore, you might almost disregard the nose, the chin, the moustache, the hair, all of which are capable of such easy alteration. But there remain some features which are more likely to persist—height, shape of head, neck, build, and fingers; the *timbre* of the voice, the colour of the iris. Even these, again, may be partially disguised or concealed; the way the hair is dressed, the amount of padding, a high collar round the throat, a dark line about the eyelashes, may do more to alter the appearance of a face than you could readily credit.'

'So we know,' I answered.

'The voice, again,' Dr. Beddersley continued. 'The voice itself may be most fallacious. The man is no doubt a clever mimic. He could, perhaps, compress or enlarge his larynx. And I judge from what you tell me that he took characters each time which compelled him largely to alter and modify his tone and accent.'

'Yes,' I said. 'As the Mexican Seer, he had of course a Spanish intonation. As the little curate, he was a cultivated North-countryman. As David Granton, he spoke gentlemanly Scotch. As Von Lebenstein, naturally, he was a South-German, trying to express himself in French. As Professor Schleiermacher, he was a North-German speaking broken English. As Elihu Quackenboss, he had a fine and pronounced Kentucky flavour. And as the poet, he drawled after the fashion of the clubs, with lingering remnants of a Devonshire ancestry.'

'Quite so,' Dr. Beddersley answered. 'That is just what I should expect. Now, the question is, do you know him to be one man, or is he really a gang? Is he a name for a syndicate? Have you any photographs of Colonel Clay himself in any of his disguises?'

'Not one,' Charles answered. 'He produced some himself, when he was Medhurst the detective. But he pocketed them at once; and we never recovered them.'

'Could you get any?' the doctor asked. 'Did you note the name and address of the photographer?'

'Unfortunately, no,' Charles replied. 'But the police at Nice showed us two. Perhaps we might borrow them.'

'Until we get them,' Dr. Beddersley said, 'I don't know that we can do anything. But if you can once give me two distinct photographs of the real man, no matter how much disguised, I could tell you whether they were taken from one person; and, if so, I think I could point out certain details in common which might aid us to go upon.'

All this was at lunch. Amelia's niece, Dolly Lingfield, was there, as it happened; and I chanced to note a most guilty look stealing over her face all the while we were talking. Suspicious as I had learned to become by this time, however, I did not suspect Dolly of being in league with Colonel Clay; but, I confess, I wondered what her blush could indicate. After lunch, to my surprise, Dolly called me away from the rest into the library. 'Uncle Seymour,' she said to me—the dear child calls me Uncle Seymour, though of course I am not in any way related to her—'I have some photographs of Colonel Clay, if you want them.'

'You?' I cried, astonished. 'Why, Dolly, how did you get them?'

For a minute or two she showed some little hesitation in telling me. At last she whispered, 'You won't be angry if I confess?' (Dolly is just nineteen, and remarkably pretty.)

'My child,' I said, 'why *should* I be angry? You may confide in me implicitly.' (With a blush like that, who on earth could be angry with her?)

'And you won't tell Aunt Amelia or Aunt Isabel?' she inquired somewhat anxiously.

'Not for worlds,' I answered. (As a matter of fact, Amelia and Isabel are the last people in the world to whom I should dream of confiding anything that Dolly might tell me.)

'Well, I was stopping at Seldon, you know, when Mr. David Granton was there,' Dolly went on; '—or, rather, when that scamp pretended he was David Granton; and—and—you won't be angry with me, will you?—one day I took a snapshot with my kodak at him and Aunt Amelia!'

'Why, what harm was there in that?' I asked, bewildered. The wildest stretch of fancy could hardly conceive that the Honourable David had been *flirting* with Amelia.

Dolly coloured still more deeply. 'Oh, you know Bertie Winslow?' she said. 'Well, he's interested in photography—and—and also in *me*. And he's invented a process, which isn't of the slightest practical use, he says; but its peculiarity is, that it reveals textures. At least, that's what Bertie calls it. It makes things come out so. And he gave me some plates of his own for my kodak—half-a-dozen or more, and—I took Aunt Amelia with them.'

'I still fail to see,' I murmured, looking at her comically.

'Oh, Uncle Seymour,' Dolly cried. 'How blind you men are! If Aunt Amelia knew she would never forgive me. Why, you *must* understand. The—the rouge, you know, and the pearl powder!'

'Oh, it comes out, then, in the photograph?' I inquired.

'Comes out! I should *think* so! It's like little black spots all over auntie's face. *Such* a guy as she looks in it!'

'And Colonel Clay is in them too?'

'Yes; I took them when he and auntie were talking together, without either of them noticing. And Bertie developed them. I've three of David Granton. Three beauties; *most* successful.'

'Any other character?' I asked, seeing business ahead.

Dolly hung back, still redder. 'Well, the rest are with Aunt Isabel,' she answered, after a struggle.

'My dear child,' I replied, hiding my feelings as a husband, 'I will be brave. I will bear up even against that last misfortune!'

Dolly looked up at me pleadingly. 'It was here in London,' she went on; '—when I was last with auntie. Medhurst was stopping in the house at the time; and I took him twice, *tête-à-tête* with Aunt Isabel!'

'Isabel does not paint,' I murmured, stoutly.

Dolly hung back again. 'No, but—her hair!' she suggested, in a faint voice.

'Its colour,' I admitted, 'is in places assisted by a—well, you know, a restorer.'

Dolly broke into a mischievous sly smile. 'Yes, it is,' she continued. 'And, oh, Uncle Sey, where the restorer has—er—restored it, you know, it comes out in the photograph with a sort of brilliant iridescent metallic sheen on it!'

'Bring them down, my dear,' I said, gently patting her head with my hand. In the interests of justice, I thought it best not to frighten her.

Dolly brought them down. They seemed to me poor things, yet well worth trying. We found it possible, on further confabulation, by the simple aid of a pair of scissors, so to cut each in two that all trace of Amelia and Isabel was obliterated. Even so, however, I judged it best to call Charles and Dr. Beddersley to a private consultation in the library with Dolly, and not to submit the mutilated photographs to public inspection by their joint subjects. Here, in fact, we had five patchy portraits of the redoubtable Colonel, taken at various angles, and in characteristic unstudied attitudes. A child had outwitted the cleverest sharper in Europe!

The moment Beddersley's eye fell upon them, a curious look came over his face. 'Why, these,' he said, 'are taken on Herbert Winslow's method, Miss Lingfield.'

'Yes,' Dolly admitted timidly. 'They are. He's—a friend of mine, don't you know; and—he gave me some plates that just fitted my camera.'

Beddersley gazed at them steadily. Then he turned to Charles. 'And this young lady,' he said, 'has quite unintentionally and unconsciously succeeded in tracking Colonel Clay to earth at last. They are genuine photographs of the man—as he is—*without* the disguises!'

'They look to me most blotchy,' Charles murmured. 'Great black lines down the nose, and such spots on the cheek, too!'

'Exactly,' Beddersley put in. 'Those are *differences in texture*. They show just how much of the man's face is human flesh——'

'And how much wax,' I ventured.

'Not wax,' the expert answered, gazing close. 'This is some harder mixture. I should guess, a composition of gutta-percha and india-rubber, which takes colour well, and hardens when applied, so as to lie quite evenly, and resist heat or melting. Look here; that's an artificial scar, filling up a real hollow; and *this* is an added bit to the tip of the nose; and *those* are shadows, due to inserted cheek-pieces, within the mouth, to make the man look fatter!'

'Why, of course,' Charles cried. 'India-rubber it must be. That's why in France they call him *le Colonel Caoutchouc!*'

'Can you reconstruct the real face from them?' I inquired anxiously.

Dr. Beddersley gazed hard at them. 'Give me an hour or two,' he said—'and a box of water-colours. I *think* by that time—putting two and two together—I can eliminate the false and build up for you a tolerably correct idea of what the actual man himself looks like.'

We turned him into the library for a couple of hours, with the materials he needed; and by tea-time he had completed his first rough sketch of the elements common to the two faces. He brought it out to us in the drawing-room. I glanced at it first. It was a curious countenance, slightly wanting in definiteness, and not unlike those 'composite photographs' which Mr. Galton produces by exposing two negatives on the same sensitised paper for ten seconds or so consecutively. Yet it struck me at once as containing something of Colonel Clay in every one of his many representations. The little curate, in real life, did not recall the Seer; nor did Elihu Quackenboss suggest Count von Lebenstein or Professor Schleiermacher. Yet in this compound face, produced only from photographs of David

Granton and Medhurst, I could distinctly trace a certain underlying likeness to every one of the forms which the impostor had assumed for us. In other words, though he could make up so as to mask the likeness to his other characters, he could not make up so as to mask the likeness to his own personality. He could not wholly get rid of his native build and his genuine features.

Besides these striking suggestions of the Seer and the curate, however, I felt vaguely conscious of having seen and observed *the man himself* whom the water-colour represented, at some time, somewhere. It was not at Nice; it was not at Seldon; it was not at Meran; it was not in America. I believed I had been in a room with him somewhere in London.

Charles was looking over my shoulder. He gave a sudden little start. 'Why, I know that fellow!' he cried. 'You recollect him, Sey; he's Finglemore's brother—the chap that didn't go out to China!'

Then I remembered at once where it was that I had seen him—at the broker's in the city, before we sailed for America.

'What Christian name?' I asked.

Charles reflected a moment. 'The same as the one in the note we got with the dust-coat,' he answered, at last. 'The man is Paul Finglemore!'

'You will arrest him?' I asked.

'Can I, on this evidence?'

'We might bring it home to him.'

Charles mused for a moment. 'We shall have nothing against him,' he said slowly, 'except in so far as we can swear to his identity. And that may be difficult.'

Just at that moment the footman brought in tea. Charles wondered apparently whether the man, who had been with us at Seldon when Colonel Clay was David Granton, would recollect the face or recognise having seen it. 'Look here, Dudley,' he said, holding up the water-colour, 'do you know that person?'

Dudley gazed at it a moment. 'Certainly, sir,' he answered briskly.

'Who is it?' Amelia asked. We expected him to answer, 'Count von Lebenstein,' or 'Mr. Granton,' or 'Medhurst.'

Instead of that, he replied, to our utter surprise, 'That's Césarine's young man, my lady.'

'Césarine's young man?' Amelia repeated, taken aback. 'Oh, Dudley, surely, you *must* be mistaken!'

'No, my lady,' Dudley replied, in a tone of conviction. 'He comes to see her quite reg'lar; he have come to see her, off and on, from time to time, ever since I've been in Sir Charles's service.'

'When will he be coming again?' Charles asked, breathless.

'He's downstairs now, sir,' Dudley answered, unaware of the bombshell he was flinging into the midst of a respectable family.

Charles rose excitedly, and put his back against the door. 'Secure that man,' he said to me sharply, pointing with his finger.

'*What* man?' I asked, amazed. 'Colonel Clay? The young man who's downstairs now with Césarine?'

'No,' Charles answered, with decision; 'Dudley!'

I laid my hand on the footman's shoulder, not understanding what Charles meant. Dudley, terrified, drew back, and would have rushed from the room; but Charles, with his back against the door, prevented him.

'I—I've done nothing to be arrested, Sir Charles,' Dudley cried, in abject terror, looking appealingly at Amelia. 'It—it wasn't me as cheated you.' And he certainly didn't look it.

'I daresay not,' Charles answered. 'But you don't leave this room till Colonel Clay is in custody. No, Amelia, no; it's no use your speaking to me. What he says is true. I see it all now. This villain and Césarine have long been accomplices! The man's downstairs with her now. If we let Dudley quit the room he'll go down and tell them; and before we know where we are, that slippery eel will have wriggled through our fingers, as he always wriggles. He *is* Paul Finglemore; he *is* Césarine's young man; and unless we arrest him now, without one minute's delay, he'll be off to Madrid or St. Petersburg by this evening!'

'You are right,' I answered. 'It is now or never!'

'Dudley,' Charles said, in his most authoritative voice, 'stop here till we tell you you may leave the room. Amelia and Dolly, don't let that man stir from where he's standing. If he does, restrain him. Seymour and Dr. Beddersley, come down with me to the servants' hall. I suppose that's where I shall find this person, Dudley?'

'N—no, sir,' Dudley stammered out, half beside himself with fright. 'He's in the housekeeper's room, sir!'

We went down to the lower regions in a solid phalanx of three. On the way we met Simpson, Sir Charles's valet, and also the butler, whom we pressed into the service. At the door of the housekeeper's room we paused, strategically. Voices came to us from within; one was Césarine's, the other had a ring that reminded me at once of Medhurst and the Seer, of Elihu Quackenboss and Algernon Coleyard. They were talking together in French; and now and then we caught the sound of stifled laughter.

We opened the door. '*Est-il drôle, donc, ce vieux?*' the man's voice was saying.

'*C'est à mourir de rire,*' Césarine's voice responded.

We burst in upon them, red-handed.

Césarine's young man rose, with his hat in his hand, in a respectful attitude. It reminded me at once of Medhurst, as he stood talking his first day at Marvillier's to Charles; and also of the little curate, in his humblest moments as the disinterested pastor.

With a sign to me to do likewise, Charles laid his hand firmly on the young man's shoulder. I looked in the fellow's face: there could be no denying it; Césarine's young man was Paul Finglemore, our broker's brother.

'Paul Finglemore,' Charles said severely, 'otherwise Cuthbert Clay, I arrest you on several charges of theft and conspiracy!'

The young man glanced around him. He was surprised and perturbed; but, even so, his inexhaustible coolness never once deserted him. 'What, five to one?' he said, counting us over. 'Has law and order come down to this? Five respectable rascals to arrest one poor beggar of a *chevalier d'industrie!* Why, it's worse than New York. *There*, it was only you and me, you know, old Ten per Cent!'

'Hold his hands, Simpson!' Charles cried, trembling lest his enemy should escape him.

Paul Finglemore drew back even while we held his shoulders. 'No, not *you*, sir,' he said to the man, haughtily. 'Don't dare to lay your hands upon me! Send for a constable if you wish, Sir Charles Vandrift; but I decline to be taken into custody by a valet!'

'Go for a policeman,' Dr. Beddersley said to Simpson, standing forward.

The prisoner eyed him up and down. 'Oh, Dr. Beddersley!' he said, relieved. It was evident he knew him. 'If *you*'ve tracked me strictly in accordance with Bertillon's methods, I don't mind so much. I will not yield to fools; I yield to science. I didn't think this diamond king had sense enough to apply to you. He's the most gullible old ass I ever met in my life. But if it's *you* who have tracked me down, I can only submit to it.'

Charles held to him with a fierce grip. 'Mind he doesn't break away, Sey,' he cried. 'He's playing his old game! Distrust the man's patter!'

'Take care,' the prisoner put in. 'Remember Dr. Polperro! On what charge do you arrest me?'

Charles was bubbling with indignation. 'You cheated me at Nice,' he said; 'at Meran; at New York; at Paris!'

Paul Finglemore shook his head. 'Won't do,' he answered, calmly. 'Be sure of your ground. Outside the jurisdiction! You can only do that on an extradition warrant.'

'Well, then, at Seldon, in London, in this house, and elsewhere,' Charles cried out excitedly. 'Hold hard to him, Sey; by law or without it, blessed if he isn't going even now to wriggle away from us!'

At that moment Simpson returned with a convenient policeman, whom he had happened to find loitering about near the area steps, and whom I half suspected from his furtive smile of being a particular acquaintance of the household.

Charles gave the man in charge formally. Paul Finglemore

insisted that he should specify the nature of the particular accusation. To my great chagrin, Charles selected from his rogueries, as best within the jurisdiction of the English courts, the matter of the payment for the Castle of Lebenstein—made in London, and through a London banker. 'I have a warrant on that ground,' he said. I trembled as he spoke. I felt at once that the episode of the commission, the exposure of which I dreaded so much, must now become public.

The policeman took the man in charge. Charles still held to him, grimly. As they were leaving the room the prisoner turned to Césarine, and muttered something rapidly under his breath, in German. 'Of which tongue,' he said, turning to us blandly, 'in spite of my kind present of a dictionary and grammar, you still doubtless remain in your pristine ignorance!'

Césarine flung herself upon him with wild devotion. 'Oh, Paul, darling,' she cried, in English, 'I will not, I will not! I will never save myself at *your* expense. If they send you to prison— Paul, Paul, I will go with you!'

I remembered as she spoke what Mr. Algernon Coleyard had said to us at the Senator's. 'Even the worst of rogues have always some good in them. I notice they often succeed to the end in retaining the affection and fidelity of women.'

But the man, his hands still free, unwound her clasping arms with gentle fingers. 'My child,' he answered, in a soft tone, 'I am sorry to say the law of England will not permit you to go with me. If it did' (his voice was as the voice of the poet we had met), '"stone walls would not a prison make, nor iron bars a cage."' And bending forward, he kissed her forehead tenderly.

We led him out to the door. The policeman, in obedience to Charles's orders, held him tight with his hand, but steadily refused, as the prisoner was not violent, to handcuff him. We hailed a passing hansom. 'To Bow Street!' Charles cried, unceremoniously pushing in policeman and prisoner. The driver nodded. We called a four-wheeler ourselves, in which my brother-in-law, Dr. Beddersley and myself took our seats. 'Follow the hansom!' Charles cried out. 'Don't let him out of your sight. After him, close, to Bow Street!'

I looked back, and saw Césarine, half fainting, on the front door steps, while Dolly, bathed in tears, stood supporting the lady's-maid, and trying to comfort her. It was clear she had not anticipated this end to the adventure.

'Goodness gracious!' Charles screamed out, in a fresh fever of alarm, as we turned the first corner; 'where's that hansom gone to? How do I know the fellow was a policeman at all? We should have taken the man in here. We ought never to have let him get out of our sight. For all we can tell to the contrary, the constable himself—may only be one of Colonel Clay's confederates!'

And we drove in trepidation all the way to Bow Street.

XII

THE EPISODE OF THE OLD BAILEY

When we reached Bow Street, we were relieved to find that our prisoner, after all, had *not* evaded us. It was a false alarm. He was there with the policeman, and he kindly allowed us to make the first formal charge against him.

Of course, on Charles's sworn declaration and my own, the man was at once remanded, bail being refused, owing both to the serious nature of the charge and the slippery character of the prisoner's antecedents. We went back to Mayfair—Charles, well satisfied that the man he dreaded was under lock and key; myself, not too well pleased to think that the man I dreaded was no longer at large, and that the trifling little episode of the ten per cent commission stood so near discovery.

Next day the police came round in force, and had a long consultation with Charles and myself. They strongly urged that two other persons at least should be included in the charge—Césarine and the little woman whom we had variously known as Madame Picardet, White Heather, Mrs. David Granton, and Mrs. Elihu Quackenboss. If these accomplices were arrested, they said, we could include conspiracy as one count in the indictment, which gave us an extra chance of conviction. Now they had got Colonel Clay, in fact, they naturally desired to keep him, and also to indict with him as many as possible of his pals and confederates.

Here, however, a difficulty arose. Charles called me aside with a grave face into the library. 'Seymour,' he said, fixing me, 'this is a serious business. I will not lightly swear away any woman's character. Colonel Clay himself—or, rather, Paul Finglemore—is an abandoned rogue, whom I do not desire to

screen in any degree. But poor little Madame Picardet—she
may be his lawful wife, and she may have acted implicitly
under his orders. Besides, I don't know whether I could swear
to her identity. Here's the photograph the police bring of the
woman they believe to be Colonel Clay's chief female accomplice. Now, I ask you, does it in the least degree resemble that
clever and amusing and charming little creature, who has so
often deceived us?'

In spite of Charles's gibes, I flatter myself I do really understand the whole duty of a secretary. It was clear from his voice
he did not *wish* me to recognise her; which, as it happened, I
did not. 'Certainly, it doesn't resemble her, Charles,' I answered,
with conviction in my voice. 'I should never have known her.'
But I did not add that I should no more have known Colonel
Clay himself in his character of Paul Finglemore, or of
Césarine's young man, as *that* remark lay clearly outside my
secretarial functions.

Still, it flitted across my mind at the time that the Seer had
made some casual remarks at Nice about a letter in Charles's
pocket, presumably from Madame Picardet; and I reflected
further that Madame Picardet in turn might possibly hold certain answers of Charles's, couched in such terms as he might
reasonably desire to conceal from Amelia. Indeed, I must
allow that under whatever disguise White Heather appeared
to us, Charles was always that disguise's devoted slave from
the first moment he met it. It occurred to me, therefore, that
the clever little woman—call her what you will—might be the
holder of more than one indiscreet communication.

'Under these circumstances,' Charles went on, in his auster-
est voice, 'I cannot consent to be a party to the arrest of White
Heather. I—I decline to identify her. In point of fact'—he grew
more emphatic as he went on—'I don't think there is an atom
of evidence of any sort against her. Not,' he continued, after a
pause, 'that I wish in any degree to screen the guilty. Césarine,
now—Césarine we have liked and trusted. She has betrayed
our trust. She has sold us to this fellow. I have no doubt at all
that she gave him the diamonds from Amelia's *rivière;* that she
took us by arrangement to meet him at Schloss Lebenstein;

that she opened and sent to him my letter to Lord Craig-Ellachie. Therefore, I say, we *ought* to arrest Césarine. But not White Heather—not Jessie; not that pretty Mrs. Quackenboss. Let the guilty suffer; why strike at the innocent—or, at worst, the misguided?'

'Charles,' I exclaimed, with warmth, 'your sentiments do you honour. You are a man of feeling. And White Heather, I allow, is pretty enough and clever enough to be forgiven anything. You may rely upon my discretion. I will swear through thick and thin that I do not recognise this woman as Madame Picardet.'

Charles clasped my hand in silence. 'Seymour,' he said, after a pause, with marked emotion, 'I felt sure I could rely upon your—er—honour and integrity. I have been rough upon you sometimes. But I ask your forgiveness. I see you understand the whole duties of your position.'

We went out again, better friends than we had been for months. I hoped, indeed, this pleasant little incident might help to neutralise the possible ill-effects of the ten per cent disclosure, should Finglemore take it into his head to betray me to my employer. As we emerged into the drawing-room, Amelia beckoned me aside towards her boudoir for a moment.

'Seymour,' she said to me, in a distinctly frightened tone, 'I have treated you harshly at times, I know, and I am very sorry for it. But I want you to help me in a most painful difficulty. The police are quite right as to the charge of conspiracy; that designing little minx, White Heather, or Mrs. David Granton, or whatever else we're to call her, ought certainly to be prosecuted—and sent to prison, too—and have her absurd head of hair cut short and combed straight for her. But—and you will help me here, I'm sure, dear Seymour—I *cannot* allow them to arrest my Césarine. I don't pretend to say Césarine isn't guilty; the girl has behaved most ungratefully to me. She has robbed me right and left, and deceived me without compunction. Still—I put it to you as a married man—*can* any woman afford to go into the witness-box, to be cross-examined and teased by her own maid, or by a brute of a barrister on her maid's information? I assure you, Seymour, the thing's not to be dreamt of. There are details of a lady's life—known only to her maid—which *cannot* be made public. Explain as much of this as you think well to Charles, and *make* him understand that *if* he insists upon arresting Césarine, I shall go into the box—and swear my head off to prevent any one of the gang from being convicted. I have told Césarine as much; I have promised to help her: I have explained that I am her friend, and that if *she'll* stand by *me*, *I'll* stand by *her*, and by this hateful young man of hers.'

I saw in a moment how things went. Neither Charles nor Amelia could face cross-examination on the subject of one of Colonel Clay's accomplices. No doubt, in Amelia's case, it was merely a question of rouge and hair-dye; but what woman would not sooner confess to a forgery or a murder than to those toilet secrets?

I returned to Charles, therefore, and spent half an hour in composing, as well as I might, these little domestic difficulties. In the end, it was arranged that if Charles did his best to protect Césarine from arrest, Amelia would consent to do her best in return on behalf of Madame Picardet.

We had next the police to tackle—a more difficult business. Still, even *they* were reasonable. They had caught Colonel Clay, they believed, but their chance of convicting him depended entirely upon Charles's identification, with mine to back it. The more they urged the necessity of arresting the female confederates, however, the more stoutly did Charles declare that for his part he could by no means make sure of Colonel Clay himself, while he utterly declined to give evidence of any sort against either of the women. It was a difficult case, he said, and he felt far from confident even about the man. If *his* decision faltered, and he failed to identify, the case was closed; no jury could convict with nothing to convict upon.

At last the police gave way. No other course was open to them. They had made an important capture; but they saw that everything depended upon securing their witnesses, and the witnesses, if interfered with, were likely to swear to absolutely nothing.

Indeed, as it turned out, before the preliminary investigation at Bow Street was completed (with the usual remands), Charles had been thrown into such a state of agitation that he wished he had never caught the Colonel at all.

'I wonder, Sey,' he said to me, 'why I didn't offer the rascal two thousand a year to go right off to Australia, and be rid of him for ever! It would have been cheaper for my reputation than keeping him about in courts of law in England. The worst of it is, when once the best of men gets into a witness-box, there's no saying with what shreds and tatters of a character he may at last come out of it!'

'In *your* case, Charles,' I answered, dutifully, 'there can be no such doubt; except, perhaps, as regards the Craig-Ellachie Consolidated.'

Then came the endless bother of 'getting up the case' with the police and the lawyers. Charles would have retired from it altogether by that time, but, most unfortunately, he was bound over to prosecute. 'You couldn't take a lump sum to let me off?' he said, jokingly, to the inspector. But I knew in my heart it was one of the 'true words spoken in jest' that the proverb tells of.

Of course we could see now the whole building-up of the great intrigue. It had been worked out as carefully as the Tichborne swindle. Young Finglemore, as the brother of Charles's broker, knew from the outset all about his affairs; and, after a gentle course of preliminary roguery, he laid his plans deep for a campaign against my brother-in-law. Everything had been deliberately designed before-hand. A place had been found for Césarine as Amelia's maid—needless to say, by means of forged testimonials. Through her aid the swindler had succeeded in learning still more of the family ways and habits, and had acquired a knowledge of certain facts which he proceeded forthwith to use against us. His first attack, as the Seer, had been cleverly designed so as to give us the idea that we were a mere casual prey; and it did not escape Charles's notice now that the detail of getting Madame Picardet to inquire at the Crédit Marseillais about his bank had been solemnly gone through on purpose to blind us to the obvious truth that Colonel Clay was already in full possession of all such facts about us. It was by Césarine's aid, again, that he became possessed

of Amelia's diamonds, that he received the letter addressed to
Lord Craig-Ellachie, and that he managed to dupe us over the
Schloss Lebenstein business. Nevertheless, all these things
Charles determined to conceal in court; he did not give the
police a single fact that would turn against either Césarine or
Madame Picardet.

As for Césarine, of course, she left the house immediately
after the arrest of the Colonel, and we heard of her no more
till the day of the trial.

When that great day came, I never saw a more striking sight
than the Old Bailey presented. It was crammed to overflowing.
Charles arrived early, accompanied by his solicitor. He was so
white and troubled that he looked much more like prisoner
than prosecutor. Outside the court a pretty little woman stood,
pale and anxious. A respectful crowd stared at her silently.
'Who is that?' Charles asked. Though we could both of us
guess, rather than see, it was White Heather.

'That's the prisoner's wife,' the inspector on duty replied.
'She's waiting to see him enter. I'm sorry for her, poor thing.
She's a perfect lady.'

'So she seems,' Charles answered, scarcely daring to face her.

At that moment she turned. Her eyes fell upon his. Charles
paused for a second and looked faltering. There was in those
eyes just the faintest gleam of pleading recognition, but not a
trace of the old saucy, defiant vivacity. Charles framed his lips
to words, but without uttering a sound. Unless I greatly mistake, the words he framed on his lips were these: 'I will do my
best for him.'

We pushed our way in, assisted by the police. Inside the
court we saw a lady seated, in a quiet black dress, with a
becoming bonnet. A moment passed before I knew—it was
Césarine. 'Who is—that person?' Charles asked once more of
the nearest inspector, desiring to see in what way he would
describe her.

And once more the answer came, 'That's the prisoner's wife,
sir.'

Charles started back, surprised. 'But—I was told—a lady
outside was Mrs. Paul Finglemore,' he broke in, much puzzled.

'Very likely,' the inspector replied, unmoved. 'We have plenty that way. *When* a gentleman has as many aliases as Colonel Clay, you can hardly expect him to be over particular about having only *one* wife between them, can you?'

'Ah, I see,' Charles muttered, in a shocked voice. 'Bigamy!'

The inspector looked stony. 'Well, not exactly that,' he replied, 'occasional marriage.'

Mr. Justice Rhadamanth tried the case. 'I'm sorry it's him, Sey,' my brother-in-law whispered in my ear. (He said *him*, not *he*, because, whatever else Charles is, he is *not* a pedant; the English language as it is spoken by most educated men is quite good enough for his purpose.) 'I only wish it had been Sir Edward Easy. Easy's a man of the world, and a man of society; he would feel for a person in *my* position. He wouldn't allow these beasts of lawyers to badger and pester me. He would back his order. But Rhadamanth is one of your modern sort of judges, who make a merit of being what they call "conscientious," and won't hush up anything. I admit I'm afraid of him. I shall be glad when it's over.'

'Oh, *you'll* pull through all right,' I said in my capacity of secretary. But I didn't think it.

The judge took his seat. The prisoner was brought in. Every eye seemed bent upon him. He was neatly and plainly dressed, and, rogue though he was, I must honestly confess he looked at least a gentleman. His manner was defiant, not abject like Charles's. He knew he was at bay, and he turned like a man to face his accusers.

We had two or three counts on the charge, and, after some formal business, Sir Charles Vandrift was put into the box to bear witness against Finglemore.

Prisoner was unrepresented. Counsel had been offered him, but he refused their aid. The judge even advised him to accept their help; but Colonel Clay, as we all called him mentally still, declined to avail himself of the judge's suggestion.

'I am a barrister myself, my lord,' he said—'called some nine years ago. I can conduct my own defence, I venture to think, better than any of these my learned brethren.'

Charles went through his examination-in-chief quite swimmingly. He answered with promptitude. He identified the prisoner without the slightest hesitation as the man who had swindled him under the various disguises of the Reverend Richard Peploe Brabazon, the Honourable David Granton, Count von Lebenstein, Professor Schleiermacher, Dr. Quackenboss, and others. He had not the slightest doubt of the man's identity. He could swear to him anywhere. I thought, for my own part, he was a trifle too cocksure. A certain amount of hesitation would have been better policy. As to the various swindles, he detailed them in full, his evidence to be supplemented by that of bank officials and other subordinates. In short, he left Finglemore not a leg to stand upon.

When it came to the cross-examination, however, matters began to assume quite a different complexion. The prisoner set out by questioning Sir Charles's identifications. Was he sure of his man? He handed Charles a photograph. 'Is that the person who represented himself as the Reverend Richard Peploe Brabazon?' he asked persuasively.

Charles admitted it without a moment's delay.

Just at that moment, a little parson, whom I had not noticed till then, rose up, unobtrusively, near the middle of thecourt, where he was seated beside Césarine.

'Look at that gentleman!' the prisoner said, waving one hand, and pouncing upon the prosecutor.

Charles turned and looked at the person indicated. His face grew still whiter. It was—to all outer appearance—the Reverend Richard Brabazon *in propriâ personâ*.

Of course I saw the trick. This was the real parson upon whose outer man Colonel Clay had modelled his little curate. But the jury was shaken. And so was Charles for a moment.

'Let the jurors see the photograph,' the judge said, authoritatively. It was passed round the jurybox, and the judge also examined it. We could see at once, by their faces and attitudes, they all recognised it as the portrait of the clergyman before them—not of the prisoner in the dock, who stood there smiling blandly at Charles's discomfiture.

The clergyman sat down. At the same moment the prisoner produced a second photograph.

'Now, can you tell me who *that* is?' he asked Charles, in the regular brow-beating Old Bailey voice.

With somewhat more hesitation, Charles answered, after a pause: 'That is yourself as you appeared in London when you came in the disguise of the Graf von Lebenstein.'

This was a crucial point, for the Lebenstein fraud was the one count on which our lawyers relied to prove their case most fully, within the jurisdiction.

Even while Charles spoke, a gentleman whom I had noticed before, sitting beside White Heather, with a handkerchief to his face, rose as abruptly as the parson. Colonel Clay indicated him with a graceful movement of his hand. 'And *this* gentleman?' he asked calmly.

Charles was fairly staggered. It was the obvious original of the false Von Lebenstein.

The photograph went round the box once more. The jury smiled incredulously. Charles had given himself away. His overweening confidence and certainty had ruined him.

Then Colonel Clay, leaning forward, and looking quite engaging, began a new line of cross-examination. 'We have seen, Sir Charles,' he said, 'that we cannot implicitly trust your identifications. Now let us see how far we can trust your other evidence. First, then, about those diamonds. You tried to buy them, did you not, from a person who represented himself as the Reverend Richard Brabazon, because you believed he thought they were paste; and if you could, you would have given him £10 or so for them. *Do* you think that was honest?'

'I object to this line of cross-examination,' our leading counsel interposed. 'It does not bear on the prosecutor's evidence. It is purely recriminatory.'

Colonel Clay was all bland deference. 'I wish, my lord,' he said, turning round, 'to show that the prosecutor is a person unworthy of credence in any way. I desire to proceed upon the well-known legal maxim of *falsus in uno, falsus in omnibus*. I believe I am permitted to shake the witness's credit?'

'The prisoner is entirely within his rights,' Rhadamanth answered, looking severely at Charles. 'And I was wrong in suggesting that he needed the advice or assistance of counsel.'

Charles wriggled visibly. Colonel Clay perked up. Bit by bit, with dexterous questions, Charles was made to acknowledge that he wanted to buy diamonds at the price of paste, knowing them to be real; and, a millionaire himself, would gladly have diddled a poor curate out of a couple of thousand.

'I was entitled to take advantage of my special knowledge,' Charles murmured feebly.

'Oh, certainly,' the prisoner answered. 'But, while professing friendship and affection for a clergyman and his wife, in straitened circumstances, you were prepared, it seems, to take three thousand pounds' worth of goods off their hands for ten pounds, if you could have got them at that price. Is not that so?'

Charles was compelled to admit it.

The prisoner went onto the David Granton incident. 'When you offered to amalgamate with Lord Craig-Ellachie,' he asked, 'had you or had you not heard that a gold-bearing reef ran straight from your concession into Lord Craig-Ellachie's, and that his portion of the reef was by far the larger and more important?'

Charles wriggled again, and our counsel interposed; but Rhadamanth was adamant. Charles had to allow it.

And so, too, with the incident of the Slump in Golcondas. Unwillingly, shamefacedly, by torturing steps, Charles was compelled to confess that he had sold out Golcondas—he, the Chairman of the company, after repeated declarations to shareholders and others that he would do no such thing—because he thought Professor Schleiermacher had made diamonds worthless. He had endeavoured to save himself by ruining his company. Charles tried to brazen it out with remarks to the effect that business was business. 'And fraud is fraud,' Rhadamanth added, in his pungent way.

'A man must protect himself,' Charles burst out.

'At the expense of those who have put their trust in his honour and integrity,' the judge commented coldly.

After four mortal hours of it, all to the same effect, my respected brother-in-law left the witness-box at last, wiping his brow and biting his lip, with the very air of a culprit. His character had received a most serious blow. While he stood in the witness-box all the world had felt it was *he* who was the accused and Colonel Clay who was the prosecutor. He was convicted on his own evidence of having tried to induce the supposed David Granton to sell his father's interests into an enemy's hands, and of every other shady trick into which his well-known business acuteness had unfortunately hurried him during the course of his adventures. I had but one consolation in my brother-in-law's misfortunes—and that was the thought that a due sense of his own shortcomings might possibly make him more lenient in the end to the trivial misdemeanours of a poor beggar of a secretary!

I was the next in the box. I do not desire to enlarge upon my own achievements. I will draw a decent veil, indeed, over the painful scene that ensued when I finished my evidence. I can only say I was more cautious than Charles in my recognition of the photographs; but I found myself particularly worried and harried over other parts of my cross-examination. Especially was I shaken about that misguided step I took in the matter of the cheque for the Lebenstein commission—a cheque which Colonel Clay handed to me with the utmost politeness, requesting to know whether or not it bore my signature. I caught Charles's eye at the end of the episode, and I venture to say the expression it wore was one of relief that I too had tripped over a trifling question of ten per cent on the purchase money of the castle.

Altogether, I must admit, if it had not been for the police evidence, we would have failed to make a case against our man at all. But the police, I confess, had got up their part of the prosecution admirably. Now that they knew Colonel Clay to be really Paul Finglemore, they showed with great cleverness how Paul Finglemore's disappearances and reappearances in London exactly tallied with Colonel Clay's appearances and disappearances elsewhere, under the guise of the little curate, the Seer, David Granton, and the rest of them. Furthermore, they showed experimentally how the prisoner at the bar might have got himself up in the various characters; and, by means of a wax bust, modelled by Dr. Beddersley from observations

at Bow Street, and aided by additions in the gutta-percha composition after Dolly Lingfield's photographs, they succeeded in
proving that the face as it stood could be readily transformed
into the faces of Medhurst and David Granton. Altogether,
their cleverness and trained acumen made up on the whole for
Charles's over-certainty, and they succeeded in putting before
the jury a strong case of their own against Paul Finglemore.

The trial occupied three days. After the first of the three, my
respected brother-in-law preferred, as he said, not to prejudice
the case against the prisoner by appearing in court again. He
did not even allude to the little matter of the ten per cent commission further than to say at dinner that evening that all men
were bound to protect their own interests—as secretaries or as
principals. This I took for forgiveness; and I continued diligently to attend the trial, and watch the case in my employer's
interest.

The defence was ingenious, even if somewhat halting. It
consisted simply of an attempt to prove throughout that
Charles and I had made our prisoner the victim of a mistaken
identity. Finglemore put into the box the ingenuous original of
the little curate—the Reverend Septimus Porkington, as it
turned out, a friend of his family; and he showed that it was
the Reverend Septimus himself who had sat to a photographer
in Baker Street for the portrait which Charles too hastily identified as that of Colonel Clay in his personification of Mr.
Richard Brabazon. He further elicited the fact that the portrait
of the Count von Lebenstein was really taken from Dr. Julius
Keppel, a Tyrolese music-master, residing at Balham, whom he
put into the box, and who was well known, as it chanced, to
the foreman of the jury. Gradually he made it clear to us that
no portraits existed of Colonel Clay at all, except Dolly Lingfield's—so it dawned upon me by degrees that even Dr. Beddersley could only have been misled if we had succeeded in
finding for him the alleged photographs of Colonel Clay as the
count and the curate, which had been shown us by Medhurst.
Altogether, the prisoner based his defence upon the fact that
no more than two witnesses directly identified him; while one
of those two had positively sworn that he recognised as the

prisoner's two portraits which turned out, by independent evidence, to be taken from other people!

The judge summed up in a caustic way which was pleasant to neither party. He asked the jury to dismiss from their minds entirely the impression created by what he frankly described as 'Sir Charles Vandrift's obvious dishonesty.' They must not allow the fact that he was a millionaire—and a particularly shady one—to prejudice their feelings in favour of the prisoner. Even the richest—and vilest—of men must be protected. Besides, this was a public question. If a rogue cheated a rogue, he must still be punished. If a murderer stabbed or shot a murderer, he must still be hung for it. Society must see that the worst of thieves were not preyed upon by others. Therefore, the proved facts that Sir Charles Vandrift, with all his millions, had meanly tried to cheat the prisoner, or some other poor person, out of valuable diamonds—had basely tried to juggle Lord Craig-Ellachie's mines into his own hands—had vilely tried to bribe a son to betray his father—had directly tried, by underhand means, to save his own money, at the risk of destroying the wealth of others who trusted to his probity—these proved facts must not blind them to the truth that the prisoner at the bar (if he were really Colonel Clay) was an abandoned swindler. To that point alone they must confine their attention; and *if* they were convinced that the prisoner was shown to be the self-same man who appeared on various occasions as David Granton, as Von Lebenstein, as Medhurst, as Schleiermacher, they must find him guilty.

As to that point, also, the judge commented on the obvious strength of the police case, and the fact that the prisoner had not attempted in any one out of so many instances to prove an *alibi*. Surely, if he were *not* Colonel Clay, the jury should ask themselves, must it not have been simple and easy for him to do so? Finally, the judge summed up all the elements of doubt in the identification—and all the elements of probability; and left it to the jury to draw their own conclusions.

They retired at the end to consider their verdict. While they were absent every eye in court was fixed on the prisoner. But Paul Finglemore himself looked steadily towards the further end of the hall, where two pale-faced women sat together, with handkerchiefs in their hands, and eyes red with weeping.

Only then, as he stood there, awaiting the verdict, with a fixed white face, prepared for everything, did I begin to realise with what courage and pluck that one lone man had sustained so long an unequal contest against wealth, authority, and all the Governments of Europe, aided but by his own skill and two feeble women! Only then did I feel he had played his reckless game through all those years with *this* ever before him! I found it hard to picture.

The jury filed slowly back. There was dead silence in court as the clerk put the question, 'Do you find the prisoner at the bar guilty or not guilty?'

'We find him guilty.'

'On all the counts?'

'On all the counts of the indictment.'

The women at the back burst into tears, unanimously.

Mr. Justice Rhadamanth addressed the prisoner. 'Have you anything to urge,' he asked in a very stern tone, 'in mitigation of whatever sentence the Court may see fit to pass upon you?'

'Nothing,' the prisoner answered, just faltering slightly. 'I have brought it upon myself—but—I have protected the lives of those nearest and dearest to me. I have fought hard for my own hand. I admit my crime, and will face my punishment. I only regret that, since we were both of us rogues—myself and the prosecutor—the lesser rogue should have stood here in the dock, and the greater in the witness-box. Our country takes care to decorate each according to his deserts—to him, the Grand Cross of St. Michael and St. George; to me, the Broad Arrow!'

The judge gazed at him severely. 'Paul Finglemore,' he said, passing sentence in his sardonic way, 'you have chosen to dedicate to the service of fraud abilities and attainments which, if turned from the outset into a legitimate channel, would no doubt have sufficed to secure you without excessive effort a subsistence one degree above starvation—possibly even, with good luck, a sordid and squalid competence. You have preferred to embark them on a lawless life of vice and crime—and

I will not deny that you seem to have had a good run for your money. Society, however, whose mouthpiece I am, cannot allow you any longer to mock it with impunity. You have broken its laws openly, and you have been found out.' He assumed the tone of bland condescension which always heralds his severest moments. 'I sentence you to Fourteen Years' Imprisonment, with Hard Labour.'

The prisoner bowed, without losing his apparent composure. But his eyes strayed away again to the far end of the hall, where the two weeping women, with a sudden sharp cry, fell at once in a faint on one another's shoulders, and were with difficulty removed from court by the ushers.

As we left the room, I heard but one comment all round, thus voiced by a school-boy: 'I'd a jolly sight rather it had been old Vandrift. This Clay chap's too clever by half to waste on a prison!'

But he went there, none the less—in that 'cool sequestered vale of life' to recover equilibrium; though I myself half regretted it.

I will add but one more little parting episode.

When all was over, Charles rushed off to Cannes, to get away from the impertinent stare of London. Amelia and Isabel and I went with him. We were driving one afternoon on the hills beyond the town, among the myrtle and lentisk scrub, when we noticed in front of us a nice victoria, containing two ladies in very deep mourning. We followed it, unintentionally, as far as Le Grand Pin—that big pine tree that looks across the bay towards Antibes. There, the ladies descended and sat down on a knoll, gazing out disconsolately towards the sea and the islands. It was evident they were suffering very deep grief. Their faces were pale and their eyes bloodshot. 'Poor things!' Amelia said. Then her tone altered suddenly.

'Why, good gracious,' she cried, 'if it isn't Césarine!'

So it was—with White Heather!

Charles got down and drew near them. 'I beg your pardon,' he said, raising his hat, and addressing Madame Picardet: 'I believe I have had the pleasure of meeting you. And since I have doubtless paid in the end for your victoria, *may* I venture to inquire for whom you are in mourning?'

White Heather drew back, sobbing; but Césarine turned to him, fiery red, with the mien of a lady. 'For *him!*' she answered; 'for Paul! for our king, whom *you* have imprisoned! As long as *he* remains there, we have both of us decided to wear mourning for ever!'

Charles raised his hat again, and drew back without one word. He waved his hand to Amelia and walked home with me to Cannes. He seemed deeply dejected.

'A penny for your thoughts!' I exclaimed, at last, in a jocular tone, trying feebly to rouse him.

He turned to me, and sighed. 'I was wondering,' he answered, 'if *I* had gone to prison, would Amelia and Isabel have done as much for me?'

For myself, I did *not* wonder. I knew pretty well. For Charles, you will admit, though the bigger rogue of the two, is scarcely the kind of rogue to inspire a woman with profound affection.